to
Wayne Schafer

In appreciation for the shared service on the USS Heron AMS-18

Bert Millspaugh, ET 2

# THE MYSTICAL VORTEX
## GATEWAY TO ANOTHER DIMENSION

BY

BERT MILLSPAUGH

Bloomington, IN              Milton Keynes, UK

*AuthorHouse™*
*1663 Liberty Drive, Suite 200*
*Bloomington, IN 47403*
*www.authorhouse.com*
*Phone: 1-800-839-8640*

*AuthorHouse™ UK Ltd.*
*500 Avebury Boulevard*
*Central Milton Keynes, MK9 2BE*
*www.authorhouse.co.uk*
*Phone: 08001974150*

*This book is a work of fiction. People, places, events, and situations are the product of the author's imagination. Any resemblance to actual persons, living or dead, or historical events, is purely coincidental.*

*© 2006 Bert Millspaugh. All rights reserved.*

*No part of this book may be reproduced, stored in a retrieval system, or transmitted by any means without the written permission of the author.*

*First published by AuthorHouse 3/29/2006*

*ISBN: 1-4259-1027-0 (e)*
*ISBN: 1-4259-1026-2 (sc)*

*Library of Congress Control Number: 2006900295*

*Printed in the United States of America*
*Bloomington, Indiana*

*This book is printed on acid-free paper.*

## Dedication and Acknowledgements

I dedicate this novel to my wife, Barbara, a constant companion during my retirement years, and for her continued encouragement through the writing, editing and rewriting.

Also to my seven adult children, Margaret, Annette, Andrew, Lori, Russell, Betsy and Barbie for their encouragement during the writing of this novel, and to my mother, Margaret, for listening to the childhood books I read. Thanks and appreciation to National Park Ranger, Roger Mansoldo, for his help in my research of the Anasazi, to Markee Cox for her excellent grammatical critique and suggestions, and to Roy King for his overall meticulous critiques.

# About the Author

Bert Millspaugh has been a successful writer for over 35 years. He has written numerous outdoor and travel articles for regional and national magazines and is the author of his first novel, *The Deadly Seeker, Humanoid from the Planet Venus*. He is an accomplished photographer with scenic photos presented in his travel articles. Mr. Millspaugh has a B. A. degree in Technical Communications from a California University. Born in the woods in the State of Idaho, he lived and worked in the logging industry, farming community, and ranch country before military service.

Mr. Millspaugh served four years in the U. S. Navy during the Korean War as Petty Officer Electronics. Following the war, he worked 35 years for Douglas Aircraft and Northrop Corporation as an electronic technician, a test equipment designer, and an engineering administrator. During that time, he spent many weekends with his wife and family in the desert and mountains of California, Nevada, and Arizona researching and photographing for his articles.

Mr. Millspaugh walked and hiked the red rock hills and canyons of Arizona. He stood on the recognized vortex sites, walked the meditation trails, and visited shops specializing in healing crystals. He also visited the cliff dwellings sites where ancient Indians mysteriously disappeared.

Following retirement, he traveled the United States with his wife, Barbara, in their motorhome. Presently, he is writing a sequel to *The Deadly Seeker*.

# 1

## SOUTH OF SEDONA

The small red Volvo hummed quietly as it sped along the desert highway in the evening darkness. *I can't believe how peaceful I feel right now,* Neanna Miller thought. *No obligations, I'm free.* She pushed the threads of blonde hair away from her left eye and glanced toward the sky. The full moon sat just on the eastern horizon.

Ahead, she noticed a large strange rock formation . . . a solid black image thrusting up from the valley floor in the dimly lit night sky.

*Odd shape,* Neanna thought, as she closed on the huge monolith resembling a giant bell sitting on a broad pedestal. Now, it was almost opposite her, coming between the speeding Volvo sedan and the deep yellow moon.

*You sure look like a bell,* she said to herself. *I wonder if you have some symbolic name, maybe an ancient Indian one.*

The dark silhouette now stood directly between her and the shining moon. Suddenly, a brilliant orange glow encompassed the unusual formation. "Wow!" Neanna shouted aloud. "Would you look at that!"

Then, just as suddenly, her eyes riveted to the stone shape. It captured her gaze and wouldn't let go. Her slim fingers gripped the wheel, trying to turn the out of control car, but the red Volvo shot off the road, out into the obscure desert valley. Dust and gravel filled the air behind and around the vehicle as it rocketed at full speed toward the luminescent bell-shaped rock.

The car with Neanna's hands frozen to the steering wheel and her foot pressing the accelerator to the floor plunged across the barren valley, through a dry creek bed, and up the talus slope toward the gleaming sandstone formation. Neanna stared in disbelief as the huge stone wall filled her vision. Her eyes, wide open, locked on the tall formation. She felt her heart beat quicken. The noise pounded in her ears. She struggled to breathe, gasping. Short gulps filled her mouth as she pulled air into her panting lungs.

Within seconds, the rear wheels began to lose traction as the tires dug into the desert sand. They screamed and sank deeper until the car could no longer turn the buried wheels, then the engine stalled and died.

As the Volvo careened over the dry creek bed, the seat belt held, but the jolt slammed the side of Neanna's head into the driver's window. The blow on the temple woke her from the trance. For a moment, she sat stunned, sucking in volumes of air.

With trembling and sweating hands, she gently touched her head. Slivers of pain shot upward from the battered flesh. "My God, what happened, what happened?" she moaned. "I know I didn't fall asleep. I could see everything."

Somewhere out of the darkness a shadow fell across the car. She jumped, her body tensed, and her eyes scanned the inky blackness outside. Then something tapped on her window, and a light shone inside.

"Who's out there?"

Someone struggled to open the door, but the lock would not let the intruder inside. As her head cleared, she heard a voice call out, "Miss, are you all right? Can you open the door?"

"Who are you?"

The flashlight disappeared.

"We're County Sheriff deputies."

Neanna carefully pushed the door open peering into utter blackness.

The light came on again. "What happened, Miss?"

"I'm not sure," Neanna replied, holding up her hand and squinting into the glare. As her eyes adjusted, she saw the two uniformed deputies, their badges reflecting in the meager moonlight. "One minute I'm driving along minding my own business. The next, something took control of my car and I couldn't take my hands off the steering wheel. The car turned off the road and I couldn't steer it back. Then I struck my head on the window and must have blacked out for a second."

"Young lady, you're lucky we happened to be driving by." Moving the light away from her eyes, the oldest officer asked, "Are you sure you didn't fall asleep? It happens quite often out here on these lonely highways."

"I know I didn't," Neanna replied, nervously tucking strands of golden hair behind her ear. "I was aware of the whole event until I hit my head. Something took control of me, keeping my hands from turning the steering wheel and my foot locked to the gas pedal. I'm sure of it."

The younger deputy looked over at his partner. "You don't think it was, you know, Bell Rock."

"Shut up, Jorge." Gabe's thick reddish face twitched. "You don't know anything."

Neanna looked up at the young tan-faced man. "What did you say? Did you say bell rock? What about a bell rock?"

"Nothing, Miss." He lowered his eyes. "I was just talking to Gabe here."

# 2

## SEDONA

Neanna sat in the white and blue ambulance trying to convince the paramedics she was not seriously injured. By now, the throbbing pain at her temple had subsided. The smell of antiseptic filled the air from the cool liquid the medics had daubed on the side of her head. Behind the medical van, a Triple A tow truck pulled her car back onto the asphalt road. The operator started the Volvo and left it running for her.

Stepping from the ambulance, she smoothed her white cotton blouse as if removing the wrinkles. She tucked it under the thin brown belt at the waist of her soft tan slacks that outlined her slim figure and walked toward her car. "I'm really feeling much better now. I'm sure I can drive on into Sedona. I'm staying in a cabin on Schnebly Hill Road. You probably know the place?"

"Yeah, I know the cabins," Deputy Gabe answered, hitching his gun belt over a large paunch. "How did you get the name of that place?"

"From the Sedona Chamber of Commerce. Why do you ask?"

"Those cabins are generally used by local residents. You know, locals," he waved a hand. "I'd find it hard to believe that the Chamber would recommend them to an outsider."

"I don't understand. What are you trying to tell me?" Neanna slid her fingers down the persistent strings of hair that fell across her cheek, then brushed them away.

The young deputy cut in. "What he's trying to say, Miss," his white teeth shining in the moonlight, "is that most of the people living there belong to a strange group."

"Do you mean a cult?"

"No. That's too strong," Gabe replied hanging onto his belt again. "We've said too much already. Anyway, if you got the name from the Chamber, I'm sure things are okay there now. Oh, here's your driver's license. How do you pronounce your first name?"

"It's Nee-anna. Don't ask me where it came from. Something my mother dug up." She shrugged and tucked the license back in her purse. "Gentlemen, if you're through, I've got a room to catch."

"Miss," the younger man stared into Neanna's eyes. "Just watch yourself. Don't tell anyone at those cabins where you might be going or what you plan to do. Here's my card. It's Deputy Jorge Carasco. Just call if you need help – any kind of help."

Neanna's green eyes glared back into the deputy's dark pupils. "I intend to take care of myself. Thank you. All of you."

*What kind of a place is this,* she thought as she crossed the pavement to her car, kicked the dust off her brown leather shoes, stepped inside, and started north toward Sedona. She shivered slightly as an eerie chill passed through her body. *What am I getting myself into coming here?*

The County Sheriff's white patrol vehicle pulled in behind her and followed the red Volvo into the night. Stars filled the moonlit sky above them.

Neanna glanced at the lighted clock in the car's dash. *Nine o'clock. I told the cabin owner I'd be there an hour ago. I guess it doesn't really matter right now,* she thought.

She had left Los Angeles a day earlier, flown into Phoenix, rented the deep red Volvo at the airport, and started north. Kenny G's mellow sax had floated to her ears as she drove.

She had daydreamed, wondering what Michael wanted. All he had said was, "Come to Sedona. I've found something exciting. I can't describe it, Neanna. I've got to show you."

Darkness had blanketed the Arizona countryside, silhouetting cathedral like rock formations against the evening sky, as Neanna had driven toward Sedona on Highway 17. The moon had slowly crested the eastern hills as she left the highway and drove onto a narrow county road, route 179, leading into southern Sedona.

Unusual stone formations profiled their images against the moonlit sky just before the strange bell shaped structure had pulled her from the highway.

*Here I go again,* Neanna reminisced, *running away from home. You're right, Mom, you said I'd be running away the rest of my life. And how about you, Dad? How often did you stick up for me? I was somebody, you know?*

*I can't believe this. I'm twenty-eight years old and still concerned about what my parents think. They never cared what happened to me. It was always my black-haired sister, Naomi, you cared for, Mom. At least, you cared for someone. Where were you, Dad? Always dreaming about the boy you never had, or working all the time. And why did you leave each other? I don't think either of you knew.*

Neanna tightened her grip on the steering wheel and tried to brush those thoughts from her mind, but they kept coming back. *When I ditched high school to live with those hippies in the desert, I at least enjoyed some happiness even if it was hidden in the pot I smoked.*

*Why did you keep dragging me back? Why did you send the cops after me? I would have come back on my own. I was no dummy. Didn't I finish high school with a 4.0 average? Didn't I finish at the university with the same average? Pretty good, Mom, for that girl you used to slap around and say wouldn't amount to anything. But I showed you. I showed you both. And I do thank you Dad for the financial support, but on top of it all, I still went out to the desert. Then I got the Master's and the Ph.D. on my own. Paid for it myself by modeling in my spare time.*

She fingered the locks of her blonde hair, letting the tips linger down to the ends and slowly released the strands that drifted over the rose blush tinting her lightly tanned cheek.

*It was out there on the desert where I first met Michael,* she recalled. *We had some great times together before he wandered away.* Now, whatever it was, Michael's unknown discovery excited her. The thought made her smile. She had taken her three weeks vacation from the aerospace company, asked the studio where she modeled some weekends to cancel her commitments, packed her suitcase, and headed for the airport.

She stared out the windshield at the empty road ahead. *Dear God, Michael, why am I coming here. Just to be disappointed again. Why didn't I have the nerve to tell you to go to hell when you called?* She banged the steering wheel with her hand and squeezed away the tears that tried to leave her eyes.

*I do hope you're here, hope you haven't disappeared again. I so need someone to talk to. Someone just to listen.* She bit her lip as tears streaked down her face.

# 3

## MICHAEL ADAMS

In his motel room, Michael Adams hunched over a small round table. His tan field jacket lay crumpled on the bed, topped by a worn felt hat. Sweat stained the back of his short-sleeved khaki shirt, and a thin layer of red dust sprinkled it, his khaki pants, and the dark brown boots.

He gingerly folded and unfolded a large piece of paper torn from a brown bag, caressing the material as if it were a woman's silk handkerchief. As he spread the brown sheet out on the small tabletop, he hummed a little ditty from his childhood.

"I'm going to find you." He smiled, tapping his index finger at a single small spot on the paper. As he stroked the surface, he followed the delicate lines of a map drawn across the wrinkled bag.

The archeologist traced a crudely marked cliff-lined canyon, where the word RED in capital letters gleamed back at him. His finger moved along, tapping small tributaries that led off to the left and right sides of the map. As Michael moved his hand across the paper, he could feel the excitement build within him. His fingers seem to tingle as he followed the map to his destination.

To the right of the canyon, he laid the palm of his right hand over a tall rock formation labeled in small crude letters "cathedral." With his four fingers pointing up the map, he extended his thumb to the left, touching the third tributary. Just as old man Jacob had told him, somewhere up that gully and over the next ridge lay the cave. Before he died, Jacob said it contained artifacts from one of the last Spanish expeditions that came through the red mountains.

Michael's fingers trembled as he gazed at the map. He took a deep breath and let it out. "Happens every time I touch it," he muttered. He ran his hand over his long brown hair, bleached almost blonde by the sun, until he reached the thin leather lacing that tied his hair in a short ponytail.

Tomorrow he would meet Neanna and together they would locate the cave. He had rented a tan hard-top Jeep Wrangler to navigate the rugged hills that surrounded Sedona, then spent a week in the little town of tourist and artist colonies just looking over the countryside. He soon realized he needed help to find the tributaries.

At first, he had tried the local tour guide services, but they were not interested. More money could be made driving tourists than taking Michael on what they called a wild goose chase. An operator from a jeep charter service had told him that people came here all the time seeking lost treasure, but none had ever been discovered. Besides, several of the treasure hunters had disappeared and were later found dead in these desert mountains. Most perished from thirst. Some fell to their deaths. For some reason, the tour agent smiled as he spoke.

As Michael strolled from the charter service, a small fellow in bib overalls had approached him.

"I couldn't help but overhear you talking to Mac."

"Oh yeah? I didn't see you." Michael looked skeptically down at the short brown-faced man.

"Never mind. I heard, and well, I can help you. I know this country better than most." Smiling, he held up a fist twisted like a dark misshapen claw.

"Whoa," Michael stepped back. "Can you start tomorrow?"

"Certainly, my time is yours."

Still staring at the man's ugly hand, he quickly answered, "Be at the Park Motel, Room 107, at eight in the morning."

As he strolled back to his jeep, Michael shook his head thinking about the man's strange hand, then realized he hadn't asked the guy about his fee.

The archeologist folded the map and looked around the room. *I'll only show the guy a small section at a time.*

He tenderly put the brown paper in his pocket and went to bed determined to call Neanna first thing in the morning. *I shouldn't have run out on her,* he thought. *We had everything going for us and I was sure it would last forever, but then that offer to go to Utah came along. Damn, I shouldn't have gone, but I thought I could earn enough money to marry her.* He sighed as reflections of the past ran though his mind. *I guess I couldn't blame her for not following me one more time.* Reminiscing about the blonde girl, he soon fell asleep.

# 4
## SCHNEBLY CABINS

Neanna stopped the Volvo sedan, and stepped out next to the faintly lit office sign. The sign didn't blink; it simply shuddered OFF and ON, hesitating at OFF before ON once again appeared. She looked for an open or closed sign before reaching for the unusual brass door handle with a little lever on top. She pressed it with her thumb and the door creaked open.

The inside looked as dim as the moonlit doorway. She tapped the silver bell, and from somewhere, a small slightly bald man in wrinkled clothes approached the rear of the wooden counter.

"Yes, Neanna," his soft and slow voice drifted to her. "We have been expecting you."

"What?" she gulped, stepping back and covering her mouth.

The man continued, "Was the traffic from Phoenix heavy this evening? I expect it was."

"You know me?" she stammered, pulling a strand of blonde hair through her fingers.

"Why yes. You made reservations for tonight." He glanced down at an immense logbook spread across check-in desk.

"You're right, of course, I did." She relaxed assuming the last guest of the evening had already arrived. "I'm very tired. Do you have my room ready?"

"Your cabin. Yes, young lady, Number Seven," he whispered in the same slow voice. His thin white fingers handed her a large bronze key. "I realize the key looks odd, but the cabins were originally built by a rather eccentric man who had some ancient locks installed on each door. The doors themselves represented something to him. You will see."

Neanna drove her car along the row of wooden-faced cabins until she reached seven. At first glance, all the buildings appeared the same until she studied the doors, each carved with a unique design including the cabin's number. The meager moonlight prevented her from discerning the different curves and whirls carved into the thick wood.

She carried her Samsonite suitcase to the door, then inserted the large key into the bronze lock and turned the handle. *It's almost like opening a castle door,* she thought. Neanna heard the mechanism inside the lock smoothly slide and click to a new position. She pushed down on the lever above the metal handle, and the heavy door squeaked inward. Reaching along the wall, she found and flipped up the switch. A lamp near the door illuminated the room in a faint yellow glow.

"There must be another light," she muttered, setting down her suitcase and peering into the dimly lighted room. Near the table, she spied a tall reading lamp, and felt under the shade for a switch. Then, without warning, the light suddenly came on, its brightness filling the room "Oh, you're one of those," she smiled at the lamp. The plain room contained a blue quilt covered bed with spiral designs cut in the headboard, a small round table, and a single padded chair. An oval rug covered the open center of the smooth wooden floor and the faint smell of cleaning fluids drifted out the open door as she stepped in.

After closing the door, Neanna eased her tired body into the soft chair, then glanced through several brochures carefully spread on the small table's surface advising visitors what to see and do and where to eat in Sedona. She fingered through the printed matter illustrating several large restaurants, along with the local fast food places. Other pamphlets pictured art galleries displaying paintings, sculptures, pottery, photography, and works of wood. The glitter of one particular leaflet caught her eye.

"Well, what do we have here?"

The long narrow card illustrated several crystals on its face. In its center, shimmered a crystal hologram, its brilliant color transforming as she tilted the card. Glowing in the light, it glimmered from fiery red to iridescent blue, then gold and on to emerald green. The title read, *The Golden Crystal Shop, Martha's Crystals for Health and Happiness.* "Now what do you suppose that means?" she mused.

Fascinated by the changing colors, Neanna wiggled the card again, running her long thin fingers over the surface, her red nails reflecting in the light. In a small way, the hologram reminded her of some of the more sophisticated holographic telescope lenses she had been developing. They reflected the same radiant colors of the rainbow.

*I've got to go to bed,* she thought, peering at her watch, *if I'm going to meet Michael in the morning. It seems so long ago when we first met at a dig in Zzxyz, where we shared the exploration of the 50,000-year old man site in San Bernardino County. My passion for ancient Indian lore almost topped the excitement of my work as an astrophysicist.*

*I really hope this trip has some meaning for both of us. That last year at the university was the beginning of a wonderful relationship. I believed I'd finally found someone to share my dreams. Yes, Mom, I did have dreams. Why do you think I went to the desert, just to get lost? Michael, you were a dreamer, too. Always looking for that elusive treasure. Always looking over the next hill. It just might be there, you said, and I loved the excitement you brought with you. I needed that and your companionship. Too bad you were such a wanderer. But here I am following you again.* She swallowed the lump that filled her throat and wiped the tears from her eyes.

As she drifted off to sleep, somewhere in the distance her senses picked up a low auhmm, auhmm, auhmmm. And it was not the air conditioner.

# 5

## INTO THE NIGHT

Michael Adams awoke to someone pounding on the door to his room.

"Who is it?" he yelled struggling from under the heavy bedding.

"Mister. It is Tony. It is time to go."

"Go where? Go away." Michael yelled at the plain white door. "Who did you say you were?"

"It's Tony. You asked me to take you into the canyons, into the sacred lands. Now is the time to leave before it gets too hot, before the time of the devil."

"Oh yes. Well, hold on." He shook his head, trying to decipher what the man at the door had said. As Michael tossed off the blankets and pulled on his pants, he called back to the door. "Why did you say it was time to go? The time of the devil? Are you crazy?"

"No." The voice outside repeated. "When the heat comes, the devil comes with it."

"Just a second." Michael opened the door.

Tony stepped into the room. His baggy blue overalls hung on a thin frame covering a faded red shirt tucked inside. From beneath a worn straw hat, the small man's eyes flittered from one place to another around the room. The narrow mouth in his tan, weather-stained face opened. "Must be something wonderful to stay in a place like this."

The archeologist studied him irritably, pulling his long hair back into the ponytail. "I told you eight in the morning, not five-thirty, and then you tell me a cock and bull story about the devil. Besides, I have a friend to take with us."

"No. We must leave now or I don't go." Tony raised his crippled hand. "You don't know this desert. My great uncle always told us, when it gets too hot out there, strange things happen."

"Yeah, I know deserts, especially in California. It was hot there, too."

"So, are you ready." He paced the floor, shaking his odd hand.

Michael sighed. "I don't like this, but I guess Neanna will have to wait. Sit down while I get dressed."

As he pulled on his field jacket over the dusty clothes he had worn yesterday, he thought about Neanna. *What am I doing, running off without her again? If only there had been another room at this motel, she would be close to me right now and I could explain it to her.* He left a detailed note at the office desk, hoping she would understand. As Michael drove away from the motel wondering whether his mission had lost all traces of sanity, he stared into the night. Darkness covered the sky and countless stars filled the black void above them. To the north, Ursus Minor circled Polaris.

"Where are we headed?" his new companion asked nervously.

"For right now, I'm just driving," Michael evaded his question as he drove through the sleepy town just waking up.

"But friend, I thought I would be guiding you to an unknown place, but you are telling me nothing."

"I know. What did you say your name is? Tony? That's it. Well, Tony, I just want to make sure no one is following us." Then to himself, *just in case little man, you told someone you were guiding me.*

"Ah. So this is a secret place!" A wide smile broke across his deeply tanned face. "Yes, Arizona has many secret places and Sedona, she has many secret places, too."

Michael glanced repeatedly in the rear view mirror as he drove north of the town through Oak Creek Canyon. The lights of Sedona disappeared behind them and oaks lined the twisting highway along the meandering stream that rushed down from the mountains above. Near a small group of tourist cabins, he pulled off the road, slowly turning in the parking lot until he faced back the way they had come, and extinguished the lights.

"Are we close, Mister?" Tony prodded, waving his twisted hand.

The archeologist didn't answer.

The bright headlights of a car shone up the highway from Sedona flashing in the darkness. Michael waited as his heart beat increased and his chest tightened. Then the car raced passed and he released the breath he had been holding. After a few minutes, he looked over at the man sitting next to him and back down the highway. Nothing moved.

"I need to find a place lined with cliffs that might be called red or maybe the cliffs are red in color. Do you have any ideas?"

"Of course I do," he eagerly answered, shifting in his seat. "It could be Red Canyon."

Michael leaned his arms against the steering wheel and gazed back toward the highway as if trying to see through the darkness. "Is there such a rock formation near it called Cathedral?"

"Yes, there is. Cathedral Rock is a famous rock formation in Sedona . . . a sacred landmark." Then he quickly added, "I can take you to it."

"What do you mean, sacred? Like an Indian burial ground?"

"No, Mister. It was sacred before the Indians ever came. It was sacred before the people who came before the Indians came. It may have been sacred when God created the Earth."

Michael smiled over at the little man. The guy had a small gaunt face, covered by a three-day stubble of whiskers. The dirty straw hat concealed most of what little gray hair Michael could see. His clothes looked worn, but appeared to be clean. Michael reached out his hand.

"My name is Michael, Tony. I'm glad you came along."

Tony scrambled to shake, with his good hand.

"Now, Tony, let's go find Red Canyon." He slapped his guide on the shoulder.

"It's on the west side of town." He pointed with the deformed hand. "Back the way we came, Mister."

Michael wheeled the tan Wrangler out from the parking lot onto the asphalt highway back toward Sedona as a tinge of color softened the eastern sky. A frown creased his face. *I'll come back for you this afternoon, Neanna. You'll soon know the importance of this expedition.*

# 6

## SCHNEBLY CABINS

Neanna woke as her internal alarm went off at 6 a.m. *Even on vacation, I can't turn it off. I'll bet Michael is still sleeping. I'll call him after I shower.*

At 7 a.m., after walking from the bathroom in a new pair of jeans and a short sleeve light blue shirt, she called the phone number Michael had given her.

"Park Motel," a sleepy voice answered.

"I would like room 107, please."

The voice hesitated, then. "There is no answer, Ma'am. Would you like to leave a message?"

"No, I wouldn't." She could feel the butterflies tickling her stomach. "Ring it again, please. I know he's there." She pulled a strand of blonde hair across her face, twisting it as she waited.

"I have been ringing, Ma'am, but there is really no answer. A message?"

The knot tightened in her stomach as she tried to calm her voice. "No message?" she swallowed. "I'll stop by. Where are you located?"

Neanna wrote down the address and directions. She closed the cabin door behind her and as she tried to insert the key, it slipped from her fingers, bouncing off the worn step. "Michael, you better be there," she muttered as her shaking hand retrieved the key. On the way to the Park Motel, her mind questioned over and over why Michael didn't answer his phone. *He must be at the motel. The sleepy night clerk hadn't done his job. I hope.*

The bright morning sun had just climbed above the eastern horizon when Neanna in her slim fitting denims slid into the front seat of the red Volvo. Subconsciously, she gently fingered the lock of hair that draped over the slightly open collar of her shirt as she drove to the Park Motel. Before leaving the car, she glanced in the mirror, checking the smooth red lipstick caressing her lips, the faint hint of rose blush on her cheeks, and the long blonde strands cascading over her shoulders, making sure everything was perfect, and then dabbed a touch of Chanel on her neck and wrist.

"Could you ring Room 107?" she asked the desk clerk as she entered the motel lobby, "I'm looking for a Michael Adams."

"You must be Miss Neanna Miller," wheezed the stout, puffy-faced man as he stared down at her slim legs, and then gazed slowly up to the open shirt.

"Why, yes." Neanna felt the same leap in her heart she had experienced at the cabins. *Are these people psychic,* she wondered. "How do you know my name?"

"Mr. Adams left a message for you," the man puffed. "He said you would come by." His eyes rose to meet the emerald ones glaring at him and then lowered.

"But I called earlier and someone from this very motel said there was no answer from his room and no message." Neanna raised her voice. "The man sounded very dull and difficult to understand. Do you know him?" She stared directly at the obese man's round face.

"Yes, Miss. That must have been Alan. He is a slow one, if you know what I mean." The clerk handed her a note clutched in his fat sweaty hand.

Without answering, the blonde girl delicately took the note, carefully avoiding the man's touch. She walked outside before reading it.

"Neanna," the message said, "Sorry I missed you. I had to leave early before the temperature became unbearable in the desert. I'll be back late in the afternoon. I'll call. Love you, Michael."

"Damn you, Michael Adams." She cried aloud as she crumpled the note in her small tight fist. "Are you doing this to me again?" Her face reddened and her green eyes flashed as she felt the anger build. Neanna glanced around, almost expecting to see him staring back at her.

"I'll give you one more day, Michael. Do you hear me? Then I'm out of here," she shouted at the sky, squinting the tears away. "And to hell with you, too, I'm going to breakfast alone." She brushed her hand across the front of her face, feeling for that elusive hair, and stomped to the Volvo.

After slowly picking through a small Spanish omelette at the Last Coyote restaurant, she wandered through the many shops along the Sedona's main drive trying to compose herself. Just ahead, she recognized the strange sign hanging from a rusty standard above her. It read the *Golden Crystal Shop.* Neanna watched the long crystal image change colors, from a golden glow to fiery red and sapphire blue. Finally, an iridescent rainbow flashed before her eyes as she stopped in front of the red and gold weathered shop door.

*This must be the place advertised in the holographic brochure,* she thought, peering through the open doorway into the dark store. *Must be difficult to see inside because it's so bright out here.*

As she stepped across the threshold, a cold hand touched her. Neanna gasped and shook the icy fingers from her arm.

"Please come in, Miss," a faint female voice spoke from the shadowy background. "You are most welcome."

"Where are you?" she blinked. "I can't see you in the dim light."

"Your eyes will become accustomed to the interior, Miss," the speaker whispered. "I was only guiding you inside. Some visitors have missed the threshold and fallen."

As her pupils widened, Neanna first noticed points of colored light flickering throughout the room. Then, her eyes adjusted to the hundreds of colorful crystals hanging from the ceiling and along the walls of the small shop. More crystals covered tables and counters . . . some shaped like spheres, long hexagons, and ovals, others cut like diamonds with many facets. She stared in wonderment at the sight.

"Welcome to my small shop," the clerk's soft slow voice spoke again. "Please come in and look around."

Neanna turned toward the sound. She saw a small chubby woman dressed in a pale blue gown with the hood of a thin silky cape covering her head. The cloak hung down between her narrow shoulders, and beneath the cowl, tiny round dark eyes peered out of a little plump face.

"I saw your brochure at the cabin where I'm staying." She tried to smile. "The hologram was very beautiful and attractive."

A tiny dimple appeared on each side of the pudgy face as the woman smiled. "Thank you, Miss. What can I help you with? Would you be interested in buying a crystal, or perhaps you would be curious enough to learn about their magical powers?" The shopkeeper's face tightened slightly and her voice raised several tones higher.

"I've heard something about the healing force of crystals," Neanna's voice calmed, "but I've always assumed it was a myth." She looked down and slid her hand along the translucent surface of a quartz gem lying on a display table.

The tubby little woman spoke more rapidly. "Not a myth at all, Miss. They have been used for centuries, no, more than centuries, for healing and spiritual guidance."

Neanna lifted her fingers from the crystal and turned to face the store clerk. "I had no idea," she said, wondering what had led her into the unusual shop, "but it does sound fascinating. Perhaps you could tell me more."

"Let me show you," the shopkeeper said, excitement rising in her voice and her eyes flashing from side to side as she led Neanna to a small room. "Please make yourself comfortable. This chair will rest your body and ease your mind as I explain the power of the crystal." Her words tumbled out quickly as she motioned for the blonde girl to sit down.

*Why am I doing this?* Neanna eased herself into the velvet-covered lounge. *Then again, I might as well kill some time here. Michael's doing his own thing.* She instinctively brushed away the strands of hair from her left cheek, allowing the locks to caress her fingers.

"You will soon know, Miss," the rapid-fire monotone continued as if she read Neanna's mind. The small woman reached her chubby hand behind her and pulled a black velvet curtain between them and the open floor of the crystal shop.

Neanna shivered as she stared into the faint light once again.

# 7

## THE CULT

    Two men, dressed in street clothes, strode to the door of Schnebly Cabin Number Five. The taller of the two inserted a large bronze key into the lock and twisted it slowly, listening to the ancient mechanism squeaking as it moved to the unlock position. The man then pushed down on the lever above the corroded bronze handle and allowed the door to creak inward. Their shadows passed over several spiral figures carved into the surface of the wooden door as they entered.

    At one time this room had been the residence of John Oliver, the original owner of Schnebly Cabins. Now, black paint covered a portion of each wall upward from the floor. From there, the color blended to a cold blue and then a pale azure tint that spread across the ceiling. Here and there, white painted spirals like tiny whirlwinds led up from the black walls into the blue above. Little stickmen figures appeared inside some of the twisting helixes.

*Gateway to Another Dimension*

The pair moved to a tall cabinet, opened the wooden doors and selected blue hooded robes. They pulled them over their street clothes in a quiet manner, crossed the room toward a square platform raised four inches above the floor, and sat cross-legged in the center with their arms outstretched, palms up. The wooden form was labeled Airport Mesa on all four sides, and each word terminated in a small spiral image carved into the floor.

Only silence filled the cabin. Even the stale air inside did not move. The two men sat quietly in their blue robes with darker blue spirals cresting the crown of each hood; then they began muttering a long, low chant, "auhmm, auhmm, auhmmm."

A miniature mockup of Sedona's red hills surrounded the two. A sculptured form labeled Cathedral Rock rose up four feet from the bare wooden floor. Additional plaques identified the other red stone monuments spread across the room, including the sandstone image of Bell Rock, while Gunt's Thumb and the Teapot, sculptured perfectly, stood near several tall red spires, encompassing Lizard Head Butte, Devils Bridge, and Coffee Pot Rock. The nameplates for Cathedral Rock, Bell Rock, and a place designated Boynton Canyon, ended in the same twisting spiral.

At times, the men lowered their arms, then raised them to the blue ceiling. Unseen faces beneath the hooded capes never spoke, but the incantation went on, auhm, auhm, auhmm.

The smaller one, sitting cross-legged next to the other man, spoke quietly. "When will we meet again, Brother Paul?" His sharp nose peeked from under the hood.

His tall bulky form tightly filling the robe, Brother Paul spoke in the same quiet tone as he pointed to the boarded window. "At the next full moon we should know, Brother Elias. The time is drawing nearer when the Chosen One arrives and the Ancient Ones return."

"I have been waiting so long for this event," whispered Brother Elias, bowing his head, "All my life."

"I know your anticipation." Brother Paul lowered his eyes. "I too have waited many years, but we had so much work to do. Just look at the number of members we now have."

"Brother, when will I be given the knowledge to receive the messages?"

"Soon." He glanced sideways at his compatriot, his flabby face peering out. "I am twenty-three years your senior and I only received the knowledge ten years ago. Since that time, our membership has tripled or perhaps quadrupled. Only the Keeper knows how many and where."

"I will receive the knowledge soon, Brother Paul." He bowed his head further striking his hand on his chest. "I know it in my heart."

"Brother Elias," the larger man said, "Go to the Golden Crystal Shop to feel the power of the crystals. Do this each day and it will prime you for the knowledge."

"Yes, Brother Paul."

"Now we must meditate."

Silence again returned to the cabin, except for the soft breathing of the two men and the scurrying of a golden yellow scorpion across the floor. Again, they fell into a meditative trance, auhm, auhm, auhmm.

# 8

CRYSTAL SHOP

As Neanna leaned back against the large velvet cushion, she realized the lights had dimmed and the temperature had dropped. She felt the chill reach inside her like an icy hand.

Tensing in the chair, she asked nervously. "Why have you lowered the lights? It was dark enough before I sat down."

"We need semidarkness to witness the glow of the crystal, Miss. You will see." Tiny fingers stroked her arm reassuringly.

"And it's colder in this room than when I first walked in the door." She raised her voice glancing around the small room. "I felt a cool breeze pass over me when I sat down."

"Oh no, Miss. You were used to the heat outside. In here, we are comfortable. You will see."

The chill slowly crept up Neanna's spine. She shivered. "Maybe I had better come back," the words choked in her throat. "Maybe tomorrow." She started to rise from the chair.

The pudgy-faced woman calmly motioned for her to sit and held before Neanna's eyes a long hexagon quartz gemstone pointed at each end. Light seemed to bend and twist inside the white jewel as the woman rotated it with her chubby fingers. "First let me show you just one crystal." Her voice was soft and low once again.

She passed the shimmering gem back and forth across Neanna's eyes as she repeated, "First let me show you just one crystal. Just one crystal. Just one crystal."

"Just one crystal," Neanna repeated. "Maybe I have time for just one," she answered in the same soft, slow monotone. Turning her head to see who was speaking, she reached up to touch the strand of hair that floated across her face, but forgot why she had raised her hand. Her eyes slowly closed, blocking her mind from the outside world.

"All of us are like the crystal. See." Again she held the pointed gem before Neanna's eyes. "The energy of the world lies in these quartz stones and within our bodies lie the centers of energy. Only the crystals can bring out this energy. Let me show you, Miss."

"Please tell me more," Neanna said softly, surprised that she was falling under the women's spell.

"Are you still cold?"

"No, I'm comfortable."

"Our bodies contain many force centers or energy points that we call our chakras. The first is located at the base of the spine over the sex organs." She held the narrow end against Neanna's lower abdomen. "The crystal brings the energy center alive and sends the power throughout the body. Can you feel the warmth?"

"Yes, I can," whispered Neanna.

"Leadership and independence are located at this center. The crystal will release and strengthen these factors within your being."

"Yes, I know," Neanna whispered, not sure how she knew.

The shopkeeper moved the crystal up to cover Neanna's spleen and then her navel. "These are the chakras of courage and intelligence." Next she moved it to Neanna's heart and her throat. "These are the chakras of relationship and communications. Can you feel it, Miss?"

"Yes, I can," Neanna muttered numbly.

The little woman in the blue cape raised the elongated gem into the air. "We are getting closer to the final energy point, Miss." She spoke in a slow monotone. Lowering the crystal to the center of Neanna's forehead, she carefully touched the sharp point to the girl's soft skin. "This is the chakra of intuition and clairvoyance."

The crystal glowed in a soft pink color. A puzzled look crossed the woman's face as she watched it slowly turn to a darker pink and then light crimson. The colors ran through the quartz from one pointed end to the other. Her fat little face twisted in disbelief. Her mind said release the gem, but her hand held it tight.

The light crimson shimmered into a brilliant fiery red glow that spread out to fill the tiny room where Neanna sat. The colors vibrated from the walls and bounced down from the ceiling and up from the floor. The little woman screamed as the hot crystal burned into her hand's soft flesh. She collapsed in a bundle of blue and the long pointed gem rolled from her fist and bounced across the thin carpet.

A tiny red circle appeared on Neanna's flesh. It lingered for seconds on her forehead and then grew dimmer until it disappeared.

Struggling to rise, the shopkeeper stared at the translucent quartz gem lying on the floor, then at the blisters on her right hand. She looked at Neanna, still in a meditative state, and tenderly picked up the crystal with her left hand. *I must continue*, she thought. "Miss, are you still with me?"

"Yes, I am," Neanna whispered, her eyes still closed.

The woman tightened her right hand into a fist to reduce the pain, then gingerly touched the crystal to the top of Neanna's head. She hesitated, as if waiting for something unusual to happen again. "This is the center of enlightenment and creativity. Can you feel it, Miss?"

"Yes, I can," Neanna answered as she fell into a deep sleep.

The little chubby-faced woman stared at Neanna for a moment, shaking her head. *Was the crystal successful,* she wondered? Then, holding her injured hand against her breast, she slipped out of the small room.

# 9

## THE ROAD TO RED CANYON

Michael and his silent passenger rode toward the western horizon, leaving long shadows as the sun's morning rays glowed above the red sandstone peaks. Not a single cloud broke the dark blue expanse of the sky above.

"I want to reach Red Canyon first," the archeologist said anxiously as he pushed the sweat-stained hat back from his brow. "From that point, I'll need you to guide me into the back country. You did say you know the canyon's location?"

The small man looked over at Michael, his forehead wrinkled. "Why are you so nervous now? Of course, I told you before I knew where Red Canyon is. Everyone in Sedona knows."

"I don't," Michael shot back. "So don't get smart."

"Sorry, Mister, I didn't mean it that way," Tony stammered as he squirmed in the brown leather seat. "Just drive west out of Sedona and I will show you the way. It is right off the main highway."

Michael jammed his dusty boot down on the gas pedal and the little jeep shot forward. Ahead of them, the lights of Sedona were blinking out as dawn approached. He drove directly through the small city and on toward the western side of town.

"When can you tell me the secret you carry in your heart, Mister? I will tell no one." A narrow smile creased his tanned face. "I will guide you to the place you seek like a red fox to its lair."

"For the last time, call me Michael and forget that Mister stuff." He tightened his grip on the steering wheel. "There is no secret, so I can't tell you something I don't know. It's an archaeological find I'm going to study. But, damn it," once again Michael's voice rose until he was shouting at the man who sat beside him. "I'll need your help to locate a hidden cave. That's all you need to know."

"You are filled with too much stress, Mister Michael." His calm soft voice reached across the car. "In Sedona, we have many places where you can go and release that tension." He motioned behind him.

"Is that right, Tony?" He lowered his voice slightly. A tiny smile teased his lips as a thought crossed his mind. *If I find the cave, I'll find the artifacts that old man Jacob saw, then I'll have at least one successful discovery, perhaps a grant from the university, and perhaps Neanna's faith in me.*

"Yes, my great aunt uses healing crystals to relax the body. She could help remove all the nervousness that fills your troubled soul."

"Sounds like one of your local superstitions," he chuckled.

"It is not funny, Mister. Once I injured myself when an iron jack slipped and the car crushed my hand. From my fingers to the wrist, the pain throbbed like the devil himself had jabbed a pitchfork in it, but my aunt used the crystals to heal the broken bones. She passed the glowing gem over the damaged flesh until the pain disappeared. It was gone just like that." He slapped the car dash in front of him. "She has healed many people in Sedona."

"You don't really believe that poppy cock do you, Tony?" Michael dropped his voice to a quieter tone, trying to calm the disbelief inside. "The part about crystal healing is all in your mind, you know."

"I don't understand."

"What I'm saying is that you must fully believe in the healing. You must have faith it will heal or nothing will happen."

"I know you must be skeptical, Mister Michael, but I also know my hand was healed. The medical doctor who wouldn't fix it because I had no money, said I would lose my hand or be crippled for life." He held up the brown misshapen claw of a hand and flexed the fingers in front of Michael's face. "You see, my great aunt and the crystals saved my hand."

For the moment, Michael felt sorry for the little man and his misfortune.

Most of the early morning traffic raced by him, heading into Sedona. Although the speed limit was forty-five, he pressed the accelerator until the speedometer needle hit fifty-five. Soon they were on the outskirts, and small red hills covered with a mix of chaparral and cactus in various shades of green lined both sides of the highway. Scattered on the higher slopes, clusters of pinyon pine and junipers reached skyward.

The archeologist stared into the blue above them. "You were right, Tony, it's going to be a warm day."

"It will be a hot day, Mister Michael." He waved the crooked hand. "Here, we work early in the mornings. The hot afternoons are for siestas away from the devil, my great uncle always said."

"Your relatives have an answer for everything," he laughed, "but don't worry, we'll be back early." He adjusted the dusty hat on his head as he glanced toward the man beside him. "Now, how far to the Red Canyon turn off?"

"Only a few more miles." Tony pointed down the highway. "I will show you."

# THE MYSTICAL VORTEX
## GATEWAY TO ANOTHER DIMENSION

### by Bert Millspaugh

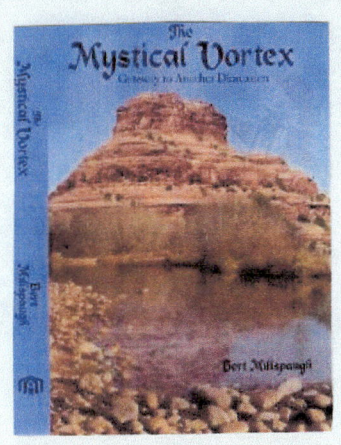

Neanna Miller drives into the sleepy red-rock artist community of Sedona to meet her treasure-hunting boyfriend only to be caught in the tentacles of a blue-robed cult seeking a way into another dimension. They claim she is the Chosen One that will give them the power to reach beyond this time. She is soon involved with believers of crystal healing, psychic meditation, and medicinal properties of mystical vortex sites. With the help of her archeologist friend and a Yavapai Indian, they discover the meaning of the revolving images glowing in the vortexes.

Bert Millspaugh has written outdoor and travel articles published in numerous regional and national magazines and he is the author of his first novel, *The Deadly Seeker, Humanoid from the Planet Venus.* He is an accomplished photographer with scenic and barn photos sold throughout Southern California and presented in his travel articles. Mr. Millspaugh has a B. A. degree in Technical Communications from a California University. He is a member of the Southern California Writer's Assn., and a graduate of the Famous Writer's School and the Writer's Digest Novel Writing School.

bnbchronicles.blogspot.com
www.bnbchronicles.com
bnbntrout@aol.com

# DEADLY SEEKER
## Humanoid from the Planet Venus

### By

### Bert Millspaugh

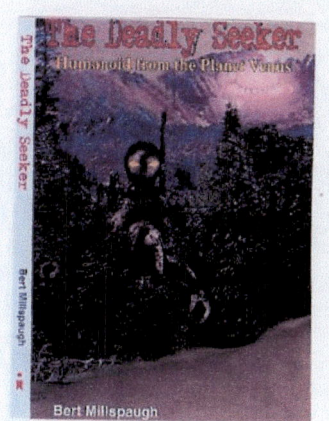

In the 1970's, a Soviet Union probe brought back a living Venusian child. Now, the Venusians want it back. They send a killing deadly seeker to find and retrieve it, but a navigational error lands the spacecraft in the Rocky Mountains. This novel takes you one step beyond the Soviet Union's landing on Venus. It takes you with rancher and ex-Army Officer Mike Jenner's fight to overcome his chronic anger and express his love for Ellen Townsend; Major John Sullivan's attempt to locate and return the Venusian child from Russia: and Mike and Ellen's battle and annihilation of the deadly seeker.

Bert Millspaugh has written many outdoor and travel articles published in numerous regional and national magazines. He is an accomplished photographer with scenic and barn photos sold throughout Southern California and presented in his travel articles. Mr. Millspaugh has a B. A. degree in Technical Communications from a California University. He is a member of the Southern California Writer's Assn., and a graduate of the Famous Writer's School and the Writer's Digest Novel Writing School.

www.deadlyseeker.com
bnbntrout@aol.com

The speed limit changed to sixty, but Michael increased the jeep's speed to sixty-five. Deep in thought about what he expected to find beyond Red Canyon, he hardly spoke to his guide. The image of the map and the treasure it held filled his mind.

After the first few miles, their car had been the only one on the highway. Suddenly, from nowhere, a large black sedan appeared behind them, slowly gaining on the jeep.

"I thought I was speeding, Tony, but that guy behind me is burning up the asphalt. He must be doing at least eighty."

Tony glanced behind them. "If he doesn't get over soon, he is going to hit us." He tightened his seat belt.

The black Lincoln Towncar pulled out as if to pass the Wrangler, then as it came alongside, Michael saw two men in the front seat, both wearing black. The thin passenger looked unsmiling at Michael and slid a finger across his scrawny throat. For a moment Michael thought how odd, until the man smiled with a mouth of uneven yellow teeth and the sedan suddenly swerved into the front fender of the jeep. A screech of metal broke the silence, as the heavier car easily shoved the Wrangler off the highway.

"Hang on Tony!" Michael yelled, gripping the wheel. The jeep plunged down into the gutter bordering the highway and out the other side into a light covering of desert brush. A large rocky outcropping appeared directly in their path. To the right of the rocky ridge, a steep drop-off plunged downward fifteen feet where a flash flood had cut through the raw desert floor. Michael made an instant decision. Risking a rollover, he yanked the steering wheel sharply to the left, back toward the highway. The tires resisted, turning as they sank deeper into the desert soil. The stone wall loomed straight ahead. Michael slammed on the brakes and with all his strength, pulled the wheel to the left.

"Come on, damn you, turn," he yelled at the car as he strained against the steering wheel.

Slowly, the jeep started to move to the left. Sweat poured down Michael's face and shoulders, soaking the back of his shirt. His tired arms ached. He glanced at the man sitting next to him.

Tony hung onto his seat belt, eyes clenched shut, and muttering prayers.

The vehicle began to slow, but Michael knew he couldn't stop it before they smashed into the rock wall. Then, suddenly, the front tires broke out of the track and swerved to the left. The jeep reared up on its left tires, tilting uneasily as he straightened the steering wheel. The Wrangler nosed back into the roadside gutter. Sand and small rocks flew up blinding the two men for a moment until the jeep jumped back on the highway. Out-of-control, it shot across the pavement, tires smoking as Michael jammed his foot on the brake pedal. The vehicle headed for the ditch on the other side.

"Come on baby, slow down," he shouted, dragging the steering wheel to the right. Finally, the tan Wrangler gradually slid to a stop, facing westward down the highway. In the far distance, the rear of the black sedan disappeared from view.

Soaked in sweat, Michael leaned back in the leather seat. He dropped his tired hands from the wheel and stared out the front window. "Damn, Tony, they did that on purpose. I don't know why the hell, but they did." He raised his arms and pounded his fists on the steering wheel. "They knew where to force us off the highway and make it look like an accident."

Tony only smiled. "Mister Michael, you were magnificent! Never in my life have I seen such driving."

Michael took off his seat belt. "I wasn't driving. I was surviving." He opened the door and stepped out. "Let's check out the jeep."

Slowly, he ran his fingers over the metal. "Just a few scratches along the left fender," he continued. "That car was so heavy it pushed us off the road like we were a kid's toy wagon. I've got some water in the ice chest. I need a cold drink. How about you?"

They were about to get back into the jeep, when Tony pointed toward the eastern sky. "Look."

The disinterested archeologist followed his gaze. "What? A few clouds."

"Look closely at them. See how they build higher and higher? Those are monsoon clouds."

Across the eastern horizon beyond Schnebly Canyon, bluish-white clouds boiled up and over the red mountain peaks. Each cloud built on the next one as they piled on top of each other in the deep blue sky.

"It's not monsoon season," Michael protested.

"Sometimes they come when there is no season. Sometimes they come when the gods are angry."

"I suppose that's your great aunt's explanation," he smiled.

"No," Tony smiled back, "it is my grandmother's belief, and she is never wrong."

"It doesn't matter, Tony." He opened the car door. "We'll be there and back before any storm hits. Let's go."

"I am only your guide, so I can just warn you. These storms strike without warning." The little man shook his head and waved his twisted hand.

They climbed back in the jeep and headed toward Michael's destination. In the distance, a small wooden sign, split through the center, appeared with a left pointing arrow.

"The turn is ahead." Tony pointed. "See, the sign tries to say Red Canyon. Turn left here, Mister."

"Tony, please, it's Michael. Just call me Michael. Back at the University, the students called me Professor Adams, but out here on an expedition, I'm just plain Michael. Okay?"

"Yes, Mister. Sorry. Yes, Michael."

Michael swung the jeep onto the partially paved road that led into a deep wide canyon. At a distance on both sides, steep red sandstone cliffs formed a vertical barrier. Ahead, the gorge narrowed until the vermilion walls rose directly above the track they followed.

"I wonder if I'll find it here?" he said quietly, patting his shirt pocket. And then more quietly, "I'd hate to die trying."

# 10
## THE CRYSTAL SHOP

The lights in the crystal shop slowly brightened, and the temperature rose a few degrees. From somewhere in the distance, a buzzer startled Neanna awake as a customer stepped into the shop. "What was that?" she cried out.

A voice beyond the black curtain spoke. "Someone has entered the shop, Miss. I will be right back."

Neanna raised her hand to her forehead. Her brow felt warm. "My God, where am I?" She quickly glanced around the semi-dark enclosure that hid her from the shopping clientele. The small room seemed to close in on her and a suffocating grip tightened around her throat. She shouted as she struggled to breathe. "Where am I?"

From out of the dim light, cold fingers touched her arm.

Neanna screamed, "Who's there?" and slapped at the strange hand.

"It is all right, Miss, you fell asleep." The soft quiet voice spoke as the small chubby woman in the blue cape pulled the black curtain away, and stood at Neanna's side. She had a white cloth wrapped around her right hand. "See. You are in my small crystal shop."

"Oh yes, I remember you. Are you quite sure I didn't fall? I can still feel the pain in my head, and besides, I never sleep during the day." She tenderly touched her forehead again.

"I am positive, Miss," a soft smile filled her face. "I was showing you some lovely crystal and you drifted into dreamland." She gently stroked Neanna's bare arm with her thick little fingers. "You looked so peaceful resting in our soft lounge chair that I could not bear to wake you."

Neanna stood and staggered unsteadily from the small enclosure into the display room. As she turned, she felt her head spin, and the crystals appeared to revolve with her. Colors flashed before her eyes until the various hues blended together. Faster and faster went the shimmering lights until they closed over Neanna's mind, but before her body crumpled to the carpet, strong hands reached out and caught her as easily as a rag doll.

"Miss, Miss," a man's deep voice penetrated her consciousness, "Are you all right?"

Neanna's weak eyes looked up into the jet-black pupils of a tall, darkly bronzed figure. She tried to speak, but lapsed back into unconsciousness.

The man carried her to a small upholstered couch on one side of the crystal shop and patted her hands. "Get me some water," the deep authoritative voice demanded. "Quick."

Someone handed him a paper cup from the cooler. The stranger wet his handkerchief and wiped Neanna's head and neck with the cool liquid. "It's time to wake up, young lady."

Neanna slowly opened her eyes, scanning the face of the man above her. "I, I must have fainted."

"Yes, Miss, you did faint." He lifted the damp handkerchief from her head. "I am grateful I was here to catch you. The floor is very hard, even carpeted."

"Thank you. I had an accident yesterday, and I may not have recovered from it." Her eyes traced the high cheekbones across his dark face to the long black hair that spread over his shoulders.

"Just rest for a few more minutes," the stranger reassured her. He placed a large hand over one of hers and squeezed gently. Neanna began to feel heat flowing from the man's hand, as the warmth moved up her arm and across her chest, radiating throughout her body.

"What did you do?" She tried to push herself up from the couch as the dizziness receded.

"You were very cold, young lady, so I added my warmth to yours." In a moment, he helped her stand. "I believe you are stronger now."

Neanna looked up into the dark eyes and collapsed against his broad chest. "Thank you. I needed someone on my side just now." A faint trickle of tears rolled down her cheeks. "It seems as if I've always needed someone." Trusting her instinct, she clung to him.

"You are a very special person. I can sense it in you."

She stepped back, her eyes transfixed on the soft smile that lightened his face. "I don't understand what has happened here, but I do feel stronger. And for some inner reason, I feel that I can trust you. What's your name?"

"First," he took her arm, "let us step outside the crystal shop, then we can talk."

"My purse." Neanna glanced anxiously around the shop. "Did you see my purse?"

The man stared down at the little pudgy-faced woman. "Where is the lady's purse?" he ordered with a sense of authority.

The pudgy-faced woman looked up at the man towering above her, then glanced around the shop. Her head slipped further back into the hood as if withdrawing into a shell like a frightened turtle, and her eyes pleaded for help, but no one spoke. "I believe she left it by the crystal display near the back room." The shopkeeper, holding her injured hand against her chest, quickly brought the purse.

Neanna looked inside for her wallet. It was there. She took out the green-rimmed sunglasses, put them on her face, and slid her fingers slowly down the errant strands of hair caressing her left cheek.

Jonathon held Neanna's arm as they stepped out into Sedona's midmorning sun, and hurried her down the street. "We could not talk in the crystal shop. It is not safe there. We must find a private place where we are alone and I can explain it to you. I believe your life is in danger, young lady."

Tourist crowds filled Sedona's sidewalks as Neanna Miller's benefactor rushed her through the throng. The midmorning sun cast shadows along the building fronts, putting small spots of darkness between narrow stretches of sunlight. The two hurried passed art galleries, antique shops, and souvenir stores. They arrived at a small outdoor restaurant where the tall stranger pulled her into a secluded corner enclosed by an artificial adobe wall. Tentacles of shade reached across the round wrought iron table as they sat down.

"Thank you for trusting me." The bronzed-skinned man spoke softly. He slid his black metal chair around to face Neanna.

*Gateway to Another Dimension*

"What did you mean?" she asked catching her breath. "I might be in danger? And who are you?" She nervously played with the long strands of blonde hair that drifted across her left eye.

"My name is Jonathon Blackeagle." He laid his hands on the table as if in a sign of friendship.

Neanna peered at the weathered face creased with lines. Her eyes followed the black shoulder-length hair down the light blue shirt tinted with turquoise, to the silver concho-laden belt around his waist. "You're Indian aren't you? I mean, Native American."

"Yes, Miss. I am Yavapai."

"Yavapai? Yes, I remember." Neanna leaned on her elbows, moving her face closer to his. "The Yavapai were originally a minor tribe living along the Colorado River until they were allowed to move inland occupying the pueblos of their ancestors. I believe they formed an alliance with the Apache when the white settlers began to take their land for farming and ranching."

"I'm surprised, Miss." A wide smile spread across his face. "You do have some knowledge about the Indians of Arizona."

"I minored in ancient Indian lore and culture at UCLA."

"Then you know the history of my ancestors."

"The Sinaqua?"

"Yes, Miss." He hesitated, then lowered his voice. "And before them, the Anasazi, The Ancient Ones."

Her eyes narrowed in puzzlement. "How could they be your ancestors? Didn't they simply disappear? Aren't they extinct?"

A young woman wearing a yellow print apron and a wide ribbon of the same color in her hair and carrying a small order pad interrupted the conversation. "Could I bring you a cool drink?" A bright smile filled her face.

Neanna hesitated, then ordered cold lemonade.

Jonathon waved the waitress away and continued. "That is what history tells us, but even more mysterious, the legends of my people tell of the existence of another world below this one. The Yavapai entered this world from the depths of what we call today Montezuma's Well, before the flood, before water filled the well."

"Now that sounds more interesting than Arizona's early man history I studied."

"I will share that story with you another time. For now, I must warn you about the danger."

"Danger?" Her fingers reached to twist the hair that blew across her face.

"Yes, of that crystal shop and the people who operate it. They are dangerous."

"What do you mean, dangerous?" Neanna repeated, releasing the blonde strands, and leaning even closer to the man across from her. She studied the lines in his face as he spoke.

"Things are not what they seem in Sedona. Several years ago, some strange people moved into town. They were secretive like those who run that crystal shop." Jonathon's face tightened. "Some members of our tribe disappeared; later, we found them associating with these people. They no longer attended tribal functions. When we questioned them, they claimed to have found a greater purpose. They believe they have found the teachings of a tribe that came before the Ancient Ones and were following that teaching."

"It sounds like a typical California cult to me." She watched the troubled expression deepen across Jonathon's face.

The big man looked across the table and held her gaze. "This movement is greater and far more dangerous than a cult, Miss." He closed his hands. "Do not go back to the crystal shop and beware of anyone who dresses like that little woman."

"Jonathon, this is unbelievable. You think for some reason they're after me. Why me?" She pulled her chair closer to the table, glancing around.

"I'm not sure, but they almost took control of you in that crystal shop just as they have some of our tribesmen."

"But I'm nothing to them. I just arrived in Sedona."

"I can't explain what I sense, but I am only asking you to beware of them."

"Thank you again for your concern, Jonathon. I'll be aware of those people," she hesitated. "By the way, I'm here from Southern California looking for a friend. His name is Michael Adams."

"Perhaps I can help you find him. Here is the address and phone number of the Indian Cultural Center." He handed her a card. "Please call or just stop by so we might share our knowledge of the past." He paused. "And your name is?"

"It's Neanna, Neanna Miller." She held out her hand to him.

"Neanna. What a beautiful name! So, what really brought you to Sedona?"

"It's a long story."

"I have some time to listen."

She toyed with the long blonde tresses that slid down her left cheek. "Like I said, I came here to meet Michael. It was probably a foolish thing to do, but I was excited to get his phone call. Perhaps I hoped to pick up where our relationship ended.' Her small mouth tightened as she gazed into the distance.

"Yes."

"Even during our days at the university, he seemed to disappear on some dig, you know the archeological kind. But then I was often lost in my own studies. After we graduated, I went to work for an aerospace firm and he was off on his discoveries. We promised to spend more time together, and sometimes we did. Those were good times," she laughed, "and I thought we were getting close."

The laughter disappeared from her voice. "Next thing I knew, he was off to Utah. About tore me apart," she hesitated, clenching her fists.

"Then I got that call to come here and suddenly I felt alive again. I got this strange inner glow like the times we stayed out in the desert. It felt good." A faint smile trickled across her face. "I couldn't wait to come here, to see Michael again.

"But when I arrived, he was gone." She sighed, shook her head. "I don't know, maybe I was partly to blame, working too many hours."

"What do your parents think about this Michael?"

"My parents? Are you kidding?" She hesitated, swallowed, and twisted her hair. "They don't care who my friends are. They don't care about me. My Mom said I would never amount to anything. She's into my sister Naomi."

"And your father?"

"Oh, Jonathon. What a question to ask." Her lip trembled. "I haven't heard from him since my PhD. I guess I'm just lonesome." She looked at Jonathon with tear filled eyes.

The big Indian grasped her small fingers and the warmth once again flowed up her arm and across her chest. "You are stronger than you think, Neanna. Come to the Cultural Center."

Before she could speak, he let her hand slip away, stepped into the shadows, and disappeared.

## 11

RED CANYON

Bluish white clouds continued to boil over the scarlet peaks on the eastern horizon, but Michael Adams never noticed. Instead, he drove the Jeep Wrangler rapidly along the canyon floor ignoring the steep, barren walls that closed in on the road. By now, the broken pavement gave way to red dirt and a large roostertail of crimson dust billowed up behind the speeding vehicle.

"Slow down just a little, Michael, and the dust will not follow us." Tony warned, motioning behind them.

Michael touched the brake lightly. "Where is Cathedral Rock from here?"

"If you wanted to go to Cathedral Rock, we are going the wrong way." He pointed with the bent fingers of his injured hand.

"I only want an answer," he grumbled. "If I wanted a comment, I'd have asked for one. And I didn't say I wanted to go there. I only want to pass it while in this canyon. Now where is Cathedral Rock?" Michael almost shouted at the little man.

"Sorry, Mister. We will see it soon as we drive deeper." Tony twisted around in his seat and looked back at the ominous cloudbank rising high above the canyon walls, then pulled his hat tighter, and stared out the windshield. A small knot of fear grew in his stomach.

Michael pressed his foot on the gas pedal. The roostertail again billowed out behind the Wrangler, now covered with the same rust colored dust that slowly seeped into the cab.

"It should not be long now," Tony coughed. "Maybe we will see Cathedral Rock around that next bend."

"You're right, Tony," he touched the brakes, "I do need to slow down."

"Michael, look behind you. The monsoon is getting closer." Black-tinged clouds loomed over the eastern cliffs of the canyon. They rolled skyward, becoming darker with each tumble. "We should return to Sedona. I can guide you another day. You do not have to pay me for this day. Okay?"

"We're not going back!" the archeologist shouted. "I've been on expeditions all over the U.S. and Canada and we never turned back. Not even for snow storms or sandstorms. And sure as hell, not for this monsoon. Do you understand?"

The little man cowered back into the seat shifting his eyes as though looking for a good place to hide and trying to ignore the lump of pain filling his tight belly. "There is no need to yell. I can hear you very plainly."

"I was just making a point." He tightened his grip on the steering wheel.

"There it is, Michael. Cathedral Rock." He aimed the brown twisted hand out the passenger window. "It's just appearing over the rim."

Michael slammed on the brakes. The dust cloud following the vehicle swarmed over it, drowning them in its fine red powder. Then it simply drifted away.

Reaching in his shirt pocket, he pulled out the wrinkled map. He studied the lines for a moment, then turned away from his passenger. Once again, he laid the palm of his right hand over Cathedral Rock, and his extended thumb touched the third tributary. He carefully folded the rough brown paper and returned the map to his breast pocket.

"I'm looking for the second tributary on our left," the archeologist lied.

"What do you mean, tributary?" His face wrinkled.

"I believe you might call it a gulch, an arroyo, or a small canyon. When the heavy rains come, water would probably run down the gully. I'll drive forward slowly and we'll both look."

Ahead to the left of the road, a smaller canyon broke off from Red Canyon. A rutted dirt track left by a four-wheeled vehicle wound its way into the wide gulch and disappeared beyond a curve in the distance.

"That must be the first tributary," Michael told Tony. "Do you know its name?"

"No. How do you know it has a name?"

"What the hell, man, if you're a guide, you should know all the names."

"I did not say I was a guide. I am just a simple man who offered to help you find your way in the desert." As he rubbed his hand across the pain in his stomach, Tony wondered, *why did I come out here with this crazy man?*

"Okay, forget the guide business. If a road goes up there, it has a name. When we get back to town, your job will be to find out the name of each tributary that runs into Red Canyon. Also, find out if there has been any mining in them."

"Why do you want to know all that?" He waved his claw-like hand, trying to remain calm.

"Never mind why. Do you want the job?"

"I will find your names, Michael. I will work for you." He sighed, tried to relax, and wondered why the pain was going away.

"Good. Now let's look for the next tributary. It should be just ahead."

*Gateway to Another Dimension*

The eastern sky darkened as the cloud mass turned from gray to black, but Michael never looked back. He turned on the headlights, pressed the accelerator, and roared down the canyon.

The road curved around a large eroded buttress that protruded into the path of the jeep and it's two passengers. Rain and wind had shaped the sandstone cliff into a medieval castle, with spires reaching skyward.

A second canyon veered away from Red Canyon on the left. Faint lines created by narrow-wheeled vehicles such as ATV's and dirt bikes, followed the small gulch into the distance.

As they passed the second tributary, Michael drove the Wrangler further into Red Canyon until the magnificent butte of Cathedral Rock slowly rose over the cliffs, reaching several thousand feet above the valley floor. The top of the butte separated into several spires, some blunt, some sharp. White limestone capped portions of the dark red sandstone structure. In the distance, a roar began to fill the air. It echoed off the red sandstone and reverberated down the canyon. Above the eastern wall, the thick billowing clouds darkened to a dreadful mass. Streams of dense black lines poured down from the clouds like a curtain pulled across the top of the rusty stone cliffs.

"I told you," Tony yelled as he made the sign of the cross. "Here comes the rain." He twisted in the seat as the knot in his stomach started growing again.

"It's just a summer storm. We'll sit it out." He glanced over and smiled at the little man.

"No! We must leave the valley now before we are trapped," Tony jabbered, his tan face paling. He squirmed in his seat and thrashed his deformed hand in desperation. *Why won't the guy listen?*

"Okay. Okay. We'll pull up on higher ground." Michael drove toward the edge of Red Canyon away from the second tributary. He maneuvered the jeep up a small rise near the cliffs and stopped.

Outside, the roar increased. Directly across from them, a wall of water poured down the second canyon, quickly covering the ATV tracks. The mud-filled stream rushed over the road Michael had followed and spread out across the valley floor. By now, the flash flood reached three feet high and surged up the slope toward the jeep and its occupants.

A sickening lump rose in Michael's throat from somewhere in his tight belly, as he stared in disbelief at the rising river of red water, filled with debris, plunged across the canyon floor toward him.

Tony tried to talk, but the words caught in his throat as he waved his twisted hand at the avalanche of mucky water racing toward them.

# 12

## STREETS OF SEDONA

Neanna remained in the small outdoor restaurant staring into the dark shadow where Jonathon Blackeagle had vanished. The sapphire sky above had disappeared behind bundles of bluish white clouds pouring across the sky from the east. The temperature slowly dropped as the clouds passed overhead. Neanna played with her cold drink and the remains of a chicken sandwich while trying mentally to resolve what had happened since she'd arrived in Sedona.

*Why am I here, Michael? I came to be with you and you're not here. It's not fair; it's just not fair.* She pushed the plate aside and glanced around. *I need you, but do you need me?* Toying with the straw, she stared into the glass looking for answers. *Besides, things are happening here that I don't understand. I feel vulnerable and I don't like the feeling.*

She turned to look beyond the cafe at the busy street, when her eyes met those of a small man with thick black hair sitting at a table near the sidewalk. He quickly averted his gaze. His companion, a large chunky-built man in a blue jacket, looked absently over Neanna's head.

*What's going on here?* flashed through her mind. She shivered. *Why are they staring at me?* Looking back at her plate, she kept one eye on the two men, when she noticed she was once again the center of their attention. This time the small man stared directly at her with a smile that crept across his whiskery face.

*Stare them down,* Neanna thought, as she looked into their faces. The straw shook in her fingers. *That's what I learned in the self-defense classes. If they know I'm onto them, they should back off.*

The two strangers rose from their seats and the chunky man bumbled through the tables toward her, easily shoving the metal chairs out of his way. The smiling one scrambled out to the street bordering the sidewalk café.

*It's time for me to leave here.* Neanna grabbed her purse and carefully strode down the crowded walkway toward the parking lot and her car.

*Don't move too fast. Stay with the crowd,* she remembered. Glancing behind her, she saw the two men following. She increased her pace; they walked faster. Ahead lay the Golden Crystal shop. Her throat tightened and pressure built inside as her heartbeat raced. *Where to go?* The stores across the highway were beyond her reach and the parking lot seemed so far away.

"Where are you, Jonathon?" she mumbled, looking around.

Just as she arrived at the crystal shop, the plump woman in the blue cape stepped out. "Welcome back, Miss."

Fingers of fear crawled up Neanna's back as she saw the little woman. She started to pass, but the pudgy-faced clerk stepped in her path. She glanced back. The chunky one closed in from the rear. Then she noticed Smiley racing across the street to block her movement in that direction. *I'm trapped.*

From somewhere inside, an inner strength emerged. *I can't believe I'm doing this.* Neanna charged directly at the little woman in blue and drove her right hand into the soft round face. The startled shopkeeper went down. Her head struck the sidewalk with a dull thud.

Neanna screamed "Fire! Fire!" *Wasn't that what she was told to do? Get the crowd's attention.*

Two beefy football player type men emerged from a nearby doorway and heard her cry. She pointed at the big man racing toward her.

"Help! That man in the blue jacket is trying to attack me. He won't leave me alone. Stop him! Stop him!"

As the beefy men wrestled with him, Neanna plunged through the crowd, past the crystal shop, and into a local new age bookstore. She hid behind a row of books and peered out at the door. *Where are they?* she wondered.

Almost immediately, Smiley slipped through the entrance. His dark eyes swept across the stacks, quickly surveying the bookstore. He glanced at the tall woman behind the counter waiting on customers, then moved to the right, hesitated and quickly raced to the left, looking down each row of books. He paused at the magazine rack to grab a periodical, then hurried to the back of the store.

As Smiley headed for the rear, Neanna streaked toward the front door. Chunky blocked her exit.

He reached out his broad hand. "We meet again, Miss. Please, come with us to the crystal shop. We have been waiting for you."

"No!" Neanna screamed. She dodged the outreached hand and wheeled to her left, where the counter blocked her. In one leap, she jumped over it, pushed the cashier aside, knocked over a cart of books, and fled back into some narrow stacks of astrological volumes. Chunky followed. He easily slammed the cashier to the floor, stumbled over the cart, righted himself, and disappeared into the store. The clerk pulled herself up and dialed 911.

As Neanna crossed the rear of the store, she saw Smiley coming toward her, his thick dark hair hung loosely over his head and eyes. The twisted smile that spread across the man's whiskery face kept getting larger as the distance between them diminished.

Gritting her teeth, Neanna never slowed her stride. Some inner instinct drove her on. She increased her speed, approaching his grinning face. From a nearby rack, she grabbed a large thin picture book and swung it in front of her. Smiley had no time to change directions. The narrow volume caught him in the throat. The sharp edge jammed his Adam's apple against his spinal column. The smile changed to a wide gaping mouth and his feet slipped beneath him as Neanna sidestepped the falling body. She dropped the book, turned, and raced back toward the store entrance.

The route to the front door appeared clear as Neanna dashed for freedom toward the opening. At the last moment, a figure suddenly filled the entryway.

Neanna collided with it.

# 13

## RED CANYON

Above the upper cliffs of Red Canyon, a mass of billowing dark clouds filled the sky. Sheets of black rain poured down over the clouded brink and the temperature dropped by twenty degrees.

Below the chasm rim, Michael Adams sat paralyzed in his Jeep Wrangler, staring at the flood of red mud and water rushing toward him. Like thick tomato soup, the flow boiled across the road he had been traveling, filling the canyon with a deafening roar.

"Do something," his companion shouted, staring wide-eyed and waving his twisted hand.

As Tony's voice broke the trance, Michael yelled back. "Let's get the hell out of here." He spun the jeep around and headed out, hugging the wall of the gorge as the water rushed toward the fleeing vehicle. An abutment ahead forced him to turn back toward the center of the canyon and into the flood. Michael could see boulders moving in the stream with a tremendous amount of debris floating on top and he faced directly into it. Then, he rounded the abutment and swung back toward the canyon wall. The flow of water had now turned and rushed in the same direction he traveled. Slowly, the distance between the water and the side of the canyon disappeared.

Ahead of them lay the first tributary and a larger river of reddish brown water and floating rubble. About ten feet lay between the immense flow and the crimson rock wall. Michael gunned the jeep, pressing the gas pedal to the floor. The ten feet shortened to eight, then five, and then three as the rushing tide of thick, muddy water hit the Wrangler broadside. Michael struggled to maintain his course, but the water slammed into the passenger side with tremendous pressure. The vehicle slewed sideways until it crashed into the side of the gorge. The metal exterior of the jeep groaned as it ground against the stone canyon wall.

Inside, the two men careened from one door to the other. Michael managed to hang onto the steering wheel and finally turned the struggling Wrangler back into the burgundy-colored stream of muck. The wall of water gushed over the wheels, the doors, and even the hood. Brush, tree limbs, and other debris slammed into the side of the vehicle jarring the occupants as mud slapped up the side, instantly painting it a mahogany red. Up from the floor, ooze seeped inside, soaking their boots in the thick syrupy gunk.

"My God," Michael moaned, "I'm going to lose it." But suddenly, the onslaught of rushing water diminished, leaving a slow moving river of sludge now rolling through the canyon. He shifted the jeep into second gear and drove slowly into the middle of the current.

"Damn, Tony, we made it! If we hadn't hit that canyon wall, we would have rolled over. We might have been under this water instead of on top of it." He reached for his felt hat resting upside down on the muddy floor.

"I told you, didn't I?" The little man frowned and rubbed his deformed hand across his forehead. He breathed a sigh, noticing the pain in his stomach was gone.

"You sure did. And I'll listen to you next time." He smiled at his companion as he carelessly plopped the burgundy stained hat on his head.

They followed the muddy stream out of Red Canyon and back onto the paved road. A trail of mud flew off the tires following them down the highway toward Sedona.

"I never thought pavement could feel so good," Michael sighed. "Let's go find Neanna."

"Who is Neanna?" Tony motioned with his crooked hand.

"You'll see, my friend," his face beamed. "You'll see."

The cloud mass drifted westward and slowly dissipated in the warm sunlight.

# 14

## STREETS OF SEDONA

Inside the new age bookstore, customers screamed, while others called for help. The cashier frantically blabbered to the 911 operator. At the rear of the store among the stacks of books, the small black haired man lay gagging on the floor, struggling to breathe, but slowly suffocating.

Neanna screamed when strong muscular arms in a tan uniform encircled her upper body. She brought her knee up, aiming for his groin, but two legs tightened on her thigh, preventing the move.

"Easy, Miss, I'm here to help you."

"Who are you?" Neanna shouted before looking into the man's face.

"Deputy Carasco."

"Thank God," Neanna sighed, grabbing the deputy and looking up into his deeply tanned face. "Thank God you're here."

"I just happened to be driving by and heard the call." His brilliant white teeth flashed behind a smile that filled his warm face. "Say, aren't you the girl we found in the car out by Bell Rock."

"Yes." She toyed with the blonde tresses that fell across her face. "You came to my rescue out there."

"So, what happened here?"

Several blue-uniformed city police officers marched into the bookstore.

"Two men attacked me, a tall heavy set one in a blue jacket and a small whiskery man with an ugly smile. The last I saw of the smiling one, he was lying on the floor in the back of the store. I hit him with a book."

One city policeman leaned out the door. "You'd better radio for an ambulance. The guy inside is in bad shape. What the hell happened to him?"

"She hit him with a book," the white teeth smiled again.

"It must have been a helluva big one. The guy can hardly breathe."

"Deputy Carasco," Neanna interrupted. "May I sit down somewhere? I'm very tired."

"Just call me Jorge, Miss," the smile never left his face. "Sure, you can sit in the SUV until I get all the details."

"A patrol car SUV?"

"Yep, sport utility vehicle. They make great police cars for the backcountry. Four-wheel drive and all."

The deputy helped Neanna into the passenger seat then hustled to the driver's side. "I'm sorry, I can't remember your name."

"It's Neanna Miller. Thanks for being there, but I think I was just about out the door when you arrived. Why would those men be after me, especially in broad daylight? You know they wanted me to go back into that crystal shop." She shivered.

"You mean the Golden Crystal?" the smile disappeared.

"Yes, that's it. Why?"

An ambulance pulled up to the front of the bookstore.

"We've had complaints about the Golden Crystal, but the people always changed their stories and wouldn't testify." He momentarily removed his beige highway patrol-style hat and wiped his brow. "Would you mind walking over there? It's just two stores down."

"I think I'm okay." She slid her hand across her left cheek searching nervously for the lengths of blonde hair. "But I've never been so scared." Her fingers twisted the light-colored strands.

The paramedics carried the small dark haired man out on a gurney and put him in the back of the ambulance. As they loaded him in, one of them remarked. "Did you see this guy? Some one gave him a karate chop right in the Adam's apple. I think the blow crushed his trachea."

Deputy Carasco looked over at Neanna. "Just a book?"

"Just a book," Neanna replied. "Let's go. I'd like you to meet that strange woman at the crystal shop."

Moments later, the deputy and Neanna stepped into the store. Crystals of all shapes and sizes decorated the shop as before. Some draped from above completely hiding the ceiling. Crystals filled cabinets lining the walls while others covered tables and counters.

The white lights in the shop passed through the prisms creating rainbows on the ceiling, on the floor, and on the walls. The colors moved in a slow hypnotic motion, mesmerizing the customers as they strolled through the store.

"Didn't I tell you the place was weird, Jorge? May I call you, Jorge? I'm not used to saying deputy."

"It's all right if I can call you Neanna?"

She smiled, then laughed. "Of course."

An older man in a dark blue business suit approached them. He had well groomed gray white hair matching his short manicured beard and deep age lines creasing his ashen face. They ran across his brow dipping at the center just above his nose. Other lines ran down his cheeks giving his face a shrunken look. Reddish purple veins faintly followed the vertical furrows down his cheeks as thin lines crinkled his lips pulling his mouth to almost a pucker. His wrinkled face seemed to pull his dark eyes back in his head and tiny red sparkles flickered in the black depth.

"May I help you, Deputy?" he asked softly, his lips hardly moving.

Jorge studied the man, blinking as he tried to make eye contact. "Yes. We would like to speak to the small woman in a blue cape who works here."

The bearded man looked at the pair with a blank face, only his eyes moved. "There is no one by that description here in the Golden Crystal. Only my assistant, David, and I work here. I have owned the shop for several years." He spoke the words in a slow high-pitched monotone.

"What do you mean, you don't know this woman?" Neanna stared at the man as her voice rose. "I must have spent an hour in this shop with her."

"Easy, Neanna," Officer Carasco grasped her arm.

"No! Look! Just a few minutes ago she tried to force me back into your shop from the street."

His cracked lips moved slightly and the cold black eyes stared at her. "There are many other crystal shops in Sedona. Perhaps you were in a different one."

As Neanna looked into those still eyes and ancient face, cold fear once again crawled up her spine like an icy spider. She took a deep breath, stepped back, and looked toward the backroom. "That woman was right there," she pointed, "just one hour ago."

"Miss, you must be mistaken."

Her gaze shifted to the deputy. "Oh, Dear God, Jorge, what's happening to me?" She covered her mouth to stifle the sob.

# 15

## SCHNEBLY CABINS

The sun had crossed the midday point and started its westward decline. A few white clouds, remnants of the monsoon, interfered with the sun's rays. In the eastern sky, the dark blue hue spread far beyond the red mountains.

The small group of clansmen had gathered in Cabin Five. They sat on the floor oblivious of the outside world. A large man in a blue cape paced between them and models of Sedona's red sandstone mountains. The clump of his heavy boots on the wooden floor echoed off the blue walls.

Suddenly, he stopped walking. "Where is the subject?" He spoke softly, but firmly looking directly at two individuals, a small pudgy woman crouching on the floor and a chunky-built man wearing a blue jacket.

Neither answered.

Brother Charles reached beneath his heavy cape and brought out a huge stick. It had been cut from a hard twisted limb of an old oak tree. A thick burl knotted one end.

He raised the club and whacked the floor in front of the little woman. Whimpering, she slithered closer to the floor, disappearing under her tiny blue cape. He then stalked over to the chunky man. Once again he raised the stick and brought it down. It struck inches from the man's foot chipping the rough wooden floorboard.

"Now, Brother John, Sister Martha, I want answers."

Brother John cowered in front of the club. A lump slid down his throat as he swallowed. "The police saved her," he whispered. "There was nothing we could do," his eyes pleaded.

"Yes," the little woman piped in, her body shaking, "the police saved her. We could do nothing."

"And where is Brother James?"

"The police took him away."

"And how was he captured?"

"It was that she-devil. She did it." Brother John gulped slowly and raised his voice. "She chopped him down like he was a rag doll." He lowered his eyes and pulled his broad chin down against his thick neck.

"She did the same to me," the little woman squeaked. "She has the energy. She does not know her own strength, but I got her with the crystal. She is marked."

"She is marked? Sister Martha, I understand you are the marked one. What is under the bandage on your hand?"

The pudgy woman slowly unwrapped her injured hand. Across the palm, the crystalline shape was burned into the flesh. She raised her limp hand to Brother Charles.

"How?" the man asked, jabbing a thick finger against the wound.

Sister Martha winced and pulled her hand away. "I was sharing the chakra with her and as usual I applied the crystal to her head. As I attempted to control her mind, the crystal became red hot. A strange light beam flashed from it and bounced around the room. I tried, but I could not release the glowing gem. It burned into my hand until I fell to the floor and jarred it loose."

"Cover your hand, Sister. I will report this to our leader. She is definitely a unique subject."

"If you had only given me time, my crystals would have brought her in."

The big man's voice softened. "Sister Martha, sometimes the crystals take too long. We wanted her now. This subject is very important. We have been waiting a long time for her."

He thrust the heavy club an inch from the chunky man's thick face. "Next time, Brother John, you will not fail."

# 16

## STREETS OF SEDONA

As Neanna Miller and Officer Carasco walked out of the Golden Crystal shop, the summer heat rose up from the sidewalk to meet them like an opened furnace door. Above their heads, the large crystal sign flickered its iridescent colors in the sunlight.

"Something is terribly wrong in that shop, Jorge. I know it. She slid her fingers down the illusive strand of hair, twisted it at the ends, and then brushed it from her eye. "That woman tried to do something to me with her crystals. I'm not sure just what. I don't remember." She wrinkled her nose at the thought.

"Are you sure it's the same shop?"

"I'm positive. I could never forget. Except," she rubbed her forehead, "I think I remember she was trying to hypnotize me, but I'm not sure." She hesitated, then shivered.

"Are you okay?"

"I don't know. I just don't know. What do you think they could have done to me?"

"I'm not sure. We've had the same complaints in the past, but we're helpless. I doubt if anyone will report this lady as missing. Not if she is involved with your attackers, but I'll check when I return to the office."

They continued walking toward Deputy Carasco's patrol vehicle.

"What about those two men who attacked me?" She nervously fidgeted with the hair behind her left ear.

"We'll question them, but they're a closed-mouth group." He glanced over at her. "They won't be talking."

"I can't believe what I've walked into." Neanna stopped and put her hand on his arm. "I need to find my friend, Michael Adams."

He nodded. "Okay, but first, let's fill out the police report regarding your complaint on the two men. It might buy us some time and with any luck, we'll catch the tall, chunky guy." The smile filled with white teeth returned. "Then, I'll drive you to your car."

"Have you ever heard of a man named Jonathon Blackeagle?"

"Jonathon?" He looked surprised. "You've met him?"

"Yes, he pulled me from the crystal shop when I fainted. He said I wasn't safe in there." The thought escaped before she could stop herself and she raised her hand to her mouth.

"Well, Jonathon was probably right." He rubbed his chin thoughtfully. "He's a respected associate of the local Nation Council. In fact, he's an influential member of the Yavapai Indian community here in Arizona."

"He was very helpful to me."

"He would be. I suggest you get some rest, Neanna. Didn't you say you were staying at the Schnebly Cabins?"

"Yes, I guess I did. The cabins are very interesting, by the way. They appear to be old, with strange carvings on the doors, almost like Indian petroglyphs. Besides, it's peaceful down there by Oak Creek."

"Notice anything else unusual or disturbing?"

"No, not really." Neanna shook her head, sat back in the patrol car, and closed her eyes. Rainbow crystals danced behind them until they stopped in the parking lot next to her red Volvo. As she pulled on the door latch to leave, he placed his hand on hers.

"Be sure to call me if anything strange occurs." Flashing his white teeth, he looked directly into her green eyes. "Even the smallest thing."

"I will," Neanna smiled her promise. "Thank you, Jorge, for being here once again." She leaned over and kissed him on the tan cheek.

# The Mystical Vortex

As an emergency code crackled heavily from his radio, the deputy picked up his microphone and answered that he was on his way. Neanna stepped out of the white patrol vehicle, and hastened to the Volvo listening to his coded response. She pulled the keys from her purse and unlocked her car as the deputy pulled away with lights flashing.

Neanna smiled and waved as Deputy Jorge Carasco drove away. Unafraid, she opened her car door and slid inside.

The deputy never heard her terrified scream.

She jerked her right arm into the air and shook it violently. The large, brown, beetle-like insects crawling on her bare skin flew through the air and smashed against the windshield. At the same instant, tiny sharp claws grasped her bare skin as they raced up her legs. Neanna screamed again.

She jumped to get away from the crawling creatures, only to slam her thighs into the steering wheel. As she fell back into the creeping mass, a pungent odor filled her nostrils.

With both hands, Neanna slapped wildly, trying to knock the insects off her legs. At the same time, she rolled to the left under the steering wheel, out the open door, and fell to the rough asphalt. The beetle-like creatures fell with her. She could no longer hear her own screams as she slapped the tiny creatures from her body and ran blindly across the parking lot. Her voice echoed from the nearby buildings, but no one came.

"My God!" she yelled, "Where did they come from?" Neanna shrieked again as she realized their tiny claws had tangled deep in the strands of her blonde hair and were now scratching her scalp. Her wildly flailing hands knocked them out and onto the dark pavement.

In the red Volvo, beetle-like insects crawled across the floor, the seats, and up the upholstered walls. They shimmered in the afternoon sun.

"Dear God!" Neanna shouted. *Why me? Why is this happening to me?* Then hysteria gave way to anger. She stomped the crawling insects into a gelatinous mass on the black asphalt. "Take that you little monsters."

Anger brought a surge of strength. She dashed back to her car, grabbed a small dust broom from the trunk, and swept the little brown creatures to the ground. The oval hard-shelled and hump-backed insects about the size of her thumb scurried away on six tiny legs. *No you don't.* The ones that crawled too slowly, she crushed under the heel of her shoe.

On the floor by the passenger seat, she noticed a gallon-sized open jar. She picked up the glass container, saw several insects still crawling inside, and heard the scraping of sharp claws on the shiny surface. At the open top of the jar, she followed a thin thread across the seat to the inside front door handle. Fear once again seeped inside. *Why? Who did this?* She shivered as a cool line of perspiration trickled down her ribs.

Neanna slowly looked around. Her eyes penetrated the shadows between the structures that lined the parking lot. Her gaze swept the roofs of the buildings and the windows that looked down into the lot. Her stare probed the street that led into the parking area and its deep shadows and doorways.

She saw no one, no one she could blame for this hideous attack.

# 17

## BACK INTO SEDONA

A slight breeze blew from the east and the temperature was rising as Michael Adams drove the mud-covered Wrangler back toward town. He turned to Tony. "Do you know where the Schnebly Cabins are?"

"Of course I do. Everyone in Sedona knows where they are. Why?"

"We're going there to meet Neanna." A warm smile drifted over his face as he caressed the muddy stubble on his chin.

"Not me." A flash of fear crossed the man's face and he squirmed in his seat. "Go, if you want to, but I am not."

"Why?" Michael threw him a curious look. "Are you actually afraid to go there?"

"No, I am not afraid." Tony grasped his crippled hand gently and held it close to his chest. "I just do not want to go anywhere near those cabins."

"Then what?" He leaned toward the little man and creases wrinkled his forehead. "What's the problem?"

"It is an evil, dangerous place," he shivered. "When people go to those cabins, strange things happen. Some just disappear and we never see them again."

A scattering of houses and shops appeared on both sides of the highway as they approached the little red rock town. Small brush-covered crimson hills interspersed the homes and small businesses as the Jeep Wrangler raced past.

Michael slowed as the speed limit dropped. Above them, a few puffy white clouds dotted the deep blue sky.

"Okay, Tony, which way to those cabins?" He slid his dust-covered hat over the light brown ponytail on the back of his head. "I need to see if I can get a lead on Neanna from the manager."

"Turn south on 179 when we reach town. I will point you in the right direction, but as I told you, I do not want to go there."

"Tell me about Schnebly Cabins? Who runs them?"

"The people are very weird, Michael." Tony again clutched his twisted hand closer. "They operate like a clan. Even the local Indians do not trust them."

"What do you mean, a clan?"

"I have heard they hold strange rituals at night around certain mountains. You know, like some kind of religious cult gathering with humming and chanting." The little man waved his claw-like hand back and forth in front of him.

"Have you seen any of these gatherings?"

"No, but my wife's Uncle Joseph has. He said they gather in circles." His hand made a circular motion. "They wear long blue robes with hoods, and they look up into the black night sky and chant."

The archeologist frowned as he turned south on 179. "Well, dangerous maybe. At the very least, interesting."

"Stop here." The little man clutched the seat as if to stop the car, his tan face paling. "The cabins are down the far lane on the left along the creek."

Wrinkles once again creased his face as he stopped the car. "What're you really afraid of, Tony?"

"I have heard that some of the people who disappear show up at night with the clan. They seem to be in a daze."

"A daze? Come on."

"Yes, and I am not going to be one of them." He fidgeted with the door handle as if to leap from the Wrangler.

"Sounds more like a superstition to me. Do they own the cabins?"

"I do not know who owns the cabins now, but my uncle says they were built years ago by a strange man." He moved his crippled hand around his face as if to draw a picture of the mysterious person.

Grabbing the swinging hand, Michael continued his questioning. "What else did he tell you about this man, Tony?"

"He said the man appeared from nowhere. One day he was not here and the next day here he was. He wandered around Sedona for several days just looking, he never spoke to anyone. Then, he hired men to build the cabins from his plans. Most of the wood came from trees close to the sacred places. He had strange metal locks shipped in from a place unknown even to the Postmaster."

"So, he's just some eccentric old bird who liked to build cabins. That's no reason to be afraid of the place. What happened to him?"

"My uncle said one day the blue robes came and he ambled off with them to the mountains where the sacred places live and never returned."

"I still say it sounds like a superstition." Michael glanced at his watch. "Meet me at my motel at 6 a.m. I want to get an early start like we did today."

"I will be there, but I still believe evil lives in those cabins."

"And I want the names of all the tributaries running into Red Canyon." His jaw tightened as he stared at the man beside him.

## Gateway to Another Dimension

"You will have them, Michael. Now, take me back to the intersection where I will be safe." He held the deformed hand against his chest like a tiny child.

Michael watched as Tony slouched away from the muddy jeep in his blue bib overalls. *Strange little man,* he thought. *I wonder if he has lived here all of his life or if he came from somewhere else in Arizona, somewhere outside of Sedona.*

He started the Wrangler and drove around the nearest block past dozens of small tourist shops to backtrack to Highway 179 and the Schnebly Cabins. The next turn brought him to a large parking lot. As he drove past, Michael noticed a young woman furiously fighting with something near the front of a bright red car.

He stopped the jeep, leaped from the seat, and rushed to the woman's rescue. By the time he reached the car, the blonde girl had stopped struggling and stared across the parking lot. "Are you okay," he called.

Neanna turned. "Michael!" she shouted. "Oh, thank God, Michael."

"Neanna! Is that really you?"

"Yes, Yes. It's me." The words choked in her mouth as she rushed the short distance into his arms. "Where on earth have you been? I've been looking for you. Oh, Michael, I need you. I need your help. Oh, Dear God." She sagged in his arms.

"Slow down, Neanna." He held her to him, wrapping his arms around her quivering shoulders. "What happened?"

"Look." She showed him the beetle infested Volvo. "Look there."

"Those are cicada nymphs. They don't belong in your car. How did they get in there?"

"Right there." She pointed at the jar with the thread attached to it. "The lid was loose and when I opened the door, it pulled the jar over covering me with those horrible things. Someone did this. Someone is trying to frighten me. This place, this town is evil. I've got to leave." Her eyes flashed in desperation. "We've got to leave."

"Easy, Neanna." He reached into her hair and pulled out a struggling brown nymph, its tiny clawed feet squirming beneath his fingers.

Neanna shivered. She slapped the creature from his hand and stomped it into the pavement.

He started to put his arm around her. "I need to know what happened."

She pulled back from him. "And where have you been?" she shouted, her green eyes tightening into narrow slits. "You left me to run off to some place in Utah, just like you always do."

"It was a great opportunity." He stepped back and raised his arms. "They called me at the university. They said they had found the remains of a lost city next to a dinosaur dig."

"So, are you famous? Did you make the biggest discovery of all time?" Her voice rose. "Is the world better for what you did?"

"The find was nothing," he snapped back, his voice louder. "Nothing but an old Indian village."

"Don't yell at me, Michael Adams. You're always shouting."

He dropped his voice and reached for her. "I'm sorry. I just get excited."

Neanna stepped back, pushing away his out stretched arms. "And look at you. You're a mess. Your clothes are filthy. That old hat! The muddy boots! Who do you think you are? All you need now is a whip and a revolver." She carefully brushed the red dust from her shirt and jeans.

"For hell's sake, I've been out in the desert all day."

"Oh, a new find, or have you just been playing in that mud covered jeep?"

"Come on," he gently touched her shoulder. "Let's go some place where we can talk."

"Talk?" She beat on his chest. "Now you want to talk." She fell against him, tears creating muddy puddles on his dusty shirt. "I wanted to talk to someone while you were gone, but you weren't there. Even my parents weren't interested. I came here because I needed you, and you weren't even here when I arrived. Why? Why, Michael, why?"

He wrapped his arms around Neanna's shoulders until the tears subsided.

"Wow! She stepped back. "Can you believe I'm doing this?" She took a deep breath and wiped her face. "What I really want right now is a shot of whiskey," she sighed. "But I'll settle for a cup of black coffee."

"Are you okay to drive your car?"

"No!" She cried out and pushed back from him. "I never want to get in that car again."

Michael locked the Volvo and helped Neanna into the Wrangler. She pulled her legs up and tightly wrapped her arms around them until she cuddled into a small ball on the leather upholstery.

He slid across the bucket seat and wrapped his arm around the small bundle she had become. "I love you, Neanna. I have always loved you and I probably will love you forever."

She looked up to him. "I know. In your own way."

He pulled her close and kissed her, first on the cheek and then on the tear-filled eyelids. "If I knew anything like this would have happened, I would never have asked you to come."

The shuddering in her body began to subside. A slow stream of hot tears ran down her cheeks and spotted her shirt as Michael drove the jeep back onto Sedona's main street.

As he drove Neanna to a small pueblo-style restaurant on Sedona's outskirts, the sun dropped further in the late afternoon sky. Long shadows stretched out on the eastern side of the small town's southwestern style buildings. Within the low adobe walls surrounding the outdoor cafe, a few tables and chairs sat on red stone tiles.

The archeologist chose an isolated corner table separating them from the few guests by a tall artificial saguaro cactus. He helped Neanna into her chair, and then tossed his dusty brown hat onto the adjacent seat. Unconsciously, he pulled his sun-lightened ponytail back and tightened the leather lacing.

Neanna clutched the tan china mug tightly with both hands and drank deeply of the strong black coffee Michael had ordered. With a heavy sigh, she set the cup down and raised her eyes to meet his.

He reached a hand across the table and grasped one of hers. "Now tell me what happened."

She squeezed Michael's fingers and took a deep breath. She slowly released it, and twisting a strand of her blonde hair, told and retold what had happened since she'd arrived in Sedona. For the next hour, she went over the nighttime car accident, the crystal shop incident, the attack by two men, and the squirming insects in her car. The waitress came by several times and refilled her cup.

Her face crinkled and her eyes squinted as she fingered the blonde tresses. "Michael, one moment I was so strong and the next I was so weak." Tears drifted down her cheeks for one minute, then her jaw tightened and fighting anger filled her green eyes, only to give way to tears again.

"My God, Neanna," Michael said more than once as she talked.

Suddenly, she became very calm and looked directly at him.

"You know," the soft face hardened, "I was going to leave this place when I first met you in that parking lot, but not now. I'm going to find out what the hell is going on here." She straightened and leaned back in her chair. "No damn town is going to drive me away."

Michael stared into the fiery emerald eyes of the girl across the table. "You're going to do what?"

"I'm going to find the people who did this to me." She banged the mug on the table. "And when I find them, they will pay." Her voice rose. "Oh Dear God, they will pay."

Michael's mouth gaped open, but the words didn't come out.

# 18

## DESERT HILLTOP

The sun slid down beyond the western horizon, casting a pale reddish orange glow on the last streaks of stratus clouds in the dark sky. Above, a few bright stars sprinkled the heavens. In the east, the evening moon glowed from behind the red sandstone peaks.

Near one of the rounded hilltops, a slow procession of hooded men and women quietly wound their way past clumps of agave and prickly pear cactus then through stunted pinion pines and junipers to the summit. The marchers moved so slowly, they often appeared to stand still. A steady low humming chant, "auhm, auhm, auhm," followed the somber queue winding up the dusty trail. A small herd of dark-skinned javelina grunted out of their way.

The rising moon lightened the evening sky. It seemed to glide upward faster than the moving procession. As the bright orange orb silhouetted the sandstone monuments, the strange gathering arrived near the summit. The marchers encircled a high flat top formation until the group formed a continuous ring. The dark red sandstone structure tapered upward in a series of concentric rings like a giant beehive to a smooth level plateau on top. Suddenly the hooded men and women ceased chanting and an oppressive silence filled the mountaintop. The nocturnal animal noises ceased. The chirping insects quieted. Even the night birds disappeared from the sky.

From out of the group, a tall hooded figure emerged and made his way inside the circle of caped followers. The man looked directly into the eyes of each member, then turned and walked to the large red rock formation in the center of the hilltop. A slight feminine figure in a crimson hooded robe followed as they disappeared into the base of the stone structure and appeared again on top.

The moonlight seemed to glow around his blue robe and it sparkled off the spiral insignia on the front of his hood. Raising his hands toward the shimmering moon, he chanted heavenward. The diminutive figure in the red robe stood passively behind him.

From the group below, a low mumble rose upward, "The Keeper, the Keeper, the Keeper." The crowd repeated over and over in unison.

On the flat plateau, the man called the Keeper shouted in a high pitched voice, "Oh Ancient Ones." A hush fell over the crowd below. "Oh Ancient Ones, we seek you. We seek you tonight as did those one hundred, no, one thousand years ago. We wait for your return. We are seeking the Chosen One to give us the energy for your return. You only need to come back to receive it." The words melted into the chant.

Below, the members' voices rose in the same incantation. "We are waiting for your return." The mantra echoed back from the nearby hillside.

As the clan leader raised his arms toward the black, star-filled heavens, the glow of the moon grew brighter. It increased slowly until it wrapped the Keeper in its light.

A hush fell over the crowd below, but the robed man above them shrieked. "Keep up the chant." He raised his arms higher as if to touch the stars. "We are waiting for your return."

His robe now emanated a deep blue aura. The glow brightened until the edges of the garment tinged in an azure golden light.

From somewhere above, yet from nowhere, the followers could see a gilded shaft of light expanding to cover the entire stone plateau. The soft radiance rotated, moving slowly at first, then faster creating a gleaming vortex. The Keeper disappeared into it.

# The Mystical Vortex

The frightened crowd below once again became silent. Many of them knelt. Many prayed to the god of their childhood.

Within the golden glow, images began to appear. With each rotation of the vortex, a different group emerged. Each came from a different cultural period. The members could see Indians from the recent past, then Indians from ancient times. As the spinning glow continued, strange beings came into view. The first wore helmets and armor. The next wore thin filmy clothing with nothing over their large heads, and the final images were glowing, floating shapes with no definite form.

By now, the crowd below crouched on their knees. Some bowed to the ground. Some stared at the rotating luminescence with mouths hanging open. A deathly silence filled them all. The stillness absorbed the hilltop and flowed down the mountain.

Below Sedona's star-filled sky, the whirling golden glow slowly dissipated. The images dissolved into the light, the light evaporated into a filmy vapor, and the vapor simply vanished.

The Keeper once again appeared, the moonlight reflecting on his blue robe and the vortex symbol glowing on his hood. He resumed his stance on the dark stone plateau and extended his shaking arms toward the glowing moon. The small feminine figure in the red cape and hood was gone.

"Oh Ancient Ones, we have seen you," he called up into the depths of the night sky. "We have received the message you sent to us in the spinning vortex and we have made the sacrifice for you, but she was not the Chosen One. We will come back again. We will find the Chosen One. We will wait for you. We will wait for your return."

Below him, the mingling blue-robed crowd picked up the sorrowful incantation, as they stood, arms straining skyward. "We will wait for your return. We will wait for your return."

After several minutes, the Keeper lowered his hands, quieting the hooded congregation. Disappearing from the towering formation, he suddenly reappeared among those below, where he walked inside the circle, staring into the eyes of each follower. Some gasped in awe . . . others bowed their heads.

Their leader broke the human ring his followers created and started a slow shuffle down the dusty trail, the members silently falling in behind. The procession wound back toward the base of the red rock hilltop under the blue-green juniper trees, around the red-barked manzanita, past the prickly pear cactus to the lower level. Those at the rear dragged leafy branches to erase their tracks. The Keeper continued at the front of the column, his hands tucked in his sleeves, and the distinctive red robe hanging over one arm like the trophy of a Roman conqueror.

The moon changed from orange to pale yellow and on to white as it rose above the chanting group. The rock formations of Sedona silhouetted black images against the night sky . . . a sky filled with a thousand stars.

# 19

## SCHNEBLY CABINS

The same bright stars shone on Neanna Miller and Michael Adams as they left the small adobe cafe. Cicadas made their mating chirps, and then they were silent, only to fill the trees outside the café once more with the incessant chirping. As they sat in the jeep, Michael related to Neanna his own misadventure in Red Canyon.

"It all began several months ago when I met an old retired prospector living in an abandoned mining town in Death Valley. I spent several days with him relating our desert adventures to each other. I really enjoyed listening to him and apparently he accepted my confidence because he gave me a most unusual gift."

"Another golden city." Neanna snickered.

"No, a map."

"Michael, not again," she turned and grasped his arm. "The lost city is here?"

He slowly reached in his breast pocket, withdrew the brown paper bag material and opened it tenderly before her.

"This is it, Neanna."

Creases wrinkled her forehead. "You've got to be kidding."

"It's real," he stammered.

She glanced down at his shaking hands and then up at the excitement pleading in his eyes. *I have never seen him so enthused,* she thought. "I believe you with all my heart. I would love to share this expedition with you, but right now I am very tired and would like to go to my cabin."

Disappointed, the archeologist nodded and carefully returned the map to his pocket. As they drove back toward town in his rented jeep, neither noticed the black sedan that pulled out from behind the café, following them.

"I feel a little stronger now, Michael. Let's stop and pick up my car." She twisted the errant strand of blonde hair and pushed it behind her left ear.

"Tomorrow, I'm going back to Red Canyon. I want you to go with me. I want you to share the discovery with me."

She touched his shoulder. "Right now, I'm not sure. Just help me into my car. I don't want to find it filled with bugs again."

Michael followed Neanna as she drove back to Schnebly Cabins. He peeked in the door. "Do you want me to come inside and check out the place before you go in?"

"Not tonight. I just want to go to bed. I'll be waiting to hear from you."

"I'll call you at six in the morning. If you feel up to it, we'll go together."

As he drove away, the black sedan followed in the distance.

* * *

Just as Neanna closed the door, she heard a noise in a dark corner of the room. "Who's there?"

"I must speak to you, Miss," a whispery voice drifted across the room.

Neanna jumped back slamming into the closed door. *It's happening again,* flashed through her mind. "Who are you?"

"An old friend who must speak to you, Dear. I want to help you."

Neanna reached out and touched the tall reading lamp flooding the room with light. Near the bed, she saw a bundle of drab clothing standing in the corner.

"Are you in there?" she asked, wondering why the fear had left her body as she strolled across the room.

A small wrinkled face peered out from the shadows created by a thick dark brown shawl. A little round mouth muttered, "Yes."

Neanna peered down. "Who are you?"

"I am called Theresa, The Old One. May I speak to you?"

Neanna eyes glanced over the small form from the tiny face to the floor and decided the diminutive ancient woman would be no threat. "Of course. You're just another stranger in this strange place that has been haunting me since I arrived. Just come out of the corner." She stepped aside to allow the small rag-covered lady to pass into the center of the room.

"Thank you," the feeble voice inside responded.

"Would you like to sit or do you prefer to stand?" Neanna motioned to one of the chairs by the small round table.

"I prefer to stand, but you may sit, Miss."

Neanna sat on the quilted cover at the edge of her bed, eye level to the wrinkled face. A faint laugh drifted from her smiling face. "You said you wanted to help me."

Two small gnarled hands shot out from the clothing. The little woman let the shawl slip down around her shoulders, revealing a head of long gray hair that disappeared down her back. The wrinkles that traced across her tan face helped to pucker her mouth up into a sly smile. She reached out with twisted hands toward Neanna's face.

"No, you don't," Neanna gasped. She grabbed the tiny wrists and pushed them back at the old woman.

"I'm sorry. I just wanted to touch your face. It is so soft and beautiful. Please," the black squinty eyes pleaded.

Folding her hands on her lap, Neanna asked, "First, tell me why you are here and what you want."

As the woman stared at her, Neanna felt a flash of panic and wished for Michael. "Why are you here?" she demanded.

The Old One nodded, her back bent under the weight of her age. "I have lived here for a long, long time. I have seen many things happen in Sedona; some are good, but some very bad. Sometimes, I know events are going to happen before they do. I knew you were coming, Miss."

"Oh, really, but how?"

"I will show you," the old woman's eyes pleaded. "Now, let me hold your hands." Again, she reached out, palms up.

Neanna stared at them for quite some time before she slowly took them in her own. The tiny crooked fingers disappeared inside Neanna's long slim white hands. A warm feeling crept out of the gnarled fingers and spread up Neanna's arms until the warmth centered on her breast. At first a fearful panic passed though her body. *Something is terribly wrong here,* she thought, as her mind tried to release the hands that were getting warmer. From there, the gentle heat fanned out like a spider web over her entire body. Neanna felt her eyes closing. The tiny hands slipped out of her limp fingers and she collapsed onto the bed.

The bright light behind the ancient woman went out as she slipped the shawl back on her head and disappeared into the darkness.

A loud scream jarred Neanna from a deep sleep. As she lurched straight up in bed, the shriek seemed to fill her streamside cabin. Her wide-open eyes stared into the darkened room as a cold line of fear filled her body, and a heavy lump in her stomach slowly squeezed its way up into her throat. *Oh, my God, what now?* Across the room, a thin ribbon of moonlight filtered through a narrow slit in the curtains and formed a white line on the far wall.

The scream came again, only softer.

"Who are you?" Neanna tried to whisper, pulling the quilt across her body. "Are you the little old lady?" *These cabins must be haunted,* she thought, shivering.

The scream died to a moan, a sobbing feminine moan.

Neanna called out again. "Where are you? In the room?"

The sobbing hesitated. "I'm here. Please help me."

Carefully, Neanna reached over and pulled the brass chain under the lampshade by her bed. The bright light illuminated the entire room for a second, then dimmed as Neanna's eyes adjusted. "What have you got me into, Michael Adams?" she murmured to herself.

She glanced around the empty room. "I don't see you."

"I'm here," the sobbing voice replied. "Right here. Please help me."

Cautiously, Neanna slid out of bed and slipped into her robe. Creeping toward the bathroom, she flipped the light switch, and peered in. A bare room filled her vision. "Keep talking so I can find you."

"I'm in a dark place. Look down. Look down. I hear your voice above me."

"I don't understand. I'm standing on the cabin floor. There is no down. There is nowhere."

"Please, I'm down here," the voice sobbed. "Please find me before they do."

Neanna stared at the wooden floor. Narrow boards ran the length of the room, interspersed by grooves where one board joined another. A colorful woven Indian rug covered a small area in the center of the floor.

Neanna rushed toward the carpet and yanked it aside. The worn floorboards stared back at her.

She knelt down and knocked on the wood.

"I hear you knocking," the voice cried. "I'm over here."

Neanna crawled over and knocked toward the bed.

"No, over here."

She knocked again toward the front door.

"Yes, yes. You're getting closer."

She tapped closer to the door.

"No, no. You passed me."

*This is crazy,* Neanna thought, moving toward the wall and tapping again.

"Yes, yes. I hear you on top of me. Please help."

Neanna slid her hands over the wooden boards searching for some crack or opening.

"Please help me," the voice pleaded.

Suddenly, Neanna stood up. "No. No I won't. It's you again, from the crystal shop. If you're trying to frighten me, I won't play your game. Go to hell," she yelled down at the floor. "Just go to hell."

The voice from below became silent.

# 20
## INDIAN CULTURAL CENTER

At 6 a.m., without any more sleep, Neanna dialed Michael's number. "Pick me up as soon as possible. I have some things to do before we go looking for lost treasure."

"I'll be there in half an hour. We may lose a day of searching, but right now you're more important."

Neanna waited outside her cabin, shivering as the cicadas burst into their ceaseless chirping. She pulled her denim jacket closer around her body to ward off the early morning chill and to put the memory of the cicada nymphs from her mind. In the east, the sky glowed pink and rose, waiting for the sun to appear.

She watched the Jeep Wrangler swing down the lane, then turn toward her cabin. Her archeologist friend opened the door.

"Good morning, Michael." She stepped inside, leaned over, and kissed him. "I'm surprised you came. I love you for that."

*The Mystical Vortex*

"I'd rather you loved me, just for me."

"I know," she nodded, fingering the wandering thread of hair that touched her cheek. "First, let's get some breakfast while I tell you a story about a little old lady who visited me just after you left last night. And you should have heard the screams in that cabin that woke me up not long after midnight. You won't believe any of it, but I'll tell you anyway. I think I've rented a haunted house."

"Whoa. What are you trying to tell me? I can't believe you didn't call last night. What were you thinking, Neanna?"

"I'll tell you when we get to the restaurant." She grabbed Michael's arm, smiled, and pulled him to her. "Afterwards, I want to go to the Indian Cultural Center, so you can meet Jonathon Blackeagle."

"Your Indian friend?"

"Yes. You'll like him. He may tell you something about that cave you're searching for."

Michael started the jeep and soon they arrived at the café. As they finished eating, Michael said, "That was quite a story about the strange little woman. Are you sure you weren't dreaming?"

"She was as real as you are, but so strange." Neanna reached across the table to grasp Michael's hands in her long thin fingers. "I almost felt I knew her from somewhere in the past, yet she left me with the most peaceful feeling.

I still feel that way." Her green eyes sparkled as she smiled at him.

His eyes narrowed as he gently squeezed her hands. "Remember, I did ask you to let me check your room, but you put me off. If she was that real, maybe you'll meet her again."

Neanna sighed. "Oh, the woman was real, all right," she shivered. "I'll never forget those little squinty eyes. No, not really the eyes, but what was deep behind them."

"And how about the person crying?"

"I thought that was real, too, but now I'm not sure where the sound originated. This is the craziest, and at times, the most terrifying place I've ever encountered." She shook her head.

"So, do you still want to stay?"

"Definitely, I need to find some answers and I will." She sighed as her soft gaze drifted across Michael's eyes, then away.

After breakfast, they knocked on the door of the Cultural Center. The sign said it opened at 9 a.m. They were early.

The door slowly swung inward and a young woman with long black hair and a big smile greeted them.

"May I help you? We are not officially open until nine."

"I know we're early, but I met a man from here yesterday. He said if I ever needed help to come see him. His name is Jonathon Blackeagle."

"You must be Neanna," the young Indian woman said.

Neanna gulped. She put her hand over her mouth and stepped back toward Michael. "You know my name?"

Brilliant white teeth flashed behind her smile. "Of course, Jonathon was very impressed by you. He told all of us." She opened the door wider.

"It seems as if everyone in this town knows me and I don't know anyone." She lowered her hand.

"My name is Laura, Laura Running Deer, and now you know me. Who's your friend?"

"I'm sorry. Laura, this is Michael Adams."

"Jonathon is here. I'm sure he'll be pleased to see you once again."

"You said your name is Laura Running Deer." A frown wrinkled Neanna's forehead. "Isn't that more of a Plain's Indian name?"

"Yes, our original surnames were taken away when our people were sent to the reservation and the Indian schools. I chose this name because it sounds more native. My real name is Martinez."

"And Jonathon?"

"I think he chose Blackeagle because it sounded romantic and appeals to the tourists. His real ancestral name is almost

## Gateway to Another Dimension

impossible to pronounce in English. Even today's Yavapai have difficulty saying it."

"Thank you," Neanna nodded.

Laura smiled, flashing the white teeth once more. "Please come inside."

They followed her into a large room filled with history of the local Indians from the time of the Ancient Ones in the past and on to the present. As the two paced along, they studied the various exhibits.

Neanna ran her hands over the displays of the ancient tribe as if to absorb their lives into hers. As she touched the artifacts, her intuition hinted that someone or something had lived here even before the Ancient Ones.

"This is amazing, Neanna. This exhibit is better than the one at the State University, and I've never heard of it." Michael gently ran his fingers over the ancient baskets, pottery, reed sandals, and many other antiquities.

"We believe it is a sacred exhibit," Laura explained. "We have preserved it for the people of the tribe. The spiritual leaders come here often for inner growth and strength and of course the visitors enjoy it."

"I can feel it," Neanna murmured, caressing each relic. "I can sense the holiness of this place and the people who lived here and used each piece. Can you feel it, Michael?"

"No. It just reminds me of a museum, but I'm intrigued with the items exhibited here. I'd give anything to run a carbon date test on some of these. I can't imagine how old they are."

"Many of the items here have been passed down through the generations," Laura explained. "Tribal members in other states have returned artifacts they rescued during the destructive period. Others claimed their ancestors brought them from this region hundreds of years ago."

"I would love to spend more time here, but first I need to see Jonathon. Where is he?"

"I'm right behind you, Neanna." His deep voice resonated through the room. "It's good to meet again."

Neanna felt a strange warmth move inside and a peaceful calm fill her body.

# 21

## DESERT HILLTOP

At the base of a hill sparsely covered with trees and peaked by a round rocky plateau, several city police cars and a paramedic vehicle were parked in a wide spot just off the narrow paved road. A small procession of uniformed men worked their way up to the rocky formation.

Ahead of the column, a sheriff's patrol SUV rumbled upward, grinding toward a camo-colored four-wheel-drive van parked just below a high flat-topped formation. The dark red sandstone structure tapered upward in a series of rings grooved in the surface by the wind and rain. Small green clumps of native brush grew out of crevices where windblown seeds had found enough moisture to germinate.

*Back Country Tours* was printed in large green letters on each side of the camouflaged vehicle. The driver leaned against the door watching the procession draw closer to the knoll. Behind him, the morning sun shone clear and bright over the eastern Sedona red rock peaks.

## The Mystical Vortex

Deputy Sheriff Jorge Carasco stopped the SUV and jumped out. His partner, Gabe Nelson, climbed out the other side.

"You the fellow that called?" Gabe asked, pulling his gun belt up and over his protruding belly.

Charlie MacKensie's grizzled face wrinkled as he spoke. "Yeah. I sent my passengers back in another tour van." He pointed down the hill. "Couldn't keep 'em out here. Going to be hotter'n hell, soon."

Charlie's face was burnt dark brown by years under Arizona's relentless sun and even his old tattered brown hat didn't give him much protection.

"We heard you found a body up here," Gabe continued.

"Yep. Right up on those rocks," he motioned with his hand, then twisted his mouth as if looking for his tongue. "This is one of our tour points. You know, one of those so-called vortex sites. The superstitious like to come here, so we oblige them. One of the tourists noticed her hanging off the top."

"Where?" Jorge cut in, his white teeth flashing in the sun and his dark eyes hidden behind black-rimmed sunglasses.

"Up there. Just follow me." Charlie led them around the side of the formation. "See, there she is." He wrinkled his face again.

"My God," Gabe muttered, staring up at the woman, her head, covered with raven hair, and one arm hanging over the rocky ledge. "How'd she get there?"

"There's a tunnel inside. Goes to the flat plateau above." Charlie stuck his tongue out the side of his mouth. "We don't tell the tourists. Hell, they'd fall off the damn thing."

Gabe and Jorge found the opening at the base of the tall formation, climbed the rock stairs, and soon emerged above. Below them, they could see the other officers and paramedics surrounding the camo-painted van. Far down the opposite side, parts of Sedona appeared as a miniature village with Oak Creek flowing through it.

"She's over here, Gabe. And look at that, she's almost naked. All she's got on is a bra, panties, and sandals."

"It's a young Indian woman," the senior deputy panted trying to catch his breath. "I wonder what she's doing up here?"

"You better call the coroner, Gabe. He's going to want to see her."

"We're not going to leave her up her in this hot sun. Get the paramedics to check her over before they take her down."

Jorge yelled down at the medical crew. "Have Charlie show you the tunnel, then get up here."

"We just want you to make a quick check, Ben," Gabe told one of the paramedics. "Then get the body out of the sun. It's been up here too long already."

"We'll take her down, Gabe. The coroner will give you the cause of death. Right now, I don't see any cuts or bruises on the body, and I don't believe there are any broken limbs."

The paramedic gently touched the Indian girl's tinted flesh. "The only thing I've noticed is this small red spot on her forehead."

## 22
## INDIAN CULTURAL CENTER

The earthy smell of ancient artifacts filled the Indian Cultural Center. Tattered baskets woven from reeds and grasses, multi-colored sculptured clay pots with chipped edges, and worn buckskin clothing added their aroma to the room. A hint of incense and rough tobacco from ceremonial pipes blended with the other fragrances giving the museum a sense of authenticity.

Neanna whirled around, blonde hair swishing across her face, toward the voice behind her.

"Jonathon! I'm so glad I found you here." As excitement filled her voice, she wrapped her arms around his large frame, her body almost disappearing into his bear hug.

"I, too, am glad to see you again, Neanna." His deep brown eyes sparkled as he smiled down at her, his grin stretching across his bronze face.

She stepped away and grasped his elbow. "Jonathon," her face beamed. "I want you to meet my very dear friend, Michael Adams."

"My pleasure," his towering frame leaned forward, his huge hand engulfing Michael's. "You must be proud to be a friend of Neanna's. In only a short time, I have found closeness to her."

"Yes. She told me much about you. Thanks for rescuing her from that crystal shop." He slid his hat back, lines creasing his forehead, wondering what Jonathon meant by closeness.

"You would have done the same," his rich voice answered. "Now what can I do for you two?" He glanced from Michael to Neanna.

"We have so many questions to ask you, Jonathon," Neanna change to a serious tone. "Can we please sit and talk somewhere?" Unconsciously, she reached for the long strands of hair that fell across her left eye and nervously twisted the golden tresses.

"Yes, of course. Come to my office," he smiled. "It is far more private." He led the way through a narrow corridor of back-lit displays.

Inside the small office, ceremonial artifacts hung artistically over the walls and lay on small burlap-covered tables beneath them. Several paintings of elderly chiefs added respect to the room. As they strolled in, Neanna noticed it was an extension of the museum.

"We have little space for the massive amount of material we have to display. We use each room to help present as much of the past and present culture as possible. Our chiefs and shamans today still use spiritual objects similar to those displayed." He motioned his guests toward the several styles of handcrafted chairs. As he took a seat behind a massive carved wooden desk, his eyes questioned her.

Neanna slowly gazed about the room, studying the many displays embracing the walls. After a few silent moments, she started. "Jonathon, I had the strangest feeling as I went into the main room."

"Yes?" The Indian nodded gravely. He clasped his big hands on the leather desk cover.

Staring intently, Neanna leaned against the dark wood in front of her. "When I first came in and touched the artifacts, I could see people, no, not actually see. I saw them in my mind. She touched her slim fingers to her forehead. "What I mean, it was like all those artifacts gave me a sense of the past, the ones who used the relics and those who lived with them."

Jonathon tightened his fingers together. A knowing smile crossed his face. "Sense is objective. At times, I have had the same sensation. Please, go on."

# The Mystical Vortex

"Well, just before you came in, I stood near that heavy wooden box with the copper hinges and locks. It gave me the strangest premonition. I felt if I touched the container, it would burn my hands."

Jonathon glanced at Michael. "Did you have the same impression?"

As the archeologist glanced up, a surprised look spread over his tanned face. "No. But Neanna has always been that way. Some kind of sixth sense."

The big Indian studied her briefly. "That box contains unique and special items, but tell me why you came," he said changing the subject. Pulling his long braid to one side, he leaned back in a tall worn leather chair and clasped his hands together in front of him.

For the next hour, Neanna and Michael related their experiences since they had arrived in the small red rock community. The archeologist told of the black sedan that drove him off the highway and how he survived the flash flood. Neanna recalled to him the crystal shop, and then of her escape from the two men and finding insects in her car.

Jonathon Blackeagle listened patiently, at times nodding his dark head. When they finished, his deep voice filled the room. "You have encountered some of the strange events that have occurred in our valley. As far back in time as anyone can recall, Sedona has been known for mystical happenings. My ancestors have shared many sacred places here. Ancient rock petroglyghs and cave paintings have portrayed mysterious events that modern man has never seen and perhaps could never conceive."

He handed them an eight by ten glossy print. "This is a photo of a petroglygh that shows a stickman rising up in what looks like a spiraling whirlwind. Below him is a rough outline of a formation not much different from what we call Cathedral Rock today."

"Here is another one." He pulled out a different photograph. "It looks similar to a formation called Bell Rock. Notice the lines leading out from it almost like rays."

Neanna gasped. Grabbing her throat, she swallowed the lump that rose from her stomach.

As he watched her face pale, Michael grabbed her arm. "Are you all right?"

"That's, that's the formation. I saw that shape glowing in the moonlight the first night I arrived. That Deputy, Gabe, told Jorge Carasco to keep his mouth shut about it."

"About what?" Jonathon queried, as the softness of his pleasant face hardened.

"About Bell Rock," her voice trembled. "They obviously didn't want to talk about it."

"Did they mention the vortex?"

"Vortex? No."

"What kind of a vortex," Michael broke in, a questioning frown wrinkled his brow.

"The whirlwind design in the cave painting could represent some kind of invisible rotating energy field, a vortex. At least, that's what the followers of this fairly new cult in Sedona believe and others before them. They apparently feel they can control this energy. Even tourists come here in hopes of witnessing or receiving some supernatural experience. They often bring crystals and leave them scattered around the vortex sites."

"What proof do they have of their actual existence?" Michael asked.

"What proof do they need?" Jonathon smiled. "They believe, that's all. Some claim to be healed of various afflictions like back pain, arthritis, and stress." He leaned across the large wooden desk. "There is no written record of the vortexes in any of the known Native American collections or even the Ancient Ones, but there is a belief or legend that mystical happenings occurred here beyond the time of the Ancient Ones. The petroglyghs and the cave paintings verify this."

As her composure returned, Neanna stared at the photographs. "You know our galaxies are spirals. Maybe that tells us something."

"Yes," Michael spoke up, "and the Mayan calendar is a spiral. Perhaps they knew something we don't."

Jonathon clasped his big hands together. "I think it is time to meditate on these happenings."

Neanna thanked him and stood up to leave when suddenly the office door burst open and Laura rushed in, her face distorted and twisted in anguish. "Jonathon! Something terrible has happened." She cried in near hysteria, tears streaming down her soft cheeks.

In two long steps, the big man rushed past his visitors to grab the frantic girl. "What is it?"

"It's Nancy. She's dead." The young Indian woman sobbed into her hands.

Jonathon tenderly wrapped his arm around the heaving body. "Dead? What do you mean? What happened? Where?"

The girl's voice trembled as she looked up. "They found her body in the foothills at Airport Mesa. She was almost naked, nude except for her bra and panties. Help me, Jonathon," she pleaded, "Help me. I can't go over there by myself."

"Who told you? How did you find out?" his voice boomed.

"A call from a deputy at the coroner's office." Laura whimpered in Jonathon's arms.

"Who's Nancy?" Neanna almost whispered.

"Laura's sister. She disappeared from home and we've spent the last two months searching for her."

As Neanna put a comforting hand on the sobbing girl's shoulder, she felt a cold chill ripple through her body. Shuddering, she jumped back. "Oh my God! It was her."

"Her! What about her?" Michael interrupted.

"It was her, Laura's sister. I heard her crying last night, asking me for help."

Laura's tear-stained face reflected the grief Neanna felt throughout her suddenly tormented body.

"That's insane." Michael shook his head. "How could you know that? You told me you thought it was a dream."

"I know, but just then as I touched Laura's arm, I felt as though an icy hand had written her sister's name on my soul. Last night in my room, I heard the girl crying, pleading for help over and over. I searched my room trying to find her, but I couldn't. Oh, Jonathon, maybe if I had found her, she would be alive today."

"You have special instincts, Neanna," Jonathon spoke softly. "I knew that when I first met you. It is possible you were called to Sedona." He took Laura's hand and led the distraught girl from the room, glancing back toward his visitors.

"Please feel free to stay as long as you wish. Perhaps you will learn why you are here, Neanna. Perhaps we have a common destiny."

# 23

## KACHINA HOTEL

James Wallace opened the door to his office suite after a large breakfast at a nearby Mexican restaurant. He carefully took the small suede bag of delicate gems from his pocket and slipped it into his desk drawer. Adjusting the knot of his dark blue silk tie as if preparing for a business meeting and patting his filled stomach, he settled back in his leather chair.

"Come in," he shouted down the hall at the closed door. Wallace sat behind his walnut desk in the window room of his business suite. He occupied the corner office on the top floor as he requested to avoid conflict with other residents. Wallace ran his fingers across the lapels of the pin stripe suit he had brought from his company office in Las Vegas, Nevada, then added one more touch to the blue tie highlighted with small red diamonds.

Two men in black clothes slouched through the door, creeping into his office.

"Well," Wallace growled as he rose from his chair. "Did you get that sneaky archeologist?"

"No, we missed the guy," the thin man in the ebony leather vest slurred.

"What the hell do you mean, you missed him? I sent you on a simple mission and you screwed up?" Wallace shoved his chair back, knocking it into the wall, and stalked around his desk. His dark eyes squinted at his two hirelings.

The two men exchanged nervous glances and started backing up.

"We thought we had him, Boss," the heavy pudgy-faced man in the wrinkled silk shirt whined as his employer approached him. "We ran his car off the highway out of town near Red Rock Canyon. We had him trapped between a rocky ledge and a deep ravine. I don't know how the guy got out of it."

"Yeah, yeah," the skinny one stammered as he retreated. "We followed him back to town. He hooked up with some woman last night. Today, we saw them at that Indian Cultural Center off Highway 117. We couldn't touch him there! He was never alone"

James Wallace grabbed the blabbering man's wrinkled throat just above the collar. His thick hand almost encircled the scrawny neck. As he slowly raised his arm, stretching the thin white skin, his deep voice escalated. "I don't want him prying around out there in the canyons. I've got too much at stake in this operation to have some desert rat screwing it up. Do you hear me?"

"Yes," the man gagged through his crooked yellow teeth, his eyes bulging. "We'll get him tomorrow, Boss, for sure."

Wallace released his grip. "Damn, you're slobbering on my best suit. Where the hell did you get this idiot, Fatso?"

"He's okay, Boss. We'll get the guy tomorrow."

"You damn right you will," he spat, wiping his hand on the slim man's black shirt. "And you'll find out who this girl is, and how she fits into his plans. And what the hell they were doing at that Indian center."

"We'll do that, Boss. We'll do all of that," Fatso answered.

"You'd better, or you might find yourselves lost out there in that hot dry desert without a drink of water." Wallace ran his fingers through his jet-black hair. "And do it to him in one of those lost canyons he loves so well so these hick cops don't find his body until only the bones are left. Do you hear?" he shouted again, and reached out toward the fat one.

"Sure, Boss. Sure, we hear you," Fatso gurgled. The two men backed toward the door and raced from the room.

Wallace picked up a small radiotelephone, keyed in the number, and waited.

"Pearson here," a gruff voice spoke.

"Scarface is that you?"

"Yeah," the man answering the call choked, as his hand nervously searched for the thick scar that crossed his cheek.

"This is Wallace. How's the mining?" He sank into his brown leather chair and leaned back.

"Better than last week, Mr. Wallace. The going is slow and Christ it gets hot out here, but we're digging 'em out."

"Listen, Scarface, if for some reason the Company gets your number, you don't know anything. You tell them to call me. You hear?"

"Sure, Mr. Wallace. That's why you told us to use the radio instead of one of them fancy cell phones. You can trust me. I told you that when you hired me and the boys."

"I just want to be sure. Don't tell anyone what you're digging up or how much." His eyes swept the room, pausing at the large geological map tacked to the wall. "Tell them to call me. Got that?"

"Sure. Like I said, Mr. Wallace, you can trust us. I'm just glad the nights are cool."

"Have you seen anyone snooping around? There's an archeologist looking for something not far from you. If he shows up, just tell him you're prospecting and you haven't found anything. If that doesn't satisfy the guy, you know what steps to take."

"Sure, like we took care of that government jerk out of Vegas. Don't worry, Mr. Wallace. We'll protect the mine. Say, where did all those bright red crystals come from? It looks like some Arabian king just sprinkled the hills and buried them a thousand years ago."

"You don't need to know the details, Scarface. Just get your job done. Call me when the next shipment is ready. And tell your men I better not catch them pocketing any."

James Wallace turned off the radio before Pearson could answer. "It won't be long before I'll have more to add to my private collection," he muttered, wiping his brow and staring out the hotel window at the red hills miles away. "The Company can sell their share overseas for counterfeit rubies."

Wallace glanced up at the large illustrated mining map of Sedona and the surrounding area hanging on one wall of his office. Yellow ink from a highlighter pen encircled several areas. "Time to make that call," he said to no one, picking up the phone, and dialing a long distance number.

"We may have a problem here," he spoke rapidly into the mouthpiece. "There's some archaeologist snooping around out in the desert. He's even hired a guide."

Wallace listened intently to the person on the other end of the line. "Yes, Sir," he repeated several times. "I'm doing my best. I've sent two men to take care of him and I expect results tomorrow."

He strolled around the room with the phone to his ear. "No, Sir, no one will discover the mine. We've almost completed preliminary screening for any precious deposits. Our men are working around the clock to remove all the surface gems, then the digging will start.

"No, Sir, no one from any government agency has been spotted in those hills. It's called the Devil's Lair. Most of the locals are either too scared to go there or afraid they'll get lost in that barren desert and never return. And the Indians believe it's sacred, so they stay away. So far, we've been able to operate without any interference."

Wallace strolled back to his chair, sat down, and leaned back. "I'm concerned about the archaeologist who's been asking too many questions about the area. He's been taking trips around Sedona looking for something. The guide claims the desert rat has a map of some kind, but he's never seen it." He stretched out, listening intently.

"Yes, we expect to begin shipments very soon. You've seen the samples . . . wait until you see the latest finds. They're beautiful."

Wallace continued, glancing at the map, "No, we don't have sufficient operating cash. Could you transfer another fifty grand to my account here in Sedona right away? It's a lousy place to live. There isn't a decent hotel here like I had in Vegas and the food's rotten. It's not to my taste. If the hot stuff doesn't burn your gut when you eat it, it'll burn your butt later."

Wallace nodded absently, "Yes, I'll let you know when the guy is taken out. I'll be making the first shipment within a week. The ones below the surface will take a little longer, you understand."

He smiled at his employer's last comment and hung up the phone. He carefully reached into his desk drawer, took out a small brown leather pouch, pulled open the drawstring, and dumped the contents into his hand. As the sparkling red gems spilled out of the bag, Wallace rolled them in his hand, caressing each one.

"One for you, one for me," he said with a strange smile.

## 24

CORORNER'S OFFICE

As Jonathon Blackeagle and Laura Running Deer raced from the reservation along the twisting highway to the Coroner's Office in Sedona, the noonday sun retreated westward in a clear blue sky. Red hills filled the sides of the winding road covered with an array of pinion pines and juniper trees interspersed with yucca and manzanita and separated by dry gullies that flowed under the pavement and down the other side. A red tailed hawk glided high across the highway in the deep azure sky, but they didn't notice. Deputy Jorge Carasco met them at the door of the adobe front building.

"Where's my sister?" Laura demanded.

"Easy, Laura." Jonathon grabbed her arm. "Give the deputy a chance."

"First, please sit down, both of you." Jorge pointed at the wooden armchairs along one wall. "I need some questions answered before we see her. She has already been identified, so you won't have to see the body unless you really want to."

"What happened to her," Jonathon cut in. "Where did you find her?" He helped Laura into one of the chairs and squeezed into one beside her.

"Yes. How did she die?" Laura pleaded, squirming in her chair.

"Please bear with me." The deputy pulled a chair up in front of them. "I need to go over some facts. When did you last see your sister, Laura? May I call you Laura?"

"Of course," Laura tried to smile. "We haven't seen Nancy for nearly two months." She twisted her hands, blinking back the tears. "In fact, we reported her missing to the police, but the man wouldn't listen. The officer said she had to be missing forty-eight hours before you would do anything. After that we tried to find her ourselves." She gazed down at the floor.

"You must have reported her disappearance to the city police, Laura. We are County Sheriff, however we do have the same forty eight-hour policy. Did you go back to the police?"

Laura looked up slowly, touching the tears that trickled down her cheek. "No. We asked them for help once and they refused. Why go back? My father was too proud to ask again. He said the tribe would find her."

"Did they?" Jorge asked as he fumbled for his handkerchief, handing it to her.

"No." Laura took the cloth, daubing at her eyes, trying to choke back the tears. "But we believe she was taken by that strange cult that chants in the night."

"Ah, yes," he nodded. "Do you have any evidence?"

"Several of our tribe have been lured into that bizarre group." Jonathon's irritated voice echoed across the room. "Some have stayed. Some have returned with empty minds. They just stare into space, especially at night. They could never provide evidence."

"Holy Jesus, man! How long has this been going on?" he exploded.

"Almost a year." Jonathon looked distraught. "The council has just recently been investigating it, but they believe it is beyond the tribal police authority. We think the civil officers are ignoring the problem. Surely others in town know of their activities."

Deputy Carasco cleared his throat, his eyes snapping away from Jonathon as he focused on the cold image of the Indian girl's lifeless body. "You can be sure the Sheriff's department will check into this immediately." He spoke directly to Laura, a sympathetic expression filling his face.

"Now, how did my sister die?" She gazed into the deputy's dark compassionate eyes searching for some meaning to such a senseless death. "Can you tell me?"

"We still don't have the full autopsy report. There were no marks on her body, except for a bright red spot on the center of her forehead. Do you have any idea what might have caused the coloration, you know, like a religious symbol?"

She shook her head, "Oh, Jonathon, we haven't found anything here and I've got to tell my father. Will you come with me?"

"Of course. We will discuss this with the tribal council."

Ignoring the deputy's outstretched hand, they stepped out into Sedona's bright sunlight toward Jonathon's van.

The heat did not warm the chill in Laura's heart.

As they left the coroner's office, Laura raised her tear filled eyes to Jonathon. "Why did this happen to Nancy? We used to be so close and shared our lives with each other almost every day until she disappeared. I don't recall her ever mentioning her involvement with any group or special organization."

"That's the way some cults work. They convince new members to keep silent until they have been brain washed enough to take control of their minds."

As the two slipped into the white minivan with Indian Cultural Center printed on the sides, a large black sedan pulled around from the back of the building. The passenger window inched down allowing the lens of a pair of binoculars to clear the opening. The optics focused intently on them as the car sped away.

Oblivious to the spy, Jonathon drove out onto the main highway heading toward the Indian Reservation several miles to the south where Laura's father lived. Lost in the silence of their own thoughts, neither of them noticed the black sedan had circled the block and now followed them out of town.

Jonathon squinted into the afternoon sun as they passed Bell Rock, an immense red mound, thrusting hundreds of feet up into the cloud-dotted blue sky.

"Jonathon," Laura wrung her hands together as if to twist some answers from them. "You have to help us find the people who killed Nancy. We have no where to turn. I know my father won't go to the police."

"Laura, believe me, we will find those responsible and bring them to justice." He stared down the highway, deep in thought. "Recently, strange things have been happening around Sedona. I believe our ancestors are getting restless. Their passing is being disturbed."

"What do you mean, Jonathon? You're talking in riddles."

"It is something I feel. I don't know where the feeling is coming from, but it is here inside me." He tapped his chest. "It is as if the Ancient Ones are talking to me."

"That's not hard to believe. I've often felt a strange sensation when I'm near you." She leaned back in the van seat, trying to relax.

"That girl, Neanna, had the same perception regarding the ancients. I know she did when she touched the artifacts. I could feel it coming from her."

Jonathon turned off the highway at the Indian Cultural Center onto a gravel road leading into the reservation. Ahead, the houses in the small community were a conglomeration of identical government-built homes lining a few narrow streets. Jonathon drove past the social services center and stopped the van at Laura's house. They rushed up the sidewalk that separated the thin lawn and both went inside.

Jonathon spoke briefly with Laura's father and then went directly outside to the large ceremonial building belonging to the tribal council and stepped through the door. Ritualistic articles lined the walls of the circular room. Above, a conical roof reached upward.

Inside, he started a small fire at the sandy center, then from a small buckskin pouch, he poured a few grains of reddish-blue granules on the flames. Colored wisps of smoke swirled up, filling the room with its pungent fragrance.

Jonathon disappeared within the dense cloud as he began to repeat the incantation of his ancient ancestors. Over and over, he chanted the words until the cloud thinned and drifted away. For several minutes, he sat in a trance, then looked up through the circular smoke vent in the top of the room. Raising his hands, arms outstretched, he prayed to some deity of his past. Lowering his arms, he quickly smothered the fire, and strode out of the building.

    Long strides carried the tall Indian back to Laura's house. "It is time for me to go," his deep voice announced at the door. "I will see you tomorrow. We have important work to accomplish." He turned and drove toward the Cultural Center.

# 25

## STREETS OF SEDONA

That evening, Neanna and Michael sat quietly in a small southwestern café. A gentle breeze blew the sweet aroma of desert blossoms across the patio.

The blonde haired girl put down her wineglass and looked across the table. "Michael, as we walked through that Cultural Center, I sensed the answer you're looking for is somewhere in that museum. I'm sure of it."

"It may be," he shrugged, "but I believe the place I'm searching for is somewhere beyond Red Canyon. I need to go there tomorrow. I want you; I need you to come with me." He reached across the table and gently stroked her hand. "I've shown you the map, so you know what I have at stake."

"Oh, Michael, I'm not sure." A half smiled crossed her face. "So much has happened to me since I arrived in this dreadful place."

"I believe the canyon will reveal what I've been looking for, and it may even hold some of your answers, too. You heard what Blackeagle said about the petroglyphs, and your intuition will guide us." Michael squeezed her hand hoping to bring a positive response from her.

She finally nodded as the little smile disappeared.

"Why don't you stay in my motel room tonight? I'd feel much better knowing you were with me."

"Come on, Michael. I'll be fine in my own room." She raised her hand searching for that annoying wisp of hair. As her fingers found the tresses, she twisted them nervously.

"Fine! But after the weird things that happened last night, I definitely don't think it's safe."

She stared up into the dark sky. "For God's Sake, Mom, you're the one that's always pushing me away. I had to keep going just to prove myself to you. And you and Dad didn't give a hell." A mist filled her eyes. "So here I am, doing it again." She glanced back across the table. "Do you understand, Michael? Do you understand? That's why I have to stay by myself. I have to know I'm strong enough to do it without help from you or anyone else." She slowly released the golden strands.

He stared back into her glistening emerald eyes. "For years, Neanna, I've said you've nothing to prove. But then you just kept coming back to the desert and I was always there. I wanted to believe I was the reason, but I guess I knew better."

"I know. I loved you for believing in me and giving me the strength I needed. Then I went home where it seemed like Mom and Naomi did their best to drive the self confidence out of me."

He caressed her hand. "If only you'll let me, I'll take those worries away."

"You've been saying that for years and every time I'm ready, you're off on another expedition." She placed her other hand on Michael's, tracing the suntanned veins across the back with her fingertips.

"It's different now," he insisted. "When this one is over, I've been offered a permanent position at the University." He pulled away from her grasp and slowly slid his hand up her arm.

"When this is over?" her voice rose.

He reached up to the girl's bare throat and leaning across the narrow table, pulled her toward him until their lips met. Michael's fingers trembled on her soft neck as they kissed.

Neanna broke the spell. "Not tonight." She removed his hand. "It's not like it used to be. Give me more time." Unknowingly, her touch lingered on the golden tresses that drifted over her cheek.

"Time is all I have."

"I'll go with you tomorrow. Besides, it sounds intriguing. Just drop me off at my room tonight." She pushed back her chair.

When Michael stopped the jeep in front of Number Seven, all of the cabins were dark except the office. In the distance, they could hear Oak Creek gurgling over the rocky streambed behind the wooden buildings.

"This time I'm coming in and checking the place first."

"Be my guest." She raised her hand toward the cabin and nodded. "I just slept in it last night, but you can walk me to the door and look around inside."

The room was as empty as she had left it that morning.

"I'll see you at six, Michael." She gave him a soft kiss and slowly pushed the door shut and turned the lock.

Shivering, Neanna crawled into bed and turned off the light. She held her breath and waited for the crying to start again. Finally, gasping for air as the silence in the dark room overwhelmed her, she slipped into an uneasy sleep.

. . . . . .

Two cabins down from where Neanna slept peacefully, people were wide-awake. Hooded members filled the large windowless building where plywood covered all outside openings, and a humming chant, "auhm, auhm, auhmm," reverberated through the room. Suddenly, the chanting stopped and the room grew silent except for the muted whispers that passed back and forth through the crowd. "The Keeper is here. The Keeper is here."

The tall clan leader entered and sat in an ornamental gold upholstered chair inside Schnebly Cabin Number Five. He looked out over the large group of followers who sat cross-legged on the floor, surrounded by the stone images of Sedona's red-crowned monuments.

From beneath his robe, the Keeper drew a long thin staff and raised it high above him. A light blue hood covered his head embroidered with a dark blue spiral insignia circling the top just above his eyes. A darker blue cape attached to the cowl overlaid his shoulders and the rest of his body. Inside, his face remained a shadow. He began a chant, swinging the staff upward and down again with the rhythm. The crowd picked up the incantation until the place vibrated from corner to corner. After several minutes, the Keeper lowered the staff and a quiet calm filled the room.

"Tomorrow night," his high-pitched voice echoed. "Tomorrow night, we go back to Airport Mesa." He pointed his staff at the model in the center the room. "Each of you will notify your people. And remember, do nothing to attract the attention of the authorities or the public. If asked, some of you will come as interested citizens, some of you will come as out-of-state tourists, and some of you will come as scientists studying strange phenomena."

"Master," a meek voice came from beneath one of the robes crouched on the floor, "today I saw the Sheriff's patrol car and several police vehicles on the road leading to the rocky mesa near the airport where we were last night. I fear they may find something."

"What they do is no concern of ours." He pointed his staff at the man.

"But what if they find evidence that we had been there?" spoke up another.

"Silence!" the Keeper screeched, raising his staff. "If you have something to say, tell us what you witnessed last night. Don't talk about your fears. You have seen the greatest strength this world has ever known. You only have to tap into this power to relieve your fears."

"Master, what did we see?" a different member spoke from the crowd. "Did we witness a great coming or was it an hallucination?"

"You saw the people that came before. The people from another dimension, from another time. They filled me with great knowledge that I will soon pass on to you."

"Yes, Master," The crowd murmured in unison.

"Stand!" The Keeper's shrill voice echoed across the room as he rose from the golden chair. "Stand and listen." He began to chant.

"You have been selected for a special purpose," his shrill tone touched their souls. "The Ancient Ones have called you. You saw them above the rock plateau, the ones from the past who left in the vortex. You have been called to meet them on their return. Is there anyone among you who does not want to meet this challenge? If so, raise your arm and you will be excused."

Not a single arm reached above the cloaked members.

"So, how many of you want to confront the unknown?"

A roar filled the room as the hooded members raised their arms and shouted at the Keeper. "We will. We are ready. Take us." They chanted on and on. "Take us with you."

"Very soon. But first, I have another task for you." He swept his staff over their heads. "The Ancient Ones are asking your help to find the Chosen One, the one filled with the spirit. The fire within her burned Sister Martha's hand and she escaped from the House of Crystals. Then she struck down Brother James like a child, and he has vanished from our midst. She has the power that the Ancient Ones seek. They want her returned to them. Who will meet this challenge?" he shrieked again raising his staff toward the ceiling.

"We will. We will," the crowd chanted, again and again.

*** 

Neanna jumped from her deep sleep and peered around the dark room. "Who's here?" she cried into the darkness, then quietly listened

In the distance, from somewhere beyond her room, she could hear rhythmic voices. Carefully slipping out of bed, she listened at the door, then walking around the room, she pressed her ear to each wall. On the side facing Cabin Six, she felt the vibration in harmony with the chanting. She opened the door a crack and listened. The voices came from the cabin beyond Six.

She quickly dressed, slipping into her denims, scooted out the door, and crept behind her cabin. Staying in the shadows, she rushed past Number Six to the back of Five over the coarse grass and fallen oak leaves. The tempo of the sound increased as she approached the rear of the wooden building.

*What am I doing here?* she thought, her heart beat racing. *I must be an idiot or just crazy. What kind of curiosity is driving me?*

Pulling her denim jacket closer about her body, she crept along the wall next to the largest window and found a tiny crack between the sill and the ragged plywood. The voices seemed quieter now as she put her eye to the slit and peered in.

"Oh, my God!" She jumped back, covering her mouth to squelch the scream that tried to escape. "Who on earth are they?" she muttered to herself. Then Deputy Carasco word's flashed through her mind about staying away from people who dressed like the lady clerk at the crystal shop. *And here was a room full of them, including their leader.*

She watched and listened as the Keeper raised his staff, silencing the crowd. "In due time we will go," his squeaky voice continued, "but do not tell the others. You have taken an oath to reveal nothing about this meeting. Now return to your homes and wait for instructions. The Ancient Ones will come soon. Remember who they are seeking, the Chosen One."

Neanna heard a creaking to her left and noticed this cabin had a back door, which was now slowly opening. Quickly, she slipped around the corner of Number Five, through the deep shadows and the fallen leaves, across to Six, and then back to her own cabin. She dashed inside, past the darkened entrance, and slammed the door shut. With trembling hands, she locked every built-in latch, then leaned her shaking body against the door as if to barricade the entrance from an attacking army.

The silent crowd slowly dissolved from Cabin Five, out the back door, and into the black of the night.

As Neanna listened, clumsy footsteps paused at her door. She felt her heart beat increase until the noise drifted into the street and evaporated in the distance.

# 26

## THE ROAD TO RED CANYON

A tired Michael Adams woke to the gentle knock on his motel door. He rolled over and strained to see the clock. "Who's there?" he yelled.

"Mr. Michael, it is me, Tony."

"What do you want?" he grumbled. The muscles of his upper arms still ached from the collision with the black sedan two days ago.

"You asked me to go with you to the desert."

"Oh, it's you, Tony. What time is it?" He snapped on the gold-trimmed bed lamp and blinked at the illuminated hands on the clock. "Why are you so early? It's like two in the morning."

"It is already five. Please let me in." He scraped his deformed hand on the door.

The sleepy archeologist staggered from under the thick quilt. He pushed away the long hair from both sides of his face and jerked the door open.

The little guide in his baggy faded blue overalls stepped into the room and glanced around. "Do you always leave your dirty clothes scattered all over your bedroom floor, Michael?" He waved his hand as a wide smile spread across his deeply tanned face, covered with a fine stubble of whiskers.

"Tony, you're my guide, not my housekeeper," he grumbled. "Did you get me the names of those canyons?"

"Yes. I have them all." He raised the tail of his faded red shirt and reached into the front pocket of his loose fitting clothes. "Do you want them now?"

"No. We'll use them later. Say, how's that hand doing," he pointed, slouching back on the bed and rubbing his hands over his face trying to wake up. "It looks pretty active."

Tony raised the twisted hand and slowly closed the fingers into a knotted grip. "See, just as I told you. My aunt and her crystals saved it. See." He flexed the deformed joints once again.

"That's great." The archeologist stood and strolled toward the bathroom. "But now I need to get dressed and call Neanna. She's going with us."

"Michael, you know that big black car that pushed us off the highway? I saw it right outside." He pointed his crooked hand at the door.

## Gateway to Another Dimension

"Why would they be here?" he frowned. "I thought it was just an irritated driver." He cracked open the pleated drape and peered out. "Where was it, Tony?"

"I can't see it now, but I swear it was right there. The paint was scraped from the fender that struck your jeep."

"Michael clapped his hand on the small man's shoulder. "We'll check around when we leave."

He showered, pulled on his worn tan shirt and pants, and tied the lacing around his sun-bleached ponytail, then called Neanna. Pacing around the small table, he waited for her to answer.

The phone rang several times before a sleepy feminine voice replied. "Is that you, Michael?" she yawned. "I'll be ready when you get here."

"We're almost on our way." He slapped the red dust from his felt hat and field jacket as he talked.

"We?" The voice was suddenly awake.

"Yes, Neanna, we're taking our guide. I told you about Tony."

"Oh, yes, I remember." The voice was sleepy again. "I'll still be ready." She raised her head and listened intently for the rhythmic sounds from Cabin Number Five, but only quietness filled her ears.

. . . . . .

*The Mystical Vortex*

The morning sun rose over the edge of the eastern horizon as the trio drove out of town in Michael's rented jeep. They had searched for the black sedan as they left the Park Motel and then the Southwest Breakfast Diner, but the car was nowhere in sight.

Neanna hesitantly broke the silence. "I saw them, Michael. I saw them last night," she chattered.

"You saw what?"

"The cult, just like Jonathon described. I saw them in another cabin after dark." Her voice rose. "They were chanting and the leader was there. It felt like my blood was turning to gelatin and getting colder. I ran to my cabin and locked the door, but I could still hear them milling around."

"And this morning?"

"They were all gone." She sighed, releasing the trapped breath. "Disappeared into the night like ghosts."

"Don't worry, Neanna," Michael raised his voice. "We will find the treasure and be gone before your ghosts return. We will be out of here and no one will frighten you again."

As the archeologist turned off Highway 89A at the broken sign marked Red Canyon, he glanced at the sky.

"Any signs of a monsoon, Tony?"

"No, today is clear. Not like the last time." He waved his deformed hand toward the blue sky.

"Is this where you almost drowned, Michael?" Neanna asked, trying to brush the fine red dust that filtered into the jeep from her denim jacket and pants.

"Not exactly. It was up this dirt road a few miles. I'll show you."

"You know, I feel so much more confident today." She smiled coyly at him.

"How's that?" A narrow grin spread across his face.

"Maybe it's the sunshine, or the excitement of going on the hunt with you once again. I'm not even mad at Mom, today." She slid closer, hugged his arm, and laid her head on his shoulder.

"I feel better myself right at this moment." He eased on the brakes, pulled her across to his seat and kissed her.

The little man in back gazed out the side window.

* * *

In the distance behind them, a black sedan pulled off the highway just before the road into Red Canyon and waited. The heavyset man rested his hands on the steering wheel while his partner played with a cobalt-blue .38 revolver. The tall skinny one in the black vest inserted bullets methodically, spun the cylinder a few times, and then slapped it shut. He leered down the sights, then repeated the process over and over.

"Dammit, Slim!" Fatso yelled, glaring at the man sitting next to him. "Stop fooling with that god damn gun."

"I'm not fooling, fat boy. I'm just getting ready to earn my pay for this job." He slammed the cylinder shut and swung his pistol toward the driver. His loose-lipped sneer revealed an uneven row of yellowish teeth.

Suddenly, the back of Fatso's thick hairy hand struck the thin guy in the left cheek. The revolver thudded to the floor as Slim's head snapped back, crashing into the passenger window. His eyes popped open and a shocked look crossed his face as a slow trickle of dark blood seeped from his mouth and dribbled onto his black vest.

"Never call me fat boy again. Next time you'll end up a dry rotten corpse in this god-forsaken desert. Are you listening?" He raised his clenched fist again.

His partner cowered against the vehicle's door. "I didn't mean anything by it, honest." Nervously, he wiped the blood from his mouth and chin with trembling white fingers.

"Then shut your face. We've got a job to do." Fatso turned and stared out the windshield at the turnoff to Red Canyon.

# 27
## INDIAN CULTURAL CENTER

Early the next morning, Jonathon Blackeagle opened the door for Laura Running Deer as they entered the Cultural Center. The smell of incense drifted toward them as the big Indian led the way through the open gallery to a storage room.

He waved his hand. "I want to see all the writings of the Ancient Ones, Laura. I want to look at all the old paintings, photographs of rock and cave art, artifacts, and any other thing that would be a record of the past. Also, the old material stored in the other rooms."

"What are you looking for, Jonathon?"

"That I do not know. I suspect the clan is looking for something and I must to find it first. It may be here."

Her long black hair swished across her face as she shook her head. "Do you know why they would want to learn about the ancients?"

"No. I hope the answer is in here."

They separated the stored material into two piles by time periods. The smaller pile contained material gathered from caves, archeological digs, rock paintings, cliff dwellings, and those relics saved over the centuries. The larger pile contained more recent artifacts.

Kneeling on the floor, Jonathon whispered. "The answer has to be here." He laid his right hand on the smallest pile of material. A warm glow crept over his palm. His fingers became warmer until he began to feel a slight tingling pain near the tips. He moved his hand in that direction. The warm feeling cooled and then warmed once more until his fingers began to tingle again. He moved his hand over the collection in that direction. This time, the mild pain centered on his palm.

"It is deeper in the pile," he shouted. "Quick, Laura, help me move some of this stuff. I need to reach further down."

Laura pulled figurines, bits of ancient moccasins, shriveled corncobs, and other debris away from the big Indian's hand.

Jonathon grasped his wrist with his left hand and forced his right to remain on the artifacts. The pain in his palm increased as droplets of sweat formed on his dark brow. "More, Laura, more," he called. "Pull more of the material from under my hand."

Laura dug deeper into pile. "I'm trying, Jonathon, I'm trying," she whispered. She tugged an old robe from beneath his palm, then slid a large flat rock with strange inscriptions on it out of the way.

"We're getting closer," he muttered as trickles of perspiration rolled down his twisted face. "The pain is less, but I have to force my hand to keep it on the pile. What is left, Laura?"

When the Indian girl pulled away a moth-eaten buckskin vest, a small fur covered pouch lay on the floor beneath Jonathon's right hand. The hot spot on the center of his palm cooled to a warm glow. The glow spread throughout his hand and then up his arm until it reached the middle of his breast. From there, it radiated over his entire body.

Laura backed away, feeling the heat flowing from her friend. A look of fear crossed her face.

Jonathon sat back on the floor, reached down and picked up the small pouch. He turned toward Laura as a wide smile crinkled over his face, "I think we have found the answer." His right hand tightened confidently around the fur-covered bag. "Where did it come from?"

"I found it in that old wooden box with the copper hinges in the display room. The pouch and several other relics have been stored there since I started working here several years ago."

Jonathon struggled to his feet. "Yes, I remember. That box was found in a cellar outside an old mission in southern Arizona. Someone recognized Yavapai artifacts in it and shipped the container to us. I never had a chance to examine all of its contents, so we just put the box on display."

"You look very tired, Jonathon," she spoke softly. "Are you sure you don't want to go home and rest for the remainder of the day?"

He smiled and laid his big hands on her shoulders, looking down into her deep brown eyes. "Once again, you know best. I do need to meditate on this little fur bag and its contents."

"I will put things away before I leave," Laura answered as she closed the door behind him, "and see you tomorrow."

## 28

IN SEARCH OF EL LOBO CANYON

A plume of crimson dust formed behind the Jeep Wrangler that Michael drove along Red Canyon Road. As the morning warmed, they removed their jackets and piled them in the back seat with the guide.

"Tony," he called, motioning to the left. "Let's hear the list of names you found for these tributaries. What's that first one we just passed?"

Tony pulled a wrinkled sheet of white paper from his overall pocket and tried to smooth it with his crooked hand. "It is called Dry Arroyo."

"And what's the next one? Just coming up on the left." Only the rutted track of a four-wheeled ATV marked the smooth red dirt in the bottom of the little canyon.

"That one is called Lost Vaquero, but don't you want to know the names of the ones on the right?"

"Not now," he snapped back. "Thanks."

"What is this about the names of all these canyons?" Neanna almost whispered, leaning toward Michael.

"I want to include them in my final journal on this expedition." He stopped the jeep, pushed his felt hat back, pulled the brown paper map from his shirt pocket, and held it on his lap away from the guide. Neanna opened her mouth to speak, but Michael touched his finger to her lips stopping the words.

He laid his right palm on the crude map covering Cathedral Rock with his four fingers pointing upward. He felt the tingling in his hand as his heart beat increased. His right thumb pointed toward the third narrow tributary roughly drawn on the brown paper. Then, using his index finger, he followed the faint tributary line until it intersected with a series of hash marks running at right angles. Neanna watched in fascination as Michael traced the lines on his crude map.

He took a deep breath and tried to calm his voice. "We almost made it here last time, but the monsoon flood took us out. Today, we'll find what lies at the head of this canyon." He tapped the map again and again as if to ensure himself that his goal was almost in his grasp. Then he turned to his quiet guide. "What's the name of the next tributary on our left, Tony?"

The baggy pants man stared at his wrinkled paper. "It is called El Lobo," his quiet voice spoke. He slid deeper in the seat as if the name alone frightened him.

Neanna grabbed Michael's hand. "What's this all about? I saw that paper you had, but what . . . ?" She hesitated as he frowned at her.

"Right now, all I can tell you is that I believe the map is accurate, very accurate." As he started the jeep and drove forward, creating a string of dust that could be seen for miles, his thoughts were on the Spanish treasure that lay hidden beyond these sandstone hills.

Farther along the road, the three riders watched in awe as the majestic Cathedral Rock rose over the side of Red Canyon into the deep blue Arizona sky. As they drove deeper, the steep sandstone wall on their right became an impenetrable fortress. Cathedral Rock hung over the cliff like a red-spired castle defying anyone to ascend its towers.

To their left, the canyon wall was not as high or insurmountable. It broke at times into wide ravines that allowed water to pour down into the main channel. The road narrowed and twisted as they drove further into the main canyon.

The archeologist pointed at the red tower above them. "That's Cathedral Rock." His heart quickened as he looked up. "When we're opposite it, we should find El Lobo."

## The Mystical Vortex

"Look, Michael, we're following the tracks of another vehicle. See, just ahead of us." Neanna motioned through the dusty windshield.

"You're right, and it seems to be the only vehicle here since the flood." He stopped the jeep to investigate the tracks imbedded in the crusted red dirt.

Neanna followed him to the front of the Wrangler and rubbed her fingers along the indentations. "They're deeper than ours. The tracks have been made by a heavy vehicle, or a heavily loaded one."

Michael called to Tony. "Have you seen any trucks or vans in Sedona that would make strange tread marks like these?"

"No, I have not." A puzzled look crossed his face as he shook his head. "They look very different to me. Do you know what made them?"

"No, but I'm sure we'll soon find out." He led his search party back to the Wrangler and, as he drove on between the red walls, a narrow crevice opened to their left.

"There it is," Neanna screamed, "just ahead. That must be El Lobo. And look, the tracks we're following turn in that direction."

Michael turned the jeep toward the gap in the red wall. As they approached, the cleft opened wide enough for a two-lane road. Both sides of the slot in Red Canyon's cliff towered over the jeep as they entered the barren, weathered landscape of El Lobo. "Have you been here before, Tony?" he called over his shoulder.

"No, I never ventured into these side canyons. I have always gone through Red Canyon to view Cathedral Rock. It is a sacred place, you know."

"Come on. Weren't you afraid to go up these ravines? Is there something forbidden about them?" He pushed for an answer.

"No one has told me to be afraid of them. Only one canyon is sacred and it is a long way from here, east of Sedona." The guide's voice quieted to a whisper.

Michael was about to answer when Neanna yelled. "Look at the tracks. They're gone. They just disappeared under the jeep."

"What the hell, where'd they go?" He jammed his foot on the brake pedal, then backed the Wrangler until the strange vehicle tracks appeared in front of them. "Let's take a closer look."

The blonde girl reached the end of the tread marks first. "See, they just slowly fade out until they're gone. It's as if the vehicle lifted off the ground and flew away."

The three members of the search party knelt to examine the tire marks. Neanna rubbed her hands over the site of the disappearing tracks pushing the red soil away revealing more indentations. She kept wiping the sandy dirt aside until the grooves appeared once more in front of the jeep.

"Here's the lost tracks, Michael. For some unknown reason, someone has covered them."

\* \* \*

From the shoulder of Highway 89A, the black sedan turned onto the road into Red Canyon. The two occupants followed the faint dust trail deeper into the narrow opening between barren sandstone walls. The thin man once again held his revolver gently in his hands. He twirled the cylinder around and around. A twisted smile covered his skinny face as the faint smell of gun oil penetrated his pinched nostrils.

\* \* \*

Michael Adams leaned against the grille of the Wrangler and glanced up and down the sandstone lined canyon. "Someone spent a lot of time and effort concealing these tracks, Neanna. I wonder why?"

She nodded, trying to brush away the crimson soil staining the knees of her slim denims, and stepped into the jeep.

El Lobo climbed higher into the upper side of Red Canyon. It narrowed to a one-lane track that turned back toward the head of the main canyon. Here and there small bushes and shrubs appeared and a variety of cacti sprouted out of the desolate, wind-creased soil.

They watched as the road dissolved into a small trail. Michael shifted the vehicle into four-wheel drive and followed the faint path until it became too steep even for the jeep.

"This is the end of the line for the Wrangler. We're going on afoot. He swung a small pack over his shoulders and handed Neanna a canteen. "Just some water and lunch. We'll be back by the middle of the afternoon. The real exploration will start tomorrow."

He eagerly took out the brown paper map and let his fingers caress the hash marks that represented the ridge they were about to climb. Beyond it, several other small lines led into the distance. Above the lines, an upside down "U" indicated a secret that only Michael knew.

Neanna pulled strings of blonde hair from the left side of her face, caressing them over and over. "Okay, Michael," a concerned look crossed her face, "Are you going to give me a hint of where we're going?" She pushed the strands under her broad-brimmed hat.

"Trust me. Just one more time."

"Trust you?" she frowned, her hands on her hips. "Like the last time in the Mojave when we looked for the end of the lost river? How many days did we look? Fifteen, twenty. And why does it always have to be in the heat of the summer?"

"I, too, would like to know where we are going," Tony chimed in.

"It's beyond this ridge." He pointed, raising his voice. "We follow the trail to the top, then I'll get my bearings. I want you to share this moment with me."

"And where do you suppose that vehicle went that made the tracks back there?" Neanna asked. "It's not up here, and I didn't see anywhere for it to go." She pointed back down El Lobo Canyon.

"We'll check on it later. Don't you understand? Right now I can't wait to see what lies on the other side of this ridge. Come on, Neanna, I'll help you." He reached out his hand.

Neanna glanced up at Michael, then behind her. She shook her head and took the outstretched hand.

As they started up the trail, a fat-bellied chuckwalla scurried out of their way trying to find a hiding place in the parched hillside. The pathway led up a steep desolate slope of red sandstone deeply grooved by desert wind and rain and devoid of any plant life. Near the top of the ridge, a few sprigs of brush and a cactus sprouted out of the hilltop.

"Look, isn't this wild," he called back to them. From the top of the lifeless crest, they looked down into a labyrinth of small twisting canyons that led off in all directions.

Tony waved his crooked hand over the maze that lay before them. "Many times I have heard of this place." A shiver swept his body. "Only evil lives down there. It is called the Devil's Lair. People have gone into there and never returned." Then he muttered words that neither Michael nor Neanna could understand.

"You can't believe that," the archeologist interrupted, "it's just a myth made up by people who were afraid."

"Yes, Tony, a lot of that is just superstition," Neanna's soft voice tried to sooth him.

"No, it is not superstition." He stepped back from them. "Look for yourself." His injured hand shook as he pointed. "You can see there is no way out. Look how the canyons merge into the deep darkness. That's the Devil's Lair."

The red Arizona sun had moved midway toward the zenith in a cloudless sky. Beneath this blue ceiling, Neanna, Michael, and Tony stood on the small desolate ridge staring down into even more desolate ridges, gullies, and hills. In the distance behind them, the towering Cathedral Rock loomed across Red Canyon.

Michael once again slid the brown paper map from his pocket. He slowly unfolded it with trembling fingers while trying not to allow their guide to view the inscriptions. As he looked down at the crinkled drawing and then into the distance, he took a small compass from his other breast pocket and placed it on the map. He slowly rotated the sketch until the bottom was positioned due south. He turned the overlaying indicator on the compass until it pointed to Cathedral Rock. Finally, he rotated the indicator to the opposite compass heading and aimed his finger in the direction it pointed. "That's the way," the words caught in his throat. "What we are looking for is in that direction?"

"Why are you so sure?" Neanna shook her head. "The ridge we're standing on could have been created recently by the wind and rain."

"Yes, that could be true, but Cathedral Rock has been there for ages. It's our guide post." With confidence, he folded the map and returned it and the compass to his shirt pocket.

Tony again pleaded with Michael to return to the jeep and not venture down into the Devil's Lair, but the archaeologist ignored him and started down a faint trail into the twisted canyons. As Neanna fell in behind him, she glanced back and saw fear in Tony's eyes. The little man watched them go, then he too started down the ridge.

* * *

Back in Red Canyon under the presence of Cathedral Rock, the black Lincoln Towncar turned up El Lobo. The two men sat quietly except for the sound of the revolver chamber spinning as the slim man whirled it again and again.

At the head of El Lobo Canyon, Fatso parked the big sedan and they raced up the slope to Michael's rented Jeep

Wrangler. The skinny man twirled his revolver as he tried the doors.

"They're locked. Go get a pry bar."

"Get the god damn pry bar yourself," Fatso yelled raising his fist and plodding around the dust covered off-road vehicle. "With a little help, I think we can release the hood."

The slim man returned from the sedan, mumbling to himself and carrying an iron lug wrench, sharpened on one end.

His partner grabbed the tool and pried the hood open. "Now, let's do a little number on this jeep and strand them out here for the night. Strange things happened to people who get lost in the desert at night. Ain't that right, Slim?"

"Sure as the sun comes up in the morning. We'll be waiting for them when it gets dark." He sneered, flashing his yellow teeth in the sunlight as he twirled the chamber in the revolver once again.

The black sedan disappeared back down El Lobo Canyon.

## 29

### INTO THE DEVIL'S LAIR

The late afternoon Arizona sun blazed down on the three explorers as they followed a faint track into the hills beyond El Lobo Canyon. Ahead of them lay a twisted series of dry gullies and bare lifeless knobs leading off in all directions. Michael Adams watched his compass as he led the exploration party deeper into the maze of winding canyons. He glanced often at the small compass and pointed them in the direction he followed. One way seemed no different from another as minute trails made by desert animals led aimlessly off in all directions.

The small group walked along quiet as the desert. Thin patches of cholla cactus blocked their progress at times, a lazy chuckwalla darted across their path to safety, and a dull yellow scorpion scurried out of their way. Michael periodically glanced toward Cathedral Rock and then back at his map. It showed nothing, but squiggly lines beyond El Lobo Canyon.

"We're on the right track," he said, pointing his hand in the direction they were following. "It's hard to stay on a trail and travel in the direction the compass is pointing."

"How far are we going today?" Neanna broke in. "Remember, we don't have supplies to stay overnight.

"Not far. I just want to get oriented." He removed his dusty hat and wiped the sweat from his forehead. "Tomorrow we can move fast and cover more ground. We'll reach the location by noon. Can't you feel the excitement, Neanna?

"I'll wait until we find it before I get too excited, if you don't mind." She started along the trail behind him.

Late in the afternoon, the trio arrived back at the red stained jeep. As Michael rotated the key, the engine turned over, but refused to start.

"What the hell," he muttered, banging the steering wheel.

"Sounds like the time you coaxed me into the Mojave Desert. Your car didn't start then, did it?" she laughed. "What did you do this time?"

"Damn, Neanna. This is different," he yelled. "Something's wrong with the jeep." He hopped out and opened the hood. "Oh Jesus. What the hell?"

"What's wrong, Michael?" She met him at the front of the vehicle.

## The Mystical Vortex

"Look. Someone pried the hood open and took the coil wire. We're stuck here until I can raise help on the cell phone and get someone out here. Damn."

Ten minutes later he gave up trying to reach anyone. "The phone's dead in these canyons," he yelled at no one. "I knew I should have bought one of those satellite phones. If you can see the sky, you can always reach a satellite." He threw the useless cell phone into the front seat.

The little guide raised his claw of a hand and waved it in the air. "I told you about the Devil's Lair," his dry voice croaked as fear passed over his face, "but you did not believe me. Now you see what happens when you tamper with the devil."

"That's just a stupid superstition, Tony," Neanna smiled at the frustrated man. "Someone followed us in here and tampered with the car, not the devil. Now let's see what we can do to fix the jeep." She peered down at the dirty engine covered with a mixture of oil and red dust.

"You know I'm no mechanic," Michael muttered back in desperation.

"But I do know a few things about the operation of a gasoline engine, especially the electrical system. Where does the coil wire connect, Michael? What size is it?"

"See," he jabbed his finger at the engine. "It goes from the coil here to the distributor cap. Someone's pulled it out and taken it with them."

*Gateway to Another Dimension*

"But we are going to find a replacement. This is a six-cylinder engine, so why can't it operate on five? We'll pull the wires off one of the plugs. A short one from a middle cylinder, use it for the coil wire, and we're on our way. It may run a little rough and we may have to travel a little slower, but we'll make it."

"You're a genius, Neanna."

"I've always known that." She smiled. "Too bad you couldn't have convinced my parents. Hey, Mom," she glanced toward the sky, "did you hear what Michael just said?"

Neanna pointed as he removed one of the spark plug wires and used it to replace the coil wire. The jeep engine quickly started, running a little rough on five cylinders. Dusk settled over El Lobo Canyon as they crawled back to the shadow of Cathedral Rock and then on into Sedona.

\*\*\*

Near the entrance to Red Canyon, two men sat in the gloom of a black sedan well hidden in the darkness. The large fat man slapped his thin partner across the face with the back of his hand. "You screwed up again," he shouted, "I told you that trick wouldn't work. Mr. Wallace is going to be very unhappy with you."

## 30

## THE MISTS

In the evening dusk, the clan gathered in the dwindling darkness behind Schnebly Cabins. Hooded figures blended into the shadowy landscape and formed in two long winding columns. Only the scuffling of shoe soles on red sandstone broke the silence of the night as the file of blue capes wound its way up into the foothills. The tall trees along Oak Creek gave way to a brief spattering of desert shrubs until stunted pinion pines and juniper trees lined the night pathway as the trail rose higher into the hills. Several feet behind the clansmen, a dark clad figure followed at a safe distance.

At the head of the column, a tall hooded leader quietly chanted. He led his followers deeper into the hills around rocky outcroppings until they arrived at a high red sandstone formation silhouetted against a dark sky. Concentric rings, cut deeply into the surface by relentless winds over the eons, narrowed upward encircling the solid beehive shaped pinnacle resting on a tree shrouded hilltop.

The clansmen ascended the faint spiraling trail as they surrounded the moonlit stone structure. The leader entered a narrow opening at the bottom, disturbing a small cloud of dark bats that winged their way skyward like shadowy specters in the night. A slight figure dressed in a red cloak followed him obediently upward through the dark passageway to the top of a wide plateau above the members. Far below, the dim lights of Sedona twinkled in the distance.

The secretive figure worked his way silently to the opposite side of the round tapered formation, hiding among the trees and shadows where he could watch the hooded gathering.

Below their leader's eyes, the crowd began to chant, "Keeper, Keeper, Keeper."

Above them, the clan leader, his face a shadow in the moonlight, raised his long wooden staff silencing the crowd. From beneath his dark blue cape, he took a worn fur skin pouch, opened the drawstring, and withdrew a minute pinch of red and green powder. He began a shrilling chant. The followers below picked up the incantation of nondescript words as the Keeper tossed the powders into the air surrounding him.

The dark clad intruder slipped behind the mesmerized crowd and seized the nearest clansman. Quickly, he placed his right hand over the victim's mouth, his other around the man's throat, and pulled him into the shadows. He dispatched him with a quick chop to the back of his neck, and as chanting continued, he donned the blue cloak of the fallen member.

Above the chanting Keeper, the powders swirled through the air. The particles whirled around and around, creating an eerie radiance. Strange representations began to appear in the iridescent glow, whirling and dancing in the rising moonlight. First the likeness of modern Indians began to emerge, and then they swirled away as images of Indians of the past appeared. They too departed as faint helmeted figures swept by. Next, the Ancient Ones floated in the sky.

The newly cloaked figure slipped through the crowd and up the cleft in the side of the red stone formation. Silently he crept to the top and, peering into the swirling mist, he could faintly see the Keeper and the small body in the red robe. He dropped the cape to blend his black clothes into the darkness as he waited for the cult leader's next move.

As the mists swirled, the Keeper reached beneath his shimmering cape and removed a large clear crystal. An intimate red glow danced at each tapered end. He held the gemstone in his left hand and his staff in his right, raising them to the heavens and increasing the chant. The figures in the rotating mist slowly changed to vaporous images without bodies, bobbing back and forth like ghostly

*Gateway to Another Dimension*

vampires. The master of the clansmen dropped his staff and grabbed the delicate red-caped body close to him. He slipped the hood from her head, revealing the calm face of a young Indian girl. She looked up into his eyes with a blank expression, as a slight smile, almost a look of happiness, crossed her face.

The Keeper lowered the crystal closer to her exposed forehead, watching the glowing tip of the quartz jewel brighten. "Oh Ancient Ones we have brought a sacrifice for you," his high pitched voice chanted as he gazed up into the vortex.

The vaporous cloud swirled faster and faster. The tip of the now blood-red gem briefly touched the girls tanned skin, when out of the mist, a dark form leaped forward. His gloved hand sliced out like a snake knocking the crystal from the cult leader's hand. Moving cat like through the vapors, the dim figure slipped an arm around the petite girl's waist and darted down the rocky stairs.

The mist above the flat-topped rock instantly disappeared. The Keeper's shrill scream crossed the plateau and thundered down on those below, "Get him; get the intruder."

As the dark figure emerged at the bottom, a swell of clan members lunged toward him. The man reached for his holster, pulled his revolver, and fired several shots into the air dissolving the menacing crowd. Officer Carasco, dressed in black clothes and carrying his prize, raced down the dark trail toward his waiting patrol vehicle.

Watching the shadow disappear down the pathway, the Keeper raised his staff heavenward. "Oh Ancient Ones, why have you left me?" he screeched. A worried look crossed his face as he stumbled over the rocky surface to peer down at his followers. "Why did you allow this infidel into our midst?"

The white moon moved westward unconcerned about the raving man below.

The crowd of hooded clansmen looked up for guidance as their loud muttering filled the air around the sandstone formation. Voices questioned each other.

"What has happened?" one whispered.

"Where did the Ancient Ones go?" muttered another.

"Why are we here?" a louder voice proclaimed.

"I must go home," cried someone else.

"Must go home," the voices grew louder.

Then from the top of the plateau a shrill voice shouted as the Keeper gained his composure. "No. We will not be denied our place in the universe. Only a moment has been stolen from us." Raising his staff to the moonlit sky, he began to chant louder and louder.

Below him, the followers picked up the incantation interspersed with, "Keeper, Keeper, Keeper."

Waving his staff, the master of the clan broke the monotone. "We will prevail against all obstacles," he screeched. "Our time is near."

He disappeared from above and entered the masses below. They treaded in his footsteps down the dirt trail toward the lights of Sedona. Dark winged bats fluttered through the sky back to their hideaway in the tall red rock mound.

# 31

## SCHNEBLY CABINS

Darkness had settled over Oak Creek and the Schnebly Cabins when Michael dropped Neanna off at Number Seven. "Do you want me to come inside and check out the place before you go in," he asked as he opened the jeep door for her.

"Not tonight. I'm too tired. All I want is to go to bed." She kissed him warmly on the cheek, stepped across the cabin threshold, and went inside.

As Neanna stepped toward her bed, she sensed a quick rap near her door. She shivered as a moment of fear swept through her. "Is that you, Michael," she whispered as she turned.

"No, I must speak to you once again, Miss." The voice drifted from the small bundle of rags standing just inside the room.

*This can't be happening again,* she thought, staring at the pile of old clothes. "Is that you in there, Theresa?"

*Gateway to Another Dimension*

The wrinkled face with tiny sparkling eyes looked up from under the ragged brown shawl and the smooth round mouth slowly spoke, "Yes, and you remembered my name."

"How could I forget, Little Grandmother," she sighed as a gentle smile crossed her lips. "The last time you were here, you left me sleeping. This time I must talk to you first." She reached out and grasped the two small gnarled hands.

"You may sit, Dear, but I prefer to stand."

Neanna sat on the edge of her bed holding the tiny palms and trying to discern the face beneath the old shawl. "Why are you here?"

"I came to warn you." The strange old woman shook her head and the shawl slid back revealing her long straggly gray hair.

"Warn me? About what?" Neanna tightened her grip on the struggling fingers.

"Please, do not go into the desert tomorrow, My Dear. Only evil resides there." Her small mouth twisted and her dark eyes pleaded as she spoke. "You must not become part of it."

Neanna laughed. "How would you know this? Did the spirits of Sedona tell you?"

"It is no laughing matter. As I said before, I have lived here for a long, long time. I have seen many strange things, good and bad.'

Neanna's smile disappeared as she looked into the tormented face of the little woman. "You're serious, aren't you?"

"Yes, Princess. You must learn the wisdom of Sedona's past. The vortex will give you that vision. Go there tomorrow. Visit the sites, not the desert. Learn."

"I don't understand."

"You will, Dear One. Now I will share some of that wisdom with you. Let me hold your hands."

Suddenly the crooked little hands slipped from Neanna's grip almost magically and grasped her long thin fingers.

The warm sensation once again crept out of the gnarled fingers and passed up Neanna's arms until the heat centered on her breast. From there, it spread across her entire body like a warm spider web. As her eyes closed, she heard the old woman warn her once more. "Please, Dear One, do not go into the desert tomorrow. Evil walks there. Visit the vortex sites."

The tiny hands slipped off limp fingers and Neanna collapsed. She imagined the thick wooden door closing behind the old woman, and the latch snapping shut.

# 32

## THE NEW AGE SHOP

A loud ringing woke Neanna from a deep sleep. The faint glow of sunrise filtered through the window into Schnebly Cabin Seven as she stared through her long hair to see the phone. "Is that you, Michael?"

"Yes, did I wake you?"

"I slept so peacefully last night. It was the best night I've had since I arrived in this dreadful town, and that little old lady was back again. I'll tell you at breakfast."

\* \* \*

The sun rose in a warm morning sky as they arrived at a small downtown restaurant.

"What the hell," Michael slammed his fist on the table after Neanna related her night visit by the little woman. "I thought we were all set for our trip to Red Canyon this morning."

"I'm sorry," she reached out her hand toward his arm. "You know something strange has been happening to me. I believe the vortex sites may provide some answers."

He jerked his arm away. "Look, don't you think this woman is a figment of your imagination. Maybe caused by the blow to your head when you ran off the road. Maybe you need to see a doctor."

"Wait a minute, Michael Adams. You invited me to this horrible place and now you want to blame me. No way." She pulled on the tresses of blonde hair that filtered over her left eye, twisting the locks into tight spirals around her fingers. "I'm going to find out what or who is behind all of this."

"Okay, we'll put it off one more day only because I want you with me. I want to share the find with you."

They continued their breakfast in silence. As they strolled out the door, Neanna asked Michael to drop her off at one of the New Age shops. A large sign in the window said *Vortex Tours - Learn the Mysteries of Sedona's Spiritual Centers.*

"Are you sure you don't want to come with me?" She managed a feeble smile.

"No, I got the jeep fixed last night. I want to try it out, then I'll do a little research at the library."

Without answering, she turned and marched into the store.

*Gateway to Another Dimension*

"May I help you?" An older woman in a rose-colored silk gown smiled as Neanna stepped through the door.

Hesitating, she almost whispered. "I came to learn about the vortex sites."

"That's why we're here." Her soft round face continued to smile as the woman played with the thin cord wrapped around her waist. "Is there something special you would like to know?" She led the blonde girl further into the shop pointing at several books.

"I would rather learn first hand than to read about them." Neanna twisted the whisper of hair that lingered across her left eye, then brushed it aside.

"I'm Nora," she held out her hand. "Perhaps I can share some knowledge of the vortex sites with you."

"Neanna," she grasped the soft hand in hers.

"Come." Nora walked to a wall with several large photographs of Sedona's red rock formations. "We believe these places are centers of energy. We call them vortexes because they appear to be swirling masses of intense power rotating about an imaginary axis that extends into the earth."

"What evidence do you have?"

"Only that Sedona is not alone. These energy sites exist elsewhere though out the world such as the Bermuda Triangle, Mount Calvary, Gold Hill in Oregon, and The Mystery Spot in California." The woman continued. "They

*The Mystical Vortex*

create a disturbance that can result in a gravitational distortion, or a time warp."

"Interesting," Neanna nodded. "And what causes this distortion," she questioned, trying to relate what she had just heard to her knowledge gained from several years of astrophysics studies.

"The vortex sites contain various sources of energy. Some electric, some magnetic."

"Have you measured this energy?" She asked as her mind streamed ahead trying to decide what equipment her company would use.

"Oh no, Miss, our bodies measure the energy. You will see. Look at Bell Rock." She pointed to the magnificent red rock tower shaped like an immense bell resting on a stone pedestal. We call it a beam vortex. It sucks up the earth's energy like a giant vacuum cleaner and beams it into outer space. Many have felt its pull on their very souls."

"My God," Neanna uttered, staggering back. An empty feeling tugged in her stomach and she felt the color drain from her face as she visualized her car being pulled off the highway toward the base of that huge structure.

"Are you all right, Miss?" Nora reached to grasp her arm. "Would you like to sit down?"

"No, I'll be okay. So many strange things have happened to me since I arrived in Sedona. But I would like a drink."

The woman handed Neanna a glass of water and motioned to someone. "I'm going to have my assistant continue. She will be very helpful."

A beautiful young woman in a lavender gown reached out her hand to Neanna. Several small jeweled rings covered her fingers.

Neanna almost gasped as her eyes traced the slender girl from the blonde hair on her head to the black high heels on her feet. *I can't believe how much she looks like me,* Neanna thought. *Her green eyes are slightly bluer than mine and she's a little shorter, but I'd guess her bust and hip sizes are exactly the same. It's like looking into a mirror, and apparently she doesn't recognize the resemblance.* "Yes," she answered, taking the thin hand in her own. "I have come to learn about the mysterious vortexes of Sedona."

"My name is Sabrina." The young woman's smiled, flashing brilliant white teeth between bright red lips, "You have come to the right place. First, I would suggest a photograph of your aura."

"Neanna, here," she smiled back flashing her own dazzling white teeth. "Whatever you suggest."

"It will tell you and us so much about your inner self," she continued. "From the photo, we will know what the next step you must take to fully benefit from your visitation to the vortex. You know, of course, there are several vortex sites. The aura will also allow us to determine which site is right for you."

"I'm here to learn the wisdom of the vortex. Can you teach me?" Neanna asked.

"Yes, we can. Please follow me," Sabrina pointed to a back room her blue-green eyes beaming.

They strolled through a maze of crystals in all shapes and sizes, then passed a myriad of racks filled with miscellaneous New Age books including those on meditation, astrology, crystal healing, spiritual transformation, guides to the vortex, and Sedona's past and future. Beyond the books, hung filmy hooded garments in many shades and hues intermingled with colorful medicine wheels. Soon the two young women entered a small room with a single chair standing in front of a Polaroid camera.

"Please have a seat, Neanna." The wide smile never left her face. "We will soon witness your aura."

*Here I go again,* she thought as she sat in the tall chair and faced the camera lens.

"To best photograph your aura, Neanna, we ask that you calm yourself. Close your eyes and concentrate on your inner self. We will be using a slow camera speed to fully record the image, but it will only take a few seconds."

"I understand," she answered, shutting her eyes and allowing her mind to clear.

After a few minutes, Sabrina spoke. "We are finished, Neanna, please feel free to visit the store while the film processes."

As Neanna wandered though the store fingering several books, she noticed the blonde girl race to a front counter where an older woman stood. She heard them mumble something to each other.

Then the older woman spoke louder, "Take another photo. The film must have been bad." They both glanced at Neanna.

She hastened over to them. "May I see the photo?"

The two woman looked at each other and then at Neanna. The young woman held up the Polaroid. A bright crimson glow filled the entire photo, emanating from an even brighter red center, to all four corners of the picture.

# 33

## INDIAN CULTURAL CENTER

Jonathon and Laura had arrived at the Cultural Center early to discuss their find of the night before. They sat in the office with their attention on a small furry pouch lying in the middle of the desk.

Suddenly, a loud banging on the front door startled them both. The big Indian looked up as if someone were spying on him and quickly hid the fur skin bag in his desk drawer. "Laura, please see who is knocking."

The Indian girl rushed to the door. "Who's there?"

"Deputy Carasco. I need to talk to Jonathon. Now!"

"Jonathon," Laura called back down the hall, "it is Deputy Carasco. I'm letting him in."

The deputy still wore the dark clothes as he struggled across the threshold with the young Indian girl in his arms. "We've got a big problem. Can you help me with her?"

"Oh no, it's Sandra. Where did you find her? What happened to her?" she stammered.

"Where I can lay her down, where you can help her? I need to talk to Blackeagle, immediately."

"In this room," she motioned. "Put her on the sofa. I'll take care of her."

"The deputy followed Laura into the room and laid the girl on the sofa. Laura covered her with a quilt.

"What happened to her?" Jonathon's deep voice resonated across the room.

Ignoring the question, the deputy looked up. "We need to talk."

"In my office," he motioned and strode down the hall and indicated a chair for deputy sheriff. "I'm ready to listen."

Jorge scooted the chair up to the desk and faced him. "I believe I saved this girl's life late last night. She was on top of that rock plateau where we found the body of that girl Nancy." Jonathon leaned across his desk, his dark eyes wide and listened as the deputy told him about the rescue. "But why did you bring her here and not to your office or the hospital?"

"First, even my office wouldn't believe me. I've been trying to get them to investigate that bunch. Their answer is, they haven't broken any law. They're just a strange group of people. Second, just look at her. She's under some kind of hypnosis. I don't think a doctor could do anything for her. Third, she is Indian. Nancy was Indian. I need help from the Indian community on the kidnapping of young Indian women to do anything against that cult. And fourth, I know you will believe me, Jonathon."

"I do believe you. I have been working on this situation myself. That is why you were able to find Laura and myself here this early. Now, let us help Sandra."

Jonathon took one of girl's small pale hands in his. He held it tightly and closed his eyes. He could feel the increased warmth flow from his palms to her hand as he waited for some reaction from the unconscious girl. He opened his eyes and glanced at Laura.

"Jonathon," Laura reached out to touch Sandra's face. "Look at her. I know something terrible has happened."

The big Indian never answered. He carefully placed his palms on the comatose girl's chest and once again closed his eyes. He could feel the warmth of his hands slowly transfer to her and waited for the heat to fill her body. Again, he opened his eyes to only observe the still unconscious young lady.

Deputy Carasco laid his hand on Jonathon shoulder. "What are you doing? Something I don't know?"

"The Great Spirit has given Jonathon special powers," Laura answered him. "He is passing them on to Sandra. He is hoping they are strong enough to overcome the evil that has infected her body."

Jonathon tenderly moved his hands from the girl's chest and placed them to the sides of her head. His fingertips pressed firmly on her temples. Again, Jonathon could feel the warmth pour from his body into the girl lying there.

The heat in Jonathon's hands slowly diminished, until the tips of his fingers chilled. He grimaced as the cold tried to enter his hands. Small beads of sweat bubbled out on his forehead. He squeezed his eyes tighter and he moved his thumbs to Sandra's forehead. The warmth once again flowed into the sleeping girl.

Laura leaned close to Jonathon's ear. "What can we do to help you?" she pleaded. "Please just tell us."

Jorge grasped her shoulders and pulled Laura away. "I know you're concerned, but I think the big man is doing everything he can."

Jonathon's fingers tingled and vibrated against the girl's temples as if some force was trying to make him release his grip. Sweat ran profusely from his forehead and streamed down his face. His countenance twisted into a distorted mask as his shoulders bent farther over the prostrate girl. He began to chant, quietly at first, then louder, struggling to pull his body upright toward the ceiling. "Oh, Great Spirit," he trolled. "Give me the strength to help this poor girl."

Laura began the sing song melody with him. "Oh, Great Spirit, Great Spirit."

Jorge gazed at the two Indians and at the girl lying on the sofa. He took a deep breath, raised his right hand, and made the sign of the cross over his body. "God help her," he whispered.

## 34

## THE MEDITATION

Neanna stared at the red photograph and then at the two women. "What does it mean, Sabrina? What does the red glow mean?"

"It means the camera or film screwed up," the clerk interrupted. "That's what it means, nothing else."

"No, Pricilla," Sabrina answered, a frown creasing the white skin above her eyes. "It doesn't mean that at all. Come, Neanna, we will take the picture again." She turned and hurried toward the back room.

Three photographs later, the same red glow filled each picture. Sabrina held all three in her hand and stared at Neanna. "I have to be honest with you. I take these photos every day and at times, I'm not sure I believe what I see, but most of the pictures do show an unusual image around the person's head and face. We take them through several polarized glass plates which help expose the person's aura."

"And you believe you can read the aura once it appears in the photo?"

"I can only relate to the customers what I feel inside and they seem to accept the explanation. I'm positive I have a gift to read the auras, but Pricilla doesn't understand any of our New Age beliefs."

"What do you read in mine?" Neanna touched the blonde's hand, her eyes penetrating the girl's dark pupils until she squirmed.

Sabrina shook her head as her mouth slowly opened and she tried to speak. Finally, "I've worked here for over ten years and I have never experienced what I saw in your aura. I can't explain it. Your physical being did not appear in any of the pictures. But I know this. There is something special about you, Neanna. Something different." She stepped closer.

"Perhaps you would be the one to take me to a vortex site. I would like to learn their meaning."

"Yes. I would enjoy giving you a personal tour," she spoke softly, caressing Neanna's arm. "There is so much we could learn about each other."

Neanna stepped back trying to give herself some space from the girl who seemed to be devouring her. "I would love to have you. What's the next step? Do we hop in a car and drive off into the hills?"

"Oh, no, we must prepare our bodies and souls for the journey."

"Of course." *Our bodies and souls?* she wondered, following Sabrina through the store.

"Come. We'll take a stroll along Oak Creek, stopping at several meditation sites to bring our soul in harmony with the earth. You will see, Neanna."

Within minutes, Neanna and Sabrina wandered along a curving path down to the trickling water of Oak Creek until they arrived at a stone sitting area. Rows of smooth round stones led to large boulders fashioned into primitive chairs or settees under the bowing limbs of massive oak trees. Rocks balanced one on top of another formed unique and unusual columns enclosing the circular meditation site. Similar cairns of balanced rocks led up and down the creek bed in groups of varying heights like the spires of some ancient Turkish city. Colorful leaves mottled in hues of red, orange, and tan floated past on the slow meandering stream as it bubbled over and around age-worn rocks and pebbles.

"Please sit." Sabrina motioned and took a seat directly across from Neanna. "First, we hold hands, close our eyes, and listen to the musical melody of the water. I will be meditating with you. As we listen, we will turn our thoughts inward and listen to our inner beings. We will start now."

She tightened her hands slightly on Neanna's fingers and relaxed the grip.

At first, Neanna's thoughts drifted back to the crystal shop and a shudder went through her until she felt the gentle touch of Sabrina's hands in hers. *Here you go again, Neanna, putting yourself in harm's way. What have you gotten yourself into this time?* She tightened her eyelids and began to visualize what was inside allowing a peaceful calm to settle over her. *Just relax, Neanna. Let your mind relax. Think about the good times you've had.*

"Listen to the water," came Sabrina poetic whisper. "Close your mind to the sound of cars passing over the bridge. Listen to the music of the water. Listen to the sounds the spirits are sharing with you."

Neanna's ears picked up the musical cadence of the dancing stream. She tried to bring her body in harmony with the sound.

"Listen to the song the birds are sharing with us. Let your soul drift upward through the leaves until you are one with the spirit of our feathered companions."

*This is amazing,* Neanna thought as her ears picked up the lyrics of the birds in the trees above her.

"Now," the soft voice of Sabrina continued, "listen to the rustle of the leaves. Listen to the gentle sound of the leaf falling, drifting through the air, down, down."

*My God, I don't believe this,* Neanna's mind cried out as she heard, no felt, the leaf drifting earthward and her with it. *I'm floating somewhere up in the trees.*

"Now is the time to enter the next dimension," Sabrina's voice whispered from the trees. "See the portal we will pass through away from this planet, out of this earthen body."

*This is eerie,* Neanna's mind reeled. *I feel so peaceful. Almost like a dream. When was the last time I felt like this? After the little old lady left last night? Yes, I was peaceful then. Wonder who she was, where she went? I know she was real. I know I didn't just imagine her like Michael said. Where are you, Little Grandmother? I could use some advice right now.*

"Listen to the breeze. It is the spirits coming to share themselves with you as we pass through the portal."

*Who are these spirits, Theresa? What portal?* As she thought, she felt her body temperature rise. *Are they real?* From her breast, the heat escaped and poured through her arms. *What's happening to me?* She opened her eyes as a painful scream irrupted from the girl holding her hands.

Sabrina released Neanna's hand yelling, "Dear Lord, my fingers are burning. They're on fire. Help me."

Neanna grasped the screaming girl's hands and thrust them into the cold water of Oak Creek. "Are you all right? What happened?"

The sobbing girl leaned back against Neanna's body as her hands cooled. "I don't know. I was just holding your hands as I meditated when I felt this extreme heat burning my fingers. Didn't you feel it?"

"I only felt the softness of your touch. I don't understand."

"It came from you, Neanna; the heat came from you. Who are you? What are you? I should have known. The answer was in the aura." She rose and staggered backward splashing into the stream.

"I only came to learn about the vortex and you promised to take me there. You will, won't you?" She glared at the young woman, emerald eyes flashing.

The girl's face contorted in fear as she stared across Oak Creek at her mirror image. "Now I see you. You are me. Yes, I will take you to the vortex sites. Maybe we will both learn something there."

# 35
## INDIAN CULTURAL CENTER

A cloud of moist air began to fill the room where the unconscious Indian girl lay. The heat within Jonathon Blackeagle's hands increased, driving away the chill that filled Sandra's head and body.

"Great Spirit, come into this girl's heart. You have the power, Great Spirit," Jonathon repeated.

His hands and arms shook as some unknown force tried to loosen his grip. Sweat poured from his brow and dripped on the girl below him. The perspiration gushed out of his flesh soaking his shirt and wetting his ribs with a cool stream of moisture.

Officer Carasco grabbed the Indian's quivering shoulders. "Jonathon, now can I help?"

"Hold my arms," his strained voice whispered. "Don't let my hands leave her head."

Jorge grasped the big Indian's arms and squeezed them together putting pressure on the girl's head. He could feel

*The Mystical Vortex*

the strange warmth pass into his body. "Holy Jesus, I can't believe this is happening. Where does the heat come from?"

"From inside," Jonathon groaned, "from inside. I don't know why, but I've always had it."

"Look, her eyes are opening!" Laura gasped, her hand covering her open mouth.

"Come, Sandra, come back to us." Jonathon gently massaged her temples. "The Great Spirit is calling you."

The small Indian girl opened her eyes and looked from side to side in fear, then around her. She tried to open her mouth, struggling for air, but nothing came out. Her fingers twitched, then moved. They reached up and clawed at Jonathon's arms as if to pull the warmth deeper inside.

"Where am I?" The words crept from frail lips.

"You're safe, Sandra. You're with us." Laura hugged the girl as tears poured down her tan face.

Jonathon released his hands. "Yes, Sandra, you are back with us again."

Jorge shook his head as he stepped back from the three Indians. "If I didn't see this, I would never have believed it, but I've got work to do now." He turned to leave the Cultural Center.

"Wait," Jonathon's deep voice called, "I would like you to come with me tonight."

"Come with you? Where?"

"To one of the sacred mountains. To one of the vortex sites."

"Of course I'll come. What's happening?"

"I found something here at the Cultural Center." His voice quieted and creases filled his brow. "I believe it is something left by the Ancient Ones. I need to bring it to sacred ground."

"Just tell me where and when. After today's experience, I'd be interested in sharing anything with you."

"We will go tonight after dark." By now he was almost whispering. "I need someone I can trust and I know you are the one. I will let you know the location." His eyelids drooped. "I must meditate first."

Jorge shook hands with the big man again. He could feel the warmth creep slowly up his arm and he released the grip before fear and disbelief took control. The deputy sheriff smiled and disappeared out the door.

## 36

### THE VORTEX SITE

Neanna and Sabrina rushed back into the New Age shop, ignoring the concerned look of the clerk as the door slammed behind them. Customers jumped aside as the two raced to the back room.

Sabrina whirled to face Neanna, "I'm not sure what you expect to receive from the vortex sites, but I will take you there. Our meditation was only the beginning of our trip. Perhaps you came here to be healed from some inner pain, mental or physical. Perhaps you came here to seek spiritual guidance for your soul. Perhaps you came here to heal a rift within your family. Perhaps the vortex will bring what seek, Neanna."

A shocked look crossed Neanna's countenance as her mother's and father's faces passed through her mind. "I'm not sure what brought me to Sedona," Neanna managed to reply, "but now that I'm here, I intend to find that reason."

*Gateway to Another Dimension*

"I must have touched a sore spot," Sabrina continued as she gathered material. "We believe a human can cure himself by concentrating the mind to arouse the awesome healing force within the body."

Ignoring Sabrina's response, Neanna fidgeted with her hair, pulling a long strand and rolling it slowly between her fingers. "I too believe the mind has more power than just thoughts."

"Often spiritual healing needs something more, such as nonphysical energies found at various places on this earth. We believe Sedona's vortex meditation sites provide a gateway to guide mysterious forces from dimensions beyond our own into our very souls."

Neanna shook her head. *This girl's belief is amazing,* she thought as she helped remove several quartz crystals from a small box and put them in a dark blue fanny pack. "Have you experienced this, Sabrina?"

"Yes, I believe I have and I have witnessed others. They said it was a wonderful and glorious experience drifting from this dimension to another with such peacefulness. You will see. First, I must change my clothes. Something more appropriate for the hills."

Soon the two of them drove through Sedona in Sabrina's small blue sedan on their way to Airport Mesa. At the narrow turnout along the hillside road, Sabrina parked the car. "It's up there," she said, pointing at the red rock trail leading to the hill above them. "This is the shortest walking route. Some jeep tours drive visitors almost to the top, but I think it dilutes the dignity of place."

Neanna followed her guide up the mountain trail, sometimes stumbling over shattered red rock beneath the branches of pinion pines and junipers, then on a dusty pathway around red-barked manzanita, sharp Spanish bayonet, and cholla cactus. As they climbed upward, she watched the little city of Sedona come in view far below them. Around the next turn, a magnificent crimson sandstone dome appeared above. The tall monument resembled a giant beehive where the wind had carved concentric rings around its tall tapering body.

"We are here," whispered Sabrina, leading them around the base of the tower.

Walking to the far side, Neanna looked down toward Oak Creek. "Look," she said, "I believe I can see Schnebly Cabins where I'm staying. I could walk down to them from this side of the mountain."

Sabrina shot her a stern gaze. "This is a spiritual place. We must respect it as such."

Neanna shrugged. "Sorry."

"We believe the vortexes are conductors of cosmic forces from some other dimension and your soul can use these conduits of extra dimensional energy to rise to new heights of healing ability. The flowing energy of the vortex can recharge the body's spirit and reinforce the immune system."

"Have you witnessed this?"

"Yes, several times. I have brought visitors who suffered from severe back pain and when we left, they said the pain was reduced or gone. Others came with emotional problems and said they felt so peaceful inside after visiting the vortex. Some claimed they had visions of ancient ancestors, witnessed past life experiences, and saw Indian spirits." She hiked around the base one more time, stopping near a cleft in the sandstone surface. "We are here. The vortex is strongest where it passes through the rock. Come lie down."

Sabrina reached into the small fanny pack strapped to her waist and withdrew several quartz crystals. She spread them on the surface of the ground and handed a few to Neanna. "Place these where your feet will contact them. The crystals boost our body's energy and thoughts, and amplify the strength of the vortex. Perhaps the vortex will reveal what you are seeking."

Neanna watched the blonde girl stretch out on the bare red soil with the tapered gems caressing the soles of her shoes, then lay down head to head with her. "What's the next step?" she whispered, nervously.

"We'll meditate as before, but we don't touch each other. Just let our minds soar as our souls drift upward and out of this dimension."

Neanna stared up into the deep blue sky looking for some form of distraction such as the errant passing of a hawk or some other bird, but nothing appeared. She slowly let her eyelids close. *What am I seeking?* she wondered. *Is this just foolishness or is there some purpose why I am here? Mom, Dad, can you sense my presence? I need to hear from you. I need to know you love me. What did Sabrina say? Just let your mind drift up and your soul flow into the next dimension. Perhaps that will help.* She tightened her eyelids and strained to see outside her physical being. A cloud seemed to drift across her mind and her body seemed to lift from the ground.

Neanna looked down at the red sandstone monument and the two bodies lying next to it. The mountaintop grew smaller as she soared upward and the beings below disappeared into tiny specks. Red rock formations jutted upward from a crimson plain that filled her view in every direction. Suddenly, her upward flight ceased and she began to float downward as images filled the land below. Bronze faced men, women, and children marched in a winding column across the plain from the desolation and ruin of cornfields and crumbling cliff dwellings. Beyond them, strange floating globular forms seemed to beckon the marchers, while behind them, men on horseback clothed in armor and helmets rode across the horizon.

*Oh Dear God,* Neanna thought. *What on earth am I witnessing? Old Woman, where are you? Tell me what this is. Tell me if this is why I came to this place. Where are you Mom? Where are you Dad? Where are you Old Woman?*

From somewhere and yet nowhere, Neanna heard the words. "Go back. This is not a place where you should be. Go back, Neanna, go back."

She sensed a calming warmth surround her thoughts and suddenly, the two physiques at the vortex site appeared below her. Then instantly, she felt herself drift back into her body and the pain of the hard surface where it rested. The soft heat flowed from her inner self outward to her arms, legs, and head. She sat up quickly as a terrified cry filled her ears.

"What happened," Sabrina screamed, jumping to her feet. "You did it again."

"I did nothing," Neanna yelled back at her as she stood. "It was your damn vortex that did it. Something came from the other dimension and attacked you."

"Go to hell. Look at my hair. It's burned to my scalp. Besides, I'm not sure there is another dimension."

"What do you mean, no other dimension? Didn't you say let your soul go there?"

Sabrina poured water on her head, cooling the pain. "Many people believe in the healing power, so we just bring them here. They say it helps their body and soul, but I have never experienced it. I have tried. I have followed my own instructions, but nothing. I was only relaxing when you burned my hair. How do you do it?"

Neanna grabbed her mirror image by the upper arms and shook her. "I went there, girl," she said, flashing her emerald eyes. "I went there just as you told me, and I didn't like what I saw. It was evil. Besides your hair is not burned. Apparently your head became overheated."

Sabrina shook her head back and forth as fear filled her pallid countenance. "No, no, you can't go there. Let me loose, let me go back to the shop."

Neanna hugged the frightened girl to her. "I'm sorry. I would never do anything to hurt you. I would give anything to help you live the vortex experience."

Sabrina slumped against Neanna. "I can't. I just can't. I don't know why. For years I've tried so hard." Tears flowed down her cheeks.

Neanna pushed her back and looked into the face of the sobbing girl. "Sabrina, perhaps your soul is at peace. Perhaps you don't need help from the spirits of the vortex, where I do, because my soul is not at rest."

A smile crossed her face. "Do you really think that could be true?" She wiped her eyes.

"Of course, you are a wonderful giving person. You don't need help."

Sabrina's face slowly beamed. She grabbed Neanna's hand. "Let's go back to the car. And please come to see me again."

Neanna tightened her grip on the young woman's hand. "I promise."

They picked up the crystals and left the vortex site. When they reached the car, Neanna glanced back at the reddish hills and shivered. *What's coming next?*

# 37

## THE CAVE

The next morning after breakfast, Neanna, Michael, and Tony rode into El Lobo Canyon. A faint spray of crimson dust filled the air behind the rented Wrangler as the jeep bounced over the uneven ruts into the narrowing gorge. Michael braked, slowing the vehicle.

"So that mysterious little old lady warned you not to go out to the desert; then why did you come?"

"So many strange things have happened in Sedona like visiting the New Age shop and the vortex site, I'm not sure what I saw or what I believe." She stroked the lock of blonde hair that strayed across her left eye, twisting it into a tight curl and finally pushing it beneath her wide-brimmed hat. "Besides, before I left town, I knew you would protect me." She smiled over at him, and gently slid her hand across his knee.

*Gateway to Another Dimension*

"See," Tony spoke up, waving his deformed hand. "Someone else has warned you of the dangers in the Devil's Lair."

"We'll take your words of caution, Tony, I promise. Right now we're here." Michael stopped the vehicle on the small ridge above the end of the road.

"The jeep ran well. You must have had it fixed." Neanna asked as she stepped outside.

"Yes. I convinced a mechanic to stay open late for double his usual fee." He shook his head. "If you want something done right, you have to pay for it."

The early morning sunlight had begun to reach down into El Lobo Canyon, but a cool desert breeze had already greeted the band of explorers as they prepared to leave the jeep. Michael put his backpack over his field jacket, handed Neanna and Tony each a canteen, and they started up the faint trail. Gusts of wind had almost erased their previous tracks.

As they hiked down into Tony's Devil's Lair, the little guide held back. "I am sorry, but I can not go down there."

"What," Michael's voice rose. "I was hoping you could help us in case we got lost."

"I can not go there. I fear I will not return." He shuddered, waving his crippled hand. "I fear it will be my last trip into the desert."

Neanna glanced back at Tony through her green-rimmed sunglasses. "Give him an extra key, Michael. Can't you see the terror in his heart? He can wait in the jeep."

"Well, it looks like you have a benefactor. Here's the key. If it gets too hot, run the air conditioner once in a while and we should be back within four hours."

As the guide wandered away, Neanna glanced at Michael, wrinkling her forehead. "Are you sure you know where we're going? Yesterday, you seemed to be lost."

"Of course I know." He quickly diverted his eyes from her's and continued on into the twisting canyons. He constantly consulted the brown paper map and his compass as he turned onto a narrow animal trail devoid of any vegetation that led them over the southern edge of the next canyon and down into a small alcove. About halfway along the winding trail, a dark form shadowed part of the cliff to their left. As the two approached it, the image slowly materialized into the mouth of a cave opening deep into the red sandstone. A thick layer of dusty soil covered the ground at the cave entrance.

Michael started to walk across it, then held up his hand to stop Neanna. "Wait. Something's wrong here." He knelt and let the dust run through his fingers. "Notice the regular pattern running through this fine dirt." Years of archeology told him something unnatural lay before him. "This soil does not belong here. It came from somewhere else. Maybe a few hundred yards away, but it didn't occur here naturally. And I'm sure no animal made those smooth lines through it."

As he took Neanna's hand, she removed her sunglasses and tucked them in her denim jacket pocket, and they stepped forward into the darkness. A musty smell filled their nostrils and the outside noises disappeared as silence surrounded them. Michael squeezed her hand as they hesitated for a moment, staring into the darkness. After a few minutes of concern, he pulled a flashlight from his backpack. The vermilion walls echoed the light back to them, but in front, the distant blackness absorbed the beam until it disappeared.

The anxious archeologist took the map from his pocket and scanned the flashlight across the ragged paper. He ran his finger along a cliff-lined canyon marked RED in bold letters. Across from the rock formation labeled "cathedral", he moved his finger up the third tributary on the left. His finger crossed a bold curvy line. "Ridge," he muttered, then he traced on to faint canyon markings that curved to the right on the map. About half way along the line an upside down "U" leaned against the graphic cliff markings. "Cave," he whispered.

He smiled as he caressed the rough paper. A graphite pencil had originally inscribed the words and pictures. Later someone had traced over the pencil with black ink.

*The Mystical Vortex*

Neanna leaned over his shoulder and touched the map. "Where are we?"

He instinctively jerked it from her touch.

"Michael, what's with you?"

"I'm sorry. I've come to believe this damn map is everything to me. You're the first person I've allowed to see it and I've always wanted to share this moment with you."

"So, where are we?"

He opened the brown paper and spread the map on the dusty cavern floor. "This is the route we have followed." His finger traced Red Canyon and then the third tributary. "This is El Lobo Canyon. These lines and the compass headings the old man gave me led us to this cave. See the upside down 'U'." He grinned. "I'm excited we've made it this far."

"I'm thrilled for you, but you never told me what you're looking for. I promised myself I wouldn't ask until you told me, but now I would like to know before I go any further into this tunnel."

Michael folded the map and put it in his pocket. He pulled Neanna to the floor close to him. "In the 1500's, the Spaniards came. Antoino de Espejo led an expedition to this country with armed soldiers to find gold, silver, copper, and other treasure they could take back to Spain. They searched for Indian mines, but disaster found them. Some of the soldiers disappeared. They simply vanished.

The others panicked and left without taking the treasure they had found."

# 38

INTO THE CAVE

The slim light from the cave entrance filtered back toward the explorers. Michael's flashlight added to the pale glow from the cave's mouth.

"And so, you believe this is where tragedy struck the Spaniards. Who told you?" Neanna reached out to grasp his arm as her voice echoed through the dark chamber.

"An old man I befriended on a trip into Death Valley," Michael spoke much quieter. "He gave me the map and directions before he died. He told me the story of the Spanish explorers. And now, I believe him because we're here just as the map said we'd be." He patted the pocket containing the sketch.

"I believe that part of the story." Her voice dropped to almost a whisper. "Let's go find the rest." She pointed into the darkness.

"We'll go only a short distance into the cave today, Neanna. We'll need lanterns, water, food and other supplies before we can go deeper. If this is an old mine, it could be dangerous. I don't want to rush into it."

Michael lifted the flashlight to trace the outline of the cave and then across the dirt-covered floor. Small stars twinkled on the cave walls where bits of embedded mica and quartz reflected the beam. Suddenly, a flight of dark cave bats swarmed off the ceiling and poured out the opening.

"Oh, my God," Neanna screamed, ducking and tugging the brim of her hat down around her hair with both hands.

"They're gone," he called, as he shielded her with his body.

Neanna straightened and shivered, "I'll always be afraid of bats, no matter how small they are."

"I'm not so fond of them myself," Michael said, as he ran his learned hands over the cave wall tracing the surface with his fingers. "Part of this cave is natural. See where the ancient patina covers a portion of the interior, then here the rock is bare with chip marks cutting into the surface." He continued to rub his fingertips over the wall. "It must have been widened by some type of cutting tool such as a rock chisel a long time ago. There's no sign of blasting."

She followed his gaze upward straining to see more bats. "Look, Michael," the excitement in her voice rose, "up near the ceiling. There seems to be a painted line. It runs into the darkness like a piece of string asking to guide us."

"You're thinking of fairy tales. I have to think with facts. If the line was made by man, it must have a purpose."

"I found it and I'm going to follow my fairy godmother into the depths of her lair. Come on." A faint smile crossed her face as she pulled on his arm, then turned and raced into the darkness.

"Wait, Neanna, don't go in there alone. Mines have vertical shafts. It may be a long way down to the next level. Do you hear me," his voice pleaded into the blackness as he followed her.

Neanna felt a strange calm settle over her as she proceeded deeper into the black cave. She could hear Michael calling behind her, but for some unknown reason she felt compelled to go further into the dark abyss. The walls of the stone cave seemed to close in on her and she began to feel warmth filling her body. Then, Neanna noticed her hands getting warmer until they were almost hot, and she needed to raise them to guide her passage. The cave curved to the right, but her raised arms propelled her to the left until her palms touched the cold surface of the tunnel. She felt along the solid rock until her hands seemed to slip through a crevice and her body fell through an opening beyond the cave wall. The warmth in her hands slowly dissipated. The warm glow around her body dissolved away. The calmness inside lifted like a vapor from her body. Suddenly she felt frightened.

"Michael, where are you? Where in God's name are you? What am I doing here?"

Neanna listened as darkness closed around her and the warmth disappeared. She felt the cold walls, waiting for a sensation on her fingertips to tell her something, but nothing happened. She laid her palms against the stone, hoping that the warmth would reappear, but the wall remained frigid. She shivered and pulled her denim jacket closer around her body as the chill pressed through her thin summer clothes.

"Michael, can you hear me." Her pleading call echoed one way down the passage and up the other, but Michael did not answer.

In desperation, Neanna placed her palms against the sides of her head. The broad-brimmed tan hat slid down her back hanging there by the thin cord around her neck and tumbling the long blonde hair over her hands. *What led me here? What pulled me to this place?* She tried to make her mind tell her the answer. *I remember following the line on the ceiling,* she thought. *I could clearly see the walls of the cave ahead of me. At that moment, I knew where to go. Something told me which passage to follow and when to turn.*

*Why can't I see or sense that now?*

"Jonathon Blackeagle can you hear me?" she yelled up at the ceiling, "Jonathon." Her solitary words came bouncing back down at her. "Jonathon, I need your warmth now," she tightened the grip on her head and screamed down the dark tunnel.

* * *

When Neanna left Michael, the dry cave air suddenly changed to dampness, and a cold chill passed over the archeologist as his eyes followed the light of his flashlight into the darkness. His call echoed down the hollow tunnel. "Neanna, wait, before you get lost."

He raised the beam to look at the faint painted line on the cave's ceiling. *What possessed her to follow it?* He raced through the cave, looking for some sign of the blonde girl. His flashlight dimmed as he ran on following the tunnel as it began curving to the right.

* * *

Neanna dropped to her knees on the rough cave floor and covered her face with cold helpless hands. As her fingertips touched her forehead, a pink glow formed beneath them. The radiance brightened from pink to pale red then dark red and the warmth from it entered her fingertips. She closed her eyelids and felt the heat flow from her fingers and stream through her arms into her chest. It centered over her heart. "The charka," she heard herself mutter.

Within her mind, she could visualize the solid cave wall as it seemed to open. Michael, her mind called as she watched him rush toward her, then instinctively she stood and reached out.

She grasped his coat sleeve and pulled him into the chamber. His flashlight clattered to the ground on the other side. She stood in the cold dark cavern tugging at Michael's tan field jacket as moist air caressed her body.

"Neanna, what the hell, is that you?"

She raised her hand and covered his lips. "Now is my time. Be quiet; be patient."

She placed open palms against her head with both forefingers pressing into her brow. Her tightly closed eyes saw nothing in the darkness that surrounded her, but they could sense the warmth that had entered her head.

As Neanna peered through the hands cupped on the sides of her head, she noticed a dim glow in the distance. She watched the glow brighten then dim again, as it flickered and danced far down the cavern. She wanted to release her hands, but feared she would loose the warmth and the intuition she had received.

She jumped as a gentle voice near her spoke. "Go Dear. Go to the light."

"What!" She whirled around. "Who are you?"

"Who are you talking to, Neanna? Michael muttered. "I can't see a damn thing. Is there someone else in this cave?"

"Go to the light, Neanna," the soft voice repeated. "Now is a time of learning."

"It's the little old woman from the cabin, Michael." Neanna dropped her hands and reached out. "Let me touch you, Little Grandmother."

"Can you see the distant glow? It is calling you."

"I know who you are. Please, touch my hand."

"I am not here, but you know where I am. I came to help you."

"Neanna, who is it?" Michael tugged at her shoulders.

"Please, Michael, give me a moment." She closed her eyes and put her hands to the sides of her head. "You're in here aren't you? I can see you now, Theresa, as plain as in the cabin. Are you the one who brought me this far? What am I looking for?"

"So many questions, Dear," the voice quietly spoke. "Go to the light. It will answer your questions. Goodbye"

"Don't go! Come back!" Neanna opened her eyes in hopes of seeing the little lady dressed in rags, but only the inky blackness stared back. Far down the cavern, the glow played its eerie light in some unknown hall.

Neanna nervously pulled and twisted the blonde strands of hair that fell across her cheek, then slid her hands inside her jacket and shirt. Her body felt strangely warm as she headed toward the flickering light. "Look, Michael, can you see it?" She grasped his arm and pulled him toward the distant glow.

## 39

THE VORTEX SCENE

Neanna strolled confidently through the moist darkness of the cave pulling a reluctant Michael with her.

"I'm right behind you," he whispered as if something or someone in the dark cave could hear.

Ahead of them, they could see the glowing light shimmer across the stone walls as it flickered through colors of white, pale yellow and gold.

Neanna stepped cautiously, glancing from side to side, toward it, watching the light play on the cavern walls leading her deeper into the bowels of the red rock mountains.

She felt strangely warm and almost peaceful as she crept along the tunnel wall approaching the dancing glow. Ahead of her, the cavern opened to a large amphitheater with yellow flakes of metal covering the walls. Multicolored crystals protruded from the rocky crusted ceiling emitting light that bounced off the walls filling the hall with a shimmering glow. Gazing from the entrance, she stood still with her mouth and eyes wide open, her blonde hair filtering across her face, and muttering over and over, "Oh, my God. Oh, my God."

"What the hell," Michael shouted, staring into the center of the huge cave room, a golden glow reflecting in his eyes.

"Oh, my God," Neanna continued to cry as she rushed toward it.

Golden objects of every description filled the center of the room. Golden goblets were stacked on top of golden plates and bowls. Golden headdresses were piled with golden necklaces, golden bracelets, and golden buckles.

"This must be your treasure, Michael, or the lost treasure of some Inca tribe. And look at these, helmets, swords, and breastplates of Spanish Conquistadors scattered around the golden treasure."

The archeologist struggled to move as if some strange force held him back until he reached the abandoned armor and picked up a metal helmet. "It's almost as history told us. When some Spanish soldiers disappeared, they left part of their armor behind." He caressed the helmet as if it were more precious than the golden treasure piled next to him.

Then, across the open room Neanna noticed them. Pictures, pictures, and more pictures pecked into the crusted yellow walls. Abandoning all caution, she raced across the dusty floor and put her hands on the figures, tracing the faint lines with her fingers. *This is the story of the Ancient Ones,* she thought. *Here is early man armed with spears, killing for food, then here are the farmers raising corn.* Her fingers touched the vertical lines with ears of corn attached. Glancing at the next scene, a look of pain crossed her face, and she pulled her hand from the solid rock. Dreadful scenes of death followed. Men, women, and children lay sprawled and twisted against the stone wall. Nearby, wavy lines represented dying corn crops, and skeletons of bighorn sheep and other animals represented their death. Only a few Indians were shown leaving the scene.

With a lump pushing up into her throat, Neanna skirted the death scene. Ahead of her, a strange hooded figure seemed to beckon the small crowd. Beyond that lay a broad mountain peak with spiraling lines above it. "My God," she gasped again, "it's the vortex with the hooded cult beckoning the people to it." She put her hand over her mouth. "This can't be true," she shouted at the walls, banging her fists against the hard surface.

Then Neanna looked above the vortex. At the top of the spiral, head dressed Indians were pecked into the surface, then people in armor stood above them, and finally faint wispy forms seemed to dance across the ceiling. Neanna reached her hands up until she touched the bizarre forms. Her fingers tingled with a strange energy that raced down her arms, across her shoulders, and into her spine. It filled her body with unusual warmth that consumed her strength until she closed her eyes and collapsed to the floor.

## 40

### THE TRAP

Holding the Conquistador's helmet gently in his hand, Michael turned to share the moment of excitement with Neanna, but she was gone from his sight in the dimly lit cavern.

"Neanna, where are you?" he called. "Damn, she must have gone back the way we came."

He raced out of the amphitheater passing the small figure lying in the dark shadows. As he reached the darkness of the stone wall, he felt for the opening, but only solid rock met his touch. "How in the hell did I get in here?" he muttered. Raising the helmet and banging it against the cave surface, the wall opened suddenly and he fell to the ground on the other side.

As Michael rose, he spotted a faint glow somewhere beyond him. He sprinted toward it, covering the distance quickly yet quietly. *She must have gone this way,* he thought. The illumination now filled the far end of the tunnel and several smaller shafts led off from the main one. He glanced at the ceiling once again and saw that the faintly painted line led straight toward the glow. Intent on what lay ahead, he never slowed his pace. Again and again, he called for Neanna.

Passing the next side tunnel, Michael heard a sharp scraping noise. Turning, he saw a large form step out of the darkness. He tried to raise his arms as a heavy blow crashed down on his felt hat driving him to the dusty floor and into unconsciousness. The metal helmet clattered across the cavern's rocky surface.

The man with the club yelled down the narrow passage for help and the two miners carried Michael to the lighted area. "Look what we found snooping in the mine shaft."

"Good work, Reynolds. I believe we've got the guy Wallace was looking for." A tall scar-faced man in a brown cowhide jacket reached down, grabbed Michael's face in his hand and twisted it toward him. "He looks like the guy. He dresses like the guy." He pushed the unconscious archeologist's head into the dirt. "Tie him up until I find out what Wallace wants us to do with him." Scarface pointed to the side of the tunnel. "And blindfold him, too. I don't want him to see what we're doing."

"Sure, Pearson. Anything else?" Reynolds sneered through his short brown beard.

"Yeah. Get back to work. We've got a schedule to make. I'll get Wallace on the radio."

They propped Michael behind some large wooden boxes at the edge of the tunnel.

Scarface Pearson ran his hand through the bag of deep red gems as he sauntered to the radio transmitter sitting on a nearby crate. He put on the headset, picked up the microphone, and pushed in several coded numerals on the keyboard and then the send button. Within seconds, he heard Wallace reply. "Yes."

"Pearson here." He ran his fingers over the thick white scar. "We got that archeologist you were looking for. We caught him snooping in the mine."

"Did he see any of you?"

"Naw," he snarled to impress the man on the other end, "Reynolds clubbed him before he knew what happened. We got him tied up and blindfolded. What's next?"

"Take him out to some remote desert spot and dump him. Don't let him see any of you or hear your voices. He'll either die or get the message that we don't want him snooping around. You got that, Scarface?"

"We gotcha, Wallace," he growled. "We'll take care of the guy. Don't you worry none."

# 41

## BEYOND THE LIGHT

Neanna Miller lay unconscious on the cold floor of the cavern when she felt a small warm hand touch her shoulder. "Wake up, Dear." Tiny fingers seemed to shake her ever so slightly. "Now is not the time to sleep. This is the time of discovery."

The blonde girl faintly opened her eyes, staring into the flickering yellow glow. "Who's calling my name? Is that you, Michael?" She leaned up, but saw no one. "Where are you?" she asked.

"You know I am here," the quiet voice replied. "It is time to go."

Neanna pressed the palms of her hands against the sides of her head. "You're in there, in my mind, aren't you?"

"Yes, my Dear. Come, it is time to go."

Neanna slowly rose from the cold floor of the cavern and shivered as the warmth that had filled her body disappeared. The shimmering gold light in the room cast weird shadows across the walls and her face. She stood and looked around.

"Now, for God's sake, where did you go, Michael Adams," she yelled at the walls of the cavern. "I'm standing in your damn cave, looking at your damn treasure, and now you're not here to enjoy it or hate it with me."

A small tunnel led off to the left of the big room and Neanna followed it. "This is where you want me to go, Old Woman. You lead the way and I will follow."

The deeper into the cave she went, the warmer it became. The faint light from the amphitheater seemed to follow, allowing her to see farther into the narrow tunnel. She walked on with the glow from behind providing her sufficient light to see.

"How much farther, Old Woman? I'm getting tired," she asked.

"Not too far," the answer seemed to come to her.

Ahead, a cool breeze crept into the tunnel and tiny spots appeared in the distance as she approached the opening. A few more steps and Neanna realized she was staring into the night sky where a myriad of stars twinkled back at her gaze. *It can't be night,* she thought. *Only a few hours ago, Michael and I entered this cave. And I'm not hungry.*

"Okay, Michael, where am I now, and by God, you better not have gone back to Utah." She pulled and twisted knots in the strings of blonde hair that fell across her left eye.

# 42

## THE DEVIL'S LAIR

A low rumbling noise resonated through the mine, and dust permeated the air as a small group of men manned a large suction hose. The tube led from a blockage in the narrow underground passage along the floor and up through a hole in the ceiling. Two men dressed in dingy work clothes shoveled the loose material from the closed end of the tunnel into a pile. A third man, equally dirty, held a suction nozzle to the heap and watched the sandy substance disappear into the hose.

The tall scar-faced man put the microphone down and turned to another who monitored the flow of material up the tube into the hole above. "Good work, Reynolds, glad you got the guy before he saw us."

"It's lucky I did," he pulled a cigarette from his pack. "I just went back in that old tunnel to take a leak. I'd just finished and there he was sneakin' up on us. He was calling some name, like there was someone else in that cave with him." He lit the cigarette and blew a puff of smoke upward. "Anyway, that old pick handle sure came in handy."

"Wallace wants us to take the guy out in the desert and dump him where he can't get back. Don't kill him. Just make sure he doesn't return."

"I'll need some help. We gotta keep him blindfolded and tied up."

"Take one of the crew from up above with you. You might drop the guy off in that place they call the Devil's Lair. Ain't nobody coming out of there." He stroked the white scar on his face. "It's noon, so the sun'll be hotter'n hell right now. And when you get back, I want you to look down that tunnel to see if anyone else came with him."

Reynolds stomped his cigarette butt into the ground and pulled the still unconscious Michael along the floor to the hole in the tunnel roof. A slim ladder led upward through the opening where the wiggling hose went. He yelled at the men above. "Mac, send me down a rope. I've got a body down here I want you to pull up."

They loaded their prisoner in the back of an old pickup truck and drove off in the direction of the Devil's Lair.

"If he wakes up, just give him another crack. I put that pick handle in the back just in case," Reynolds told the man beside him.

Reynolds followed the top of the desert ridges and in less than an hour, the men pulled Michael from the truck.

## Gateway to Another Dimension

They carried him, one by the feet, and the other under the armpits, toward the edge of a steep cliff.

"You must of hit this jerk pretty hard. He ain't moved since we threw him in the truck."

"Guess I don't know my own strength, Mac, but I can still feel the guy breathing. He'll come around."

"Sure he will, but it won't do him no damn good. He's goin' be dead in a little while anyway."

"You're right, Mac. Take off the ropes and blindfold. We'll just dump him down there. He'll roll over that cliff and no tell'n what will happen then. Make sure you throw his hat with him. We don't want any evidence."

The two men untied Michael and removed his blindfold. As the sunlight struck his eye lids, he blinked just in time to feel his body plunge down the steep grade toward the cliff below. His body flopped from side to side as it bounced over sandy mounds and rocky outcroppings. Gravel and sand cut into his bare face and hands as he rolled and slid down the steep hill, sometimes sideways, sometimes face down.

Above him, Reynolds and his partner dragged an old blanket behind them to cover their tracks.

Consciousness crept back into Michael's senses. He grabbed at the ground to slow his descent, but only loose rocks and rough gravel filled his bleeding hands. An abrupt rocky ledge lay only a few feet below his tumbling body.

The white-hot Arizona sun beat down on the barren hills surrounding the Devil's Lair, but Michael Adams never felt its warmth as he bounced over coarse sand and gravel toward a sheer cliff below. Blood spread across his bare palms and battered face as his body picked up speed on the plunge down the steep grade. His clothes and boots quickly filled with loose sand. The rocks shredded his tan field jacket and tore holes through the knees of his pants. He clawed his bloody fingers on the rough stone surface of the cliff before he slid over the edge.

Just beneath the ledge where Michael's body tumbled, the sandstone hills had eroded into upright spires resembling the cone shaped steeples of a medieval church. These spires had been carved into various heights with troughs running between them where massive runoff from flash floods carried water and debris to the bottom. The troughs sloped from the higher pinnacles to shorter ones as the erosion cut into the soft sandstone.

As the barely awake archeologist slipped over the precipice, he slid into one of the upper troughs instead of falling directly to the bottom. The wide groove in the sandstone curved behind a tall cone and then dropped down to a shorter one. He rolled like rag doll on a roller coaster track, and as the incline decreased, his forward motion slowed. Around the next turn, harder material in the sandstone had resisted erosion and set up a barrier to the flow of erosive water. The deluge of sand and gravel had carved a small indentation into the edge of the spire on its downward plunge.

Michael crashed into the barrier and slammed to a stop. His limp form jammed into the small cave cut into the wall of the cliff. He had remained conscious as he dropped over the edge, but the fall drove him into oblivion once again.

Above the Devil's Lair, the fiery western sun moved across the sky. Its relentless rays beat down on his unconscious body until a nearby spire cast a cool shadow across him.

As the sun dropped beyond the horizon, the cold desert air slid down into the canyons of the Devil's Lair. A chill brushed across Michael face and he reached a feeble hand to his blood stained cheek. His raw fingertips touched the battered and bruised skin. "Ow," he muttered, "that hurts like hell. How in the devil did I get here?"

He edged out of the small cave and looked down. *My God,* he thought, *if I'd tumbled down there, I'd be buzzard food right now.* He eased himself into the next trough that led from behind the sandstone cone above down to a smaller one below. From there, he worked his way to the canyon bottom. He looked up. *If I'd fallen over the cliff just a few feet to the left, I wouldn't be standing here.*

He gazed at the stars that faintly filled the sky. *Within an hour, they'll be bright enough for me to follow,* he reasoned.

Collapsing against the wall, he slid his back down one of the tapered sandstone spires until the seat of his ripped pants rested on the ground and then tried to remember what had happened. As memory slowly trickled back into his consciousness, Michael jumped to his feet.

"Neanna," he yelled, "where are you?"

A flash of pain rushed through his injured head as he stood. He reached up and touched the back of his skull where his fingers felt a large painful lump. *Someone hit me. It was in the cave. Yes, that's it. Neanna had disappeared and I was trying to find her. I saw a light ahead and I started for it when something or someone bashed me in the head. Who ever did it dumped my half-dead body out here to finish the job.*

Michael looked up. The bright stars filled the heavens. He picked out the Big Dipper, then found the North Star. As a sense of direction took over, he turned and started walking northeast.

## 43

AIRPORT MESA

Darkness crept over Sedona's red rock hills as Deputy Sheriff Jorge Carasco followed Jonathon Blackeagle's directions toward Airport Mesa. He was still in his tan uniform without the tie and his beige Stetson rested on the seat beside him. The warm autumn sun had disappeared in the west and the yellow moon had not risen in the east. White pinpoints of light in the dark sky above shone where the night stars lay. Jorge rolled down the window on the County Sheriff's SUV and peered into the night sky and then at his watch. He was almost one hour early.

"Just wanted to make sure I got here on time, Jonathon," he muttered to himself. In the distance, anxious coyotes started their nightly howling and dark gray bats from some hidden cave winged past him and off into the night. Jorge sat patiently and peacefully watching the bright stars above and the faint lights of Sedona blinking in the distance when a hand touched his arm. He whirled his head around and at the same time, jerked his revolver from the holster.

"Jonathon! You startled the hell out of me," his loud words broke the silence.

The big man laughed softly. "You looked so peaceful just staring out the window. I could not help but sneak up on you."

"You sure did," his voice dropped. "I might have shot you."

"I had no fear, my friend; I would have disappeared as I had come."

"Are you alone?" Jorge tried to see beyond him into the blackness.

"Yes." Jonathon released his arm. "Come, we will start tonight's work."

"This is the place where the first Indian girl was killed and where I saved Sandra. Did you know that?"

"Yes. The Great Spirit told me."

The deputy stepped from his vehicle and they hurried into the darkness. Neither spoke until they passed through the hidden passageway to the top of the red rock formation. In the east, a pale yellow glow silhouetted the distant sandstone monuments.

Jonathon took a small ceremonial blanket from his pack and handed it to Jorge. "Spread the blanket on the ground with the design side up. Face the pattern toward the east, toward the moon's glow."

Jorge stared at the fringed blanket until he could see the faded design. He laid the blanket on the surface of the stone plateau as instructed.

"Step behind me," Jonathon's deep voice called. Facing east, he placed his feet on one edge of the blanket.

Jorge stood behind him watching the moon rise above the rocky peaks. The golden-yellow orb glowed in the east, casting a pale light on the two men standing on the red rock plateau. In the distance, coyotes sang their lonely song at the moon and nearby nocturnal rodents and insects rustled, chittered, and chirped in the darkness of the night.

Jonathon stood facing the eastern horizon on the raveled border of the small worn and ragged ceremonial blanket belonging to one of his ancestors. He took the small fur-covered pouch from his pocket, loosened the leather drawstring, and poured a small amount of the contents into his left hand. He tightened the pouch with his teeth, then dropped it back into his pocket.

The tall Indian looked skyward, raised both hands clenched into fists, and began to chant. "Oh Great Spirit," his deep voice filled the air, then continued in his native tongue.

Deputy Carasco watched in fascination as the big man's words echoed into the night sky and his arms rose toward the stars. He wondered what purpose Jonathon had in petitioning the Great Spirit and why he had asked Jorge to come with him.

Suddenly, Jonathon stopped chanting and opened his left hand. Multicolored powders drifted down; some were caught in the slight breeze and swirled upward. The breeze carried the dust particles around the two men, wider and upward creating a shimmering mist in colors of pink and blue covering Jorge and Jonathon.

The colors whirled about them intermingling in a vortex of circling streams until images began to appear in the mist. The forms faded in and out as if trying to materialize. First, recent Indians, then those of the past, and the ones of ancient times appeared. Next, people in armor, then those wearing robes came forth, and finally whispy figures with no definite bodies. Finally, just globs of radiant light accompanied with a shrill musical sound circled over the sandstone formation.

The nighttime insects and animals quieted as the darkness fell silent.

Jorge stared in amazement at the phenomenon until the mists dissolved and the lights evaporated into nothing. "My God, Jonathon, what was that?"

"Not your God, Jorge." He lowered his arms. "Mine. The Great Spirit."

"What do you mean?"

"At this moment, I do not know the meaning. I will meditate on it and try to tell you tomorrow."

"Then why did you ask me to come?"

"I needed a witness. Even I was not sure the Great Spirit would come. I only had the feeling within. I needed the strength of another to help bring it out. Some one I trusted. Some one who believed in me, Jorge."

"Well, I'm a believer now. Can we call it a night?"

"Yes, my friend," Jonathon rested his hand on Jorge's shoulder. "Let us go home."

The lonely coyotes picked up their calling and the nocturnal animals chittered and scurried to their burrows beneath the meager brush on the hilltop.

# 44

## BEYOND THE CAVE

Neanna looked ahead at the night sky and the twinkling stars, then back the way she had come. *I've got to go back,* she thought. *This is the wrong way. This is a way to nowhere. I can sense it.* She whirled in her steps and moved quickly back to the lighted amphitheater. The warmth and the faint light of the cave followed her.

She raced past "Michael's Treasure" and on down the tunnel. The cavern curved to the left and she burst around the corner only to find a blank wall and the warmth within her dissipating. She looked up for the telltale line near the ceiling, but the faint light revealed nothing.

*There must be a way out,* her mind told her. *I came in this way.* "Old Woman, where are you?" she yelled at the solid stone obstruction facing her, but only the echo answered her call.

"Michael, this is your cave. Did you bring me here just to lose me again? Why, Michael, why?" She banged her fists against the stone wall. "Where are you?"

Exhausted, Neanna slowly slid down the cavern wall and squatted on the dusty floor. She wrapped her arms around her knees pulling them against her upper body as the chilling air slowly seeped into her flesh. Closing her eyes to squeeze away the tears, she noticed a dim glow inside. She tightened her eyes and searched for it. A red spot slowly appeared within her forehead. She placed her hands on her head with the fingertips centered over the spot and pressed, the glow behind her eyes brightened. She pressed harder, visualizing the cave. The hard rock shimmered in an ethereal glow, appeared, then disappeared.

"No, no. Don't go away. Please, come back."

She pressed harder and the walls appeared again. With her eyes still closed, she stood and reached her hands toward the side of the cave. It shimmered in her mind as her hands passed through the stone, then her body followed until emptiness lay ahead of her outreaching arms.

Suddenly, the chill returned and Neanna opened her eyes, but only darkness filled the air as she felt for something solid. To her right, the cold rock wall met her touch. "I'm back, Michael. Don't leave without me," she pleaded, and rushed through the blackness toward the cave entrance she knew would be there.

Strong arms snaked out of nowhere and encircled her narrow shoulders. A large rough hand cupped over her open mouth, stifling the scream that lodged in her throat. Reynolds bound and blindfolded Neanna and pulled her body into the main gallery.

"I found her back in the tunnel. She appeared out of nowhere calling for that archeologist. Looked like she was trying to find her way out," he sneered, "but I got her."

"Wallace will be pleased with this one." Pearson rubbed his hand over the white scar that ran down his left cheek. "Well pleased, I'd say."

"So, what do you want me to do with Blondie here? I can think of several things I'd like to do," Reynolds lips curled across his black teeth.

"Don't touch her," he shouted back, "until I get in touch with Wallace." Pearson carried one of the lanterns near the radio and made his call.

"Mr. Wallace, Pearson here. Guess who we've got," he spoke into the microphone.

"Yeah, we got rid of the stupid archeologist and the bony little guy that waited at the jeep. They're probably buzzard food by now."

"No," screamed Neanna. "Where is he? What did you do?"

Pearson turned off the microphone. "Muzzle her, dammit, right now."

When Reynolds finished wrapping his dirty bandanna around Neanna's mouth, Pearson picked up the radio mike. "You still there, Mr. Wallace? It was the girl who screamed. You know, the skinny one you said was hanging around with the treasure hunter.

"Yeah, Reynolds caught her back in the tunnel. No telling what she saw.

"The cult, huh." A wide smile filled Pearson's face. "Yeah, we can do that. Sure, the mining is right on schedule. I'll personally bring you a shipment tonight when we deliver the girl." He hung the mike back on the radio and took off the headphones.

"Reynolds, get the girl in the rover with that last bag of gems. Wallace says he's going to trade her to that blue-robed cult for some information. He says they're very interested in her."

"What about us?" Reynolds protested." We've been doing all the dirty work."

"He says we're all due for a bonus, a big one." Pearson smiled as he rubbed the thick scar etched across his face.

A few minutes later, Neanna lay bound and gagged in the back of an ancient stripped down British Land Rover as it bounced through the night under a field of dancing stars.

# 45
## OUT OF THE DEVIL'S LAIR

Michael hiked northeast shivering in the cold night air as a slight glow in the east told him the moon would soon be shining on his path out of the Devil's Lair.

As he rounded the foot of a large eroded spire, he stumbled over a soft object in the shadows. Reaching down to feel his way around, he realized it was another person. He pulled the body into the faint light and looked down into Tony's pallid face. He shook the limp form. "Tony, wake up. Come on. It's Michael." He felt for a pulse. "Oh, my God," he yelled at the night sky. "They've killed him. I've got to get out of here before they find I'm alive."

Michael stumbled back and forth as he worked his way through the labyrinth of dry canyons trying to find a path up the barren hills. Each one looked the same in the faint starlight, but the moon was his beacon and the North Star his guidepost. He soon found a narrow animal trail that followed the contour of the hills and led upward.

Eventually, he reached the hilltop that looked down into El Lobo Canyon. To his amazement, the dirty dust-covered Wrangler sat there like a waiting sanctuary. He reached for the key only to find his pants pocket had been ripped away.

*The map* flashed through his mind as he grabbed his shirt pocket. *Still there,* he sighed, *the jacket must have protected it.*

A tired Michael Adams jerked open the Wrangler door hoping to find the key he had given Tony, but only an empty ignition switch met his gaze. He leaned his beaten body against the red dust covered vehicle, wondering what his next move would be. *If Neanna were here,* he thought, *she would figure a way to get this jeep started. Maybe I should have taken mechanics that semester instead of Thailand Jungle Exploration.*

He raised the hood and peered inside at the engine when he heard a noise. It came from below where the road ended. He stared into the darkness when a faint light flickered out of the canyon wall. Then he saw the figure of a man who appeared to be moving some object on the side of the hill. Michael hustled down the ridge, trying to be quiet at the same time. He watched in amazement as the man pulled a camouflage net aside revealing an opening into the hill with a road across the sandy surface. Slipping closer and watching headlights creep in his direction, he soon saw a shadowy gray vehicle emerge and stop while the person at the net pulled the camouflage back in place. The man ran forward and climbed into an old Land Rover. Before it started, Michael jumped on the back bumper, and dragged himself to the top, hanging onto the roof rack.

"Did you just feel something?" Pearson asked, glancing at Reynolds.

"Naw, must have been me getting into the cab. Let's get the hell out of here. I want to go into town so I can find a decent drink."

"So, you don't like what Wallace serves?"

"That stinking warm beer we get at the job site. I hate it."

"Then why drink it?" Pearson laughed.

"When that's all you got," he slammed his fist against the dash, "you take what you can get."

"You're right, Reynolds, I agree. Let's go find some good stuff and maybe a girl for the night."

The beat up Land Rover bounded on down Red Canyon, collecting crimson dust.

"Damn, Pearson, slow down a little. This piece of crap is jarring the fillings outa my teeth. Where the hell did Wallace get it?"

"I heard he had it shipped over from South Africa," Scarface muttered. He jammed his boot down forcing the gas pedal to the floor as the old vehicle roared out of the canyon, then onto the highway and into Sedona.

# 46

## STREETS OF SEDONA

Scarface Pearson slowed the Land Rover as he drove into the night-covered city of Sedona. The pale moon had climbed higher in the star filled sky, casting moonlight shadows from the vehicle as the miners drove toward the Katrina Hotel.

On the hard floor behind the seats occupied by Pearson and Reynolds, Neanna twisted and turned, trying to loosen the ropes that held her hands together. She rubbed the bandana covering her mouth on the rough carpet until it slid from her face, but the blindfold that hid her eyes remained tightly bound.

*I've got to be ready to jump out of here when we stop,* she thought, as she struggled with the ropes. She strained against the cotton cord until little by little it stretched enough to release her hands from the bonds.

She quickly untied her feet and then removed the blindfold, blinking to see in the dimly lit vehicle. She tried

## Gateway to Another Dimension

to visualize where she lay, but her prone position and the darkness, prevented it. She quietly rolled to her right side on the coarse carpet, pulling her left leg up to make a quick escape.

"We're here," the scar-faced man announced as he pulled the old Land Rover onto the gravel behind the Katrina Hotel.

Michael quietly escaped from the roof and started toward the edge of the building. He limped around the far side and hobbled into the dark street beyond.

Pearson turned off the engine and looked over at Reynolds. "Watch the girl, I'll be right back."

Neanna heard the door slam.

"Are you okay back there, girly?" Reynolds deep nasally voice echoed through the dark vehicle. "Too bad Wallace wants you. We could have some fun." He turned and reached through the open space between the seats until he felt one of Neanna's legs and slid his hand up toward her waist. "Yep, lots of fun," he snickered.

Neanna lashed out with her other leg. The sharp toe of her shoe caught Reynolds directly in the nostrils, jamming his broad nose up between his eyes.

"Bitch," Reynolds screamed and grabbed for his face.

Neanna lashed out with her other foot, driving him against the dash.

Reynolds howled, holding his nose and falling forward to the floor.

Neanna could hear him threshing around in the front of the vehicle as she tried to find the door latch. Her fingers touched the metal on the stripped down door frame. Next, she found and tugged on a connecting rod to no avail. By now, she was kneeling on the floor desperately feeling across the door for some locking mechanism.

*Where are you?* her mind pleaded, as she slid her fingers slowly over the metal surface.

Then she noticed Reynolds body rising in front blocking the meager light coming through the windshield. Her eyes glanced furtively from the dark shadow back to the door, trying to see something in the darkness.

"Where are you girly?" snarled Reynolds, righting himself on the passenger seat. He twisted around and grabbed into the dark van. "You hurt the hell out of me and I'm going to get you for it," he growled.

Neanna's fingers desperately searched for some type of door handle. *Where is it?*

*Dear God, it must be here somewhere.*

"I'm going to get you, girly." Reynolds' hand reached across the empty space above Neanna's body. "I'm going to get you."

Suddenly, Neanna found the latch beneath the torn remains of the cloth inner door covering. She ducked under

Reynolds clawing hand, jerked the door handle upward, and leaped out the door.

Behind her, she heard Reynolds cussing, screaming, and threshing in the Land Rover. The street lights cast a faint glow to the rear of the Katrina Hotel.

Neanna raced to the back of the building and crouched near the corner debating which way to turn. *Where did the other man go?* She listened in the silent night for some sound, then crept along the rear wall toward a large dumpster resting in the gloom. From there, she rounded the back wing, looking for a door.

A dark form blocked her way.

Neanna raised her arms to protect herself as the side of Scarface's broad hand slammed into her neck. Darkness closed over her mind as she slumped to the rocky ground.

# 47

## THE CULT

Scarface Pearson lifted the limp body of Neanna in his arms and carried her back to the Land Rover.

"Reynolds, for Christ's sake, where are you?" he yelled through the open door.

"In here," he moaned. "The bitch broke my nose. I'm bleeding like a stuck pig."

"Then get your butt outside before you make a bloody mess in there and go take care of it." He threw Neanna in the back, slammed the door shut, and then grabbed Reynolds by the neck of his shirt and jerked the groaning man out of the passenger seat. "I'll be at the bar in about an hour."

As Reynolds rolled to the gravelly parking lot, Scarface drove toward Schnebly Cabins. He stopped the gray Land Rover in back of Cabin Five and quietly tapped on the door.

"Who's there," the soft voice inside spoke.

"I'm from Wallace. I've got a package for you."

The door opened slowly and a large chunky man in a blue coat stepped out. "We heard you were coming. Where is she?"

"In the Rover," Pearson jerked his thumb. He sauntered over and pulled the door open. "There she is."

An elated smile crept over the big man's face. "She is the one. I will take her with pleasure." He reached inside and threw Neanna's limp body over his shoulder.

"She's all yours," Pearson sneered as he stepped back in the Land Rover and leaned out the window. "I'd watch her if I were you. She's a hellion."

Brother John continued to smile as he carried Neanna inside the cabin, closed the door, and dumped her on the floor. "We now have her. Call the Keeper," he said softly to the others inside.

When Neanna Miller awoke, she lay crumpled on the floor among the replicas of Sedona's red rock monuments. A red welt swelled across her neck just above her right shoulder. She tried to touch the painful spot, but the cords binding her hands prevented her reaching it.

A man in a blue robe sitting in a golden chair looked down at her, his face hidden in the shadow of a hood. "Do you know who I am, Chosen One?" the man's soft high-pitched voice crept out of the hood.

"You're called the Keeper and I'm not your chosen one," she growled back.

"Ah, but you are the One."

"I would suggest you release me right now or the Sheriff will soon be here to do it," she spoke louder twisting her hands, trying to loosen the bonds.

"As I understand it, the authorities believe you are out in the desert. Perhaps lost in a terrible place called the Devil's Lair and I have been assured your archeologist friend is now dead," the Keeper said in his slow shrill monotone.

"Unless you saw him dead, I'm sure Michael is alive," she shouted, then calmed her voice. "Now, why do you want me?"

"Because you are the Chosen One," he squeaked as he stood, leaned over Neanna, and peered into her emerald eyes. "The Ones Before, who were here prior to the Ancient Ones, have asked for you. They need the Chosen One to make their journey back to this time."

Neanna shivered as she gazed into his black eyes and wrinkled face leering out of the shadowy hood. "Who are these people you're talking about?" she imitated his slow drawl. "Are they in some other place?"

"Yes. Time is but a figure of speech. The vortex is more like a dimensional warp. It took them from here before the Ancient Ones came."

"And where did the Ancient Ones go?" she softly replied squirming in her bonds, trying to motivate the Keeper to continue his tale.

"You ask too many questions, Chosen One," he wiggled a crooked finger at her, "but I will tell you. The Ones Before came and took away most of the Ancient Ones. That is why you can only find their ruins today and no trace of them," his shrill voice continued. "The Indians today are too ignorant to read the ancient writings and symbols or they too would know."

"How did you learn about me?" she whispered. "How did you know I was coming?"

"The light in the vortex told me you were about to arrive. It said now was the time and we have been waiting so many years. Then you called the Chamber and we knew." He wandered back to his chair and slumped down, sighing at the effort.

Neanna stopped struggling and concentrated on the man in dark blue robe. She could barely see the wrinkled face under the shadow of his hood. "How did you learn of the Ones Before?"

The Keeper looked up at the ceiling. "Many years ago," his high pitched and tired voice spoke, "I became lost and stumbled aimlessly across the desert near Tucson, Arizona and happened upon this old Indian site. Nearby, I found a spring of fresh water and rested for the night, but when the stars came out and the moon rose, I noticed a strange light on the far side of the ancient ruins."

The hooded man shifted in his seat and continued on in his slow shrill monotone. "I walked to the illumination and traced the light back to an oval opening in a facing wall. At a certain time of night with the moon in an exact position, the light strikes the center of those remains. I noted the location, went back to sleep, and the next morning, I dug into the clay wall. Inside, I found a mass of vines wound around a cylindrical object."

Neanna broke his concentration. "Why are you sharing this with me?"

"You are the Chosen One. You need to learn about the source before your time runs out." His voice trembled as he continued.

"Anxiously, I tore away the vines," the tempo of his voice increased, "only to find a cluster of strange looking sticks made of wood not grown in that area. I cut the bindings and unrolled the bundle to find a dried animal hide wrapped around some artifact. The thick rawhide bound the hidden article so tightly. I cut it away only to reveal a decayed rabbit skin pouch, but inside of it, I found the future."

# 48

## STREETS OF SEDONA

On the tall hill above the little red rock town, Jonathon and Jorge said their good-byes. The big Indian climbed into the Cultural Center's white van and drove down the dusty track to the highway below. Deputy Carasco watched the red taillights disappear, then stepped into the County Sheriff's SUV and followed him toward Sedona.

When Jonathon reached Highway 89A, he turned south at the 'Y' and drove toward the Indian Cultural Center on his way home. Jorge continued on into town deciding to check the streets and the Schnebly Cabins, hoping to observe any unusual activities of the blue-robed cult.

As he drove past Cabin Seven, he wondered how peaceful Sedona's newcomer was sleeping. Reaching the edge of Oak Creek at the lower end of the cabins, he turned and retraced his route toward the western side of town. In the pale moonlight, he watched Coffeepot Rock appear off to the right, when suddenly a strange figure flashed into view. The form hobbled ape-like from a side street onto the main drag. Jorge rapidly swung the SUV around until the headlights enveloped the creature, a creature that now turned to face him waving its arms in the air. Jorge jammed on the brakes, leaped from the vehicle, and raced toward the form.

"Aren't you Michael Adams, Neanna's friend? What are you doing out here?"

Michael fell against him, trying to stand.

"Holy Mary, your clothes are ripped to shreds and your hands and face are cut to pieces. What happened?"

"Neanna, you've got to help Neanna." He struggled to stand.

"Where is she?" He pulled Michael over to the SUV and sat him on the seat, feet dangling outside. "Come on, Michael, talk to me."

"Water, do you have some water?" He lifted his blood caked face to the deputy. "I need a drink."

Jorge pulled a plastic water bottle from an old ice chest, handing it to Michael.

"Now, where is Neanna?" He shook the tattered man.

"Out in the desert, in a cave at the head of El Lobo," he stammered. "Do you know where that is?"

"Yes. Are you well enough to come with me?"

"I'll make it. Just give me the water and let's get out there." He poured some of the water on the cloth Jorge handed him and washed his bloody face. They killed Tony and they damn near killed me."

"No, not that little guy who hangs around town looking for tourists to guide. Who are they?" He swung the county vehicle around and drove west on Highway 89A, then called for backup.

Michael splashed more water on his face, wiped the cloth over it, and dried on what remained of his shirt. "I don't know who they were. I was blindfolded, but they're in the cave."

"And Neanna?" Jorge looked beyond the shining headlights, watching for coyotes and other wild animals.

"I don't know. We were in the cave together, then we got separated. I never saw her again."

As they turned off the highway into Red Canyon, Michael told the remaining pieces of his story including the finding of Tony's body and riding back into town on the roof of a Land Rover. He tried to find a soft spot in the bouncing SUV as they raced up Red Canyon.

"El Lobo Canyon is just ahead on the left." He leaned forward and pointed into the darkness ahead of the SUV lights. "We'll turn up there."

"I see it." Jorge swung the sheriff's vehicle into the walled canyon. The headlights flashed eerie shadows ahead of them.

"Have you seen a big black sedan driving around Sedona?" The archeologist asked settling back in his seat. "They ran me off the road once and I'm sure they sabotaged my jeep another time. In fact, it may have been them that struck me on the back of my head and they may have Neanna right now."

"We'll soon know, Michael," he said straining to see ahead as the darkness absorbed the light. "You said that old Land Rover came out the side of the canyon up here."

"Yes, we were following tire tracks and then they just disappeared. Someone covered them. It must have been the same vehicle that I rode into Sedona. They could have hid it in some hole along the canyon wall." Michael waved his hand toward the dark side of the nearby cliff. "I doubt if I could find where it came out in this darkness."

"How much farther?"

"The road's narrowing. It won't be long until we see my rental jeep."

"You're right." Jorge pointed to a reflection in the headlights. "It's up there, just ahead!"

"If that's the jeep, then the hole in the wall must be over there." He pointed to their right.

The deputy swung the SUV in the direction Michael indicated. A reddish sandstone wall reflected back from the headlights. Jorge stopped the vehicle, grabbed a flashlight from the holder under the dash, and jumped out. "Come on, Michael, if you can make it."

As they reached the canyon wall, only rough sandstone met their touch. Michael slowly ran his cut fingers over the rough stone surface, grimacing at the pain. "It has to be some place right here."

Jorge flashed the light across the cliff side. "Looks like plain old red sandstone to me," he observed. "Are you sure this is the place?"

"I'm positive. It has to be here somewhere." He continued, hobbling along, dragging his hand over the surface. "Jorge, bring the light closer. Look." He pushed against the rough surface and watched as it moved away from his hand.

"It looks the same color and feels like the same texture," Jorge shouted as he touched the surface. "There must be an edge somewhere." He rushed on ahead of the injured archeologist.

Michael struggled to follow. "Find anything?"

"Over here," the excited deputy yelled. "Can you make it this far?"

"I'm right behind you," he wheezed. "What did you find?"

By now, Jorge had pulled the phony wall aside. "This is a great camouflage job," he called in amazement. "Now I know why you never saw it. Can you give me a hand?"

They grasped the thick canvas like material coated with a layer of dull red sand and pulled it away from the wall. Beyond the curtain, a tunnel led into the darkness. Jorge shone his light on the sandy ground.

"See those tracks. Are they like the ones you saw coming up the canyon?"

"Yes, I believe they are. They were easier to see in the damp surface outside than in the dry sand here."

"Let's get back to my car and see where they go." He took Michael by the arm to help him into the county vehicle. "By the way, how many men do you think are in there?"

"I only heard the two that threw me over the cliff and the two in the rover. I don't know if there were others." He slumped back against the seat trying to rest.

Jorge drove deeper into the dark tunnel. Ahead, they could hear the faint rumbling of machinery.

The deputy turned off the lights and followed the faint road up a small draw. At the top, the terrain leveled to a broad plain with the headstock of a vertical mine protruding in the distance. Beneath the framework, they could see a faint light shining up from the shaft and could hear the mechanical noise vibrating through the air

Jorge stopped the SUV. "I think we should go on foot from here." He pointed at the headstock silhouetted in the moonlight.

"I agree," Michael nodded and carefully stepped to the ground.

The two men crept toward the opening and the faint sound from below. Jorge touched the archeologist's shoulder. "Hold it. There's some kind of a pipe coming from the shaft and running down the hill on the other side."

"You're right. It looks like a dust cloud is billowing from the end of it," he whispered. "Let's sneak a little closer."

Hunching over, they slipped forward when a head popped up from the shaft. Both men fell prone trying to hide on the bare plain. Michael slithered behind a small stunted greasewood bush as Jorge removed his hat and willed his body into the ground.

A dark clothed man with a thick beard emerged from the mineshaft, checked the vibrating pipe, and crawled back inside. The deputy eased his revolver from the holster and crept closer to the hole. Michael followed until they both peered down into the opening.

"Look," Michael whispered, "it's like a giant vacuum hose coming out of there."

"Yeah, and it goes to that wooden box with the screen on top. The men below are sucking something out of there. Let's check it out."

They crouched over the bin and looked inside.

*The Mystical Vortex*

"Look, Jorge, do you see what I do? Even in this dim light, I can see some kind of shiny rocks, almost like gems." He reached inside, filling his hand.

Jorge snapped a wooden match on his thumbnail and watched the glow illuminate the glistening red stones in Michael's hand. "What are they?"

"They appear to be natural grown garnet crystals with a few ground smooth by the elements. If these people kill to hide this place, I'd guess they're worth a bundle"

The match went out. "Let's see what we can find down that hole."

They had just started to crawl around the bin when they heard voices.

"What the hell are you doing down here again? Scarface will be on your ass if you don't get up there and monitor the end of hose."

"Screw you, Joe. I was just coming down for a beer."

"Well, take your beer and get back up there. If Scarface doesn't rip your butt apart, that big guy Wallace will do it if you let some of those gems spill into the tailings pile. Have you got the bag up there?"

"You know damn well I do. You guys got it made down here. During the day, I've got to sit up there in the blasted hot sun and tonight it's getting colder'n a polar bear's butt."

"Just git outa here. We're all doing our job and the pay is the same. We work like gophers down here in this dusty hell hole and all you do is sit up there on your fat ass."

Jorge and Michael watched as a head and then the body appeared from the shaft. The man stumbled toward them dragging his feet. When he reached the bin, Jorge jammed his gun in the man's rib and covered his mouth. "Make a sound and you're dead."

## 49

KACHINA HOTEL

Pearson gently knocked on James Wallace's business suite door several times before he heard a movement on the other side.

"Who's out there?" Wallace shouted

"It's me, Pearson," Scarface half whispered to the door.

"That you, Scarface?" Wallace called back peering through the tiny peephole.

"Yeah, let me in. I just dropped off that blonde girl."

Wallace quickly opened the door and pulled his mine foreman inside as he glanced down the hall. "Anyone see you come up here?"

"No, Mr. Wallace," he stumbled back against the closed door as the big man leaned closer. "For God's sake, I was just following your orders. I came by earlier, but you were gone."

"Where I go is none of your damn business," his mouth wrinkled in a snarl. "Do you have the delivery?" He held out a thick hand.

Pearson reached inside his brown cowhide jacket and pulled out a leather bag. "Here it is, just like I said. There must be a small fortune in there."

James Wallace took the leather bag, pulled the drawstring open and peeked inside, shaking the bag. As he watched in fascination, a mesmerizing smile trickled over his round face. "The actual value of these garnets is not much, but the syndicate sells them to an Asian buyer. He ships them overseas where they're cut like rubies, mounted in rings and broaches, and sold back here in the states and in Europe to ignorant buyers for big bucks."

"No kidding?" A big grin filled Pearson's face.

"Yes and the more we dig out, the bigger the fortune for all of us." The smile broadened on his face as he continued to gaze into the bag.

"Mr. Wallace," the foreman interrupted the interlude. "You mentioned we might be up for a little bonus. You know, something extra. After all, we delivered the girl to that sneaky cult and we got rid of that desert rat and that other little guy. We dumped their bodies out in that desert wilderness."

Wallace wheeled toward him, an angry look flashing across his face. "Who the devil do you think you are asking me for a bonus? We haven't got paid yet. I haven't got paid! You're getting your monthly wage. That's what you agreed to work for, including side jobs like that snoop."

Pearson started backing toward the door as Wallace pressed forward. "I ain't asking for any more. Right now I'm here in town and I need a drink and I ain't got any money."

A sly smile crossed James Wallace's face. "What the hell, Scarface, you're all doing a good job. Just wanted to let you know who the boss was." He walked back to his desk, reached inside, and handed the man a packet of bills. "Stay in town for tonight. I'll call the mine and tell them where you are."

He closed the door behind the man with the scar on his face.

## 50

**THE KEEPER**

Neanna listened intently to the blue-robed man as he told his story. "Yes, go ahead," she said, leading him on.

"I knew there was something special about the sand, but I was not sure. I found an old Indian shaman in Tucson and asked him. He only wanted to keep the fur pouch, said it was sacred and should be kept with other sacred items, but I disagreed. I owned nothing at that time and since they would not pay me, I kept it. A few years later, I happened to be in Sedona and realized this is a sacred place itself. I began to hear about the vortexes, the powerful crystals, mystic valleys, and the special waters of Oak Creek."

"How long ago was that?"

"Over thirty years," his high pitched words continued. "Thirty years of waiting for the right moment. Thirty years of building a group of followers. Thirty years of anticipation. But now you are here and the waiting is over."

"How did you find the power of the pouch?" she kept him talking.

"One evening, Chosen One, I was at the airport vortex site. The full moon glowed white in the night sky when it came to me. I raced home and returned with the pouch. It was late and no one was around as I took a few grains from it and tossed them at the moon. That's when it happened."

"What happened?" Neanna worked to release the rope as she faced the Keeper.

"It was unbelievable," his shrill voice raised with excitement. "Suddenly, the sky between the bright moon and me filled with a cloudy mist that swirled above me, then it slowly drifted away. So I threw more of the grains into the air and watched in utter amazement as the mists returned and images began to appear in the swirling clouds. I was frightened beyond imagination and ran down from the hill."

"What were the images?" Neanna spoke softly as she strained at the ropes that held her. *I've got to keep him talking until I can get loose.*

"The first ones I saw that night appeared to be Indians in strange clothing. A week later, I became brave enough to try it again. The moon was losing its brilliance as I climbed to the top of a rock platform at the same vortex site. I opened the pouch to reach inside when the mist suddenly appeared out of nowhere. There was no wind, but the vapor swirled upward and images of ancient Indians appeared, then warriors in helmets and armor, then those who came before."

"Are you sure you weren't hallucinating on some Indian poppy seed?"

"No. Never. I saw it that night and at full moons, night after night. I tried to stay that night, but when the floating heads without faces appeared, I ran like a frightened puppy with my stomach in my throat."

"No guts."

He kept talking in his high-pitched monotone as if oblivious to Neanna's presence. "At the next full moon, I went back and opened the fur pouch again. I was much braver and as I watched the headless bodies float above, I could hear voices talking to me. Telling me to gather followers and the time would come when they would once again come from the past to be with me."

"Didn't I tell you? You were hallucinating! You were really hearing yourself, not some image in the sky."

"No!" he shouted down at her. "You lie. They told me the Chosen One was coming and here you are."

"How long did you say you've been hearing these voices? Thirty years? You must be insane by now." She prodded him as the rope loosened on one wrist.

"Yes, thirty years now I have heard them and followed their instructions. I have gathered a group of followers. We have taken over the Schnebly Cabins, the Golden Crystal shop, other businesses in Sedona, and some members of the Chamber. It was the builder of the cabins who came from the past to prepare a place for us." He eased the hood back from his head.

Neanna gasped as she saw the wrinkled face of the elderly man in the blue suit who had said he owned the crystal shop. She choked the lump back down and worked to release her arms. *I've got to keep him talking.*

"You're the man in the crystal shop? The one who talked to Deputy Carasco and me?"

"Of course I am, Chosen One. If that big stupid Indian had not appeared, Sister Martha would have used the crystals to finish the controlling, but you became too strong. We knew then that you had the power to help return the Ancient Ones."

"Do you know who put the cicada nymphs in my car?" she continued to quiz him.

"Yes, one of the brothers did that to test you. At first you were weak, but then your true nature overcame the weakness, and you fought the insects as the Chosen One would have."

Neanna closed her eyes and silently asked the little lady for help. *I know you're in here. Please help me. I don't know how, but just help me.* Warmth spread over her from the pit of her stomach in all directions. She could feel the strength return to her tired body as she struggled with the ropes. She flexed her fingers and the muscles in her lower arms until the bindings slipped from her wrists. She stopped struggling and hid her hands from the Keeper. "Who are the heads with no bodies floating in the mists?"

"They are the ones who put man on Earth, the Ones Before. They left first through the vortex, and then others followed, including the Ancients Ones, before they died in this desolate land. I intend to bring them back. I intend to lead them to a fuller life here in this dimension." He looked away from her as he spoke.

Neanna saw her opportunity. She dropped the rope from her wrists, leaped to her feet, and dashed toward the back door. Her first jump carried her past the stone images of Sedona's red mountain monuments. As she raced toward the back wall, she noticed the open lock on the rear entrance and struck the wooden door running. Although the latch was loose, the door did not yield to her thrust.

Across the room, the man in the blue cape screamed. "Stop! You can't get away. We need you."

Neanna hit the door with outstretched hands only to see them crumble beneath her attack. A moment of fear past through hr body, but she shifted to one side as her arms bent under the weight of her forward movement and her shoulder struck the door. It swung wide and the darkness of night met her eyes as she flew across the sill to the ground outside.

I'm free, she thought, as her feet hit the earth running. Her eyes flashed from side to side as she tried to see in the darkness. *My cabin, which way is my cabin,* flashed through her mind. She dashed around the corner toward Cabin Six only to run into a soft body in the darkness. She felt the large arms wrapping around her, lifting her off the ground.

Neanna raised her arms in the air and dropped to the ground, falling from the grip that held her. From a crouched position, she leaped up and raced toward Cabin Number Four. As she passed the rear door of Number Five, she saw the outline of the old man calling at his cult members to catch her. *I'm free now, almost to the highway.* Ahead, the office light blinked on and off, as she crossed the walkway to the street. Suddenly, the office door burst open and the clerk stepped out.

"Help me," Neanna gasped, staggering toward the man.

"Quick, inside."

As Neanna stepped through the door, a flood of blue robes appeared from behind the counter. She turned only to find her way blocked by the clerk.

"Your escape is over." He tightened his grip on her arms and handed her over to a large blue robed man.

"I am sure, Chosen One, the Keeper would prefer you stayed in the cabin," Brother John's deep voice growled down at her.

"Not on your life," Neanna shouted and beat on the broad chest that confined her as the cult member pulled her outside. When her eyes became accustomed to the darkness, she could see the thick leering face inches in front of hers. She lowered her hand and brought it up rapidly, palm open, until the heel of her hand struck the huge man in the open nostrils. He yelled in pain, releasing his grip on her. She turned and raced toward the highway, only to run directly into a horde of blue capes. *My God, they are everywhere.* Kicking and fighting, she was swept back into the cabin and the presence of the Keeper.

The Keeper raised his wooden staff over Neanna's head and started to swing it down. "No, Chosen One," he shrilled, "you will not provoke me. Your time will come." He turned to a follower, "Lock her in the storeroom and post a guard. If she escapes, the wrath of the ancients will be on you until the pain is unbearable."

## 51

THE GEM MINE

White pinpoints of light from the distant stars hardly illuminated the three men crouched by the sand-filled bin. Deputy Carasco's hand tightened on the bearded man's mouth as he pulled the miner away from the shaft.

"I'm only going to ask you this once. If you yell out when I loosen my hand, you're a dead man," the deputy spoke softly. "Where's the blonde girl?" He lifted his hand slightly from the man's mouth.

"What girl? Who are you guys?"

"You know what girl." He jammed the gun deeper into the man's ribs and pulled the hammer back.

"Dammit, man. You're hurting me."

"Not as hard as a bullet in your gut. Do you want me to drop this hammer? Where's the girl?"

"Okay, man, okay. Take it easy with the gun. Scarface took her to town in the Land Rover."

"Where in town?" He raked the barrel upward toward the man's armpit.

"Hey, you're tearing my ribs apart," the man moaned. "To some hotel. I don't know the name of it. I heard Scarface talking? He said Wallace was selling her to some kind of a cult. Now take it easy."

"We're just starting," Jorge growled. "Michael, do recognize this guy as one of the men who threw you over the cliff?" He twisted the man's face upward.

The prisoner winced. "It wasn't me. It was Mac and Reynolds that done it. I helped pull you out of the cave, but they took you, not me."

"I was unconscious, Jorge. I didn't wake up until they threw me off the truck. I don't know what any of them look like, except maybe the guy who pulled back the camouflage." Suddenly, a startled looked passed over Michael's face. "Oh no, it can't be," he groaned.

"What is it?" the deputy asked.

"Neanna must have been in that Land Rover I rode into town. And I sure do know where that hotel is. Let's get out of here."

"Yes, and we're taking this one with us." Jorge eased the hammer back on the revolver and pulled the bearded man to his feet. "Remember, one sound and you're a goner."

They slipped quietly down the flat top hill to the deputy's waiting vehicle. He handcuffed his prisoner and put him in the back seat, then quickly drove back through the secret tunnel, into El Lobo, then out into Red Canyon.

Michael glanced out the rear window to see if they were followed, but no lights appeared in the distance behind them. The blackness of night covered the cloud of red dust that sucked up behind the racing Sheriff's patrol vehicle.

"Come on, Jorge, pour it on," Michael urged. "I've got to get there and save Neanna. I never should have asked her to come to this god forsaken country."

"Easy, Pal," he increased the pressure on the accelerator. "You can't blame yourself just because some hoodlums decided to rob an abandoned mine. We'll get her back. I'm pretty fond of her myself."

The bright headlights stabbed out into the darkness as they plunged toward the entrance of Red Canyon. Shadows danced along the bare sandstone walls as they passed Dry Arroyo and then Lost Vaquero.

"The way out of here is just ahead," Michael motioned.

The canyon walls gave way to the open desert as the lights pierced the outside landscape. Just as the SUV passed the last ridge, a black shadow moved in front of them, materializing into the form of a large dark sedan. Deputy Carasco slammed on the brakes, and the tires gripped the broken asphalt, trying to slow the forward motion of the vehicle. As the lights of the SUV bathed the black car, a window rolled partially down and the barrel of a steel blue revolver glinted through the opening.

"Down, Michael, they've got a gun." Jorge rotated the steering wheel to the right, swinging his side of the patrol vehicle between them and the sedan. He ducked below the thin door as bullets shattered the glass window above his head. The dust cloud following the SUV enveloped it and the black sedan in an instant. "Out your door," he shouted pushing Michael and following him out the passenger side.

As the SUV swerved to a stop, the two men fell to the ground. Jorge jerked his gun from the leather holster and rolled to the rear of the vehicle. Lying on his belly, he gripped his revolver with both hands, and rapidly fired two shots into the tinted window of the sedan as the dust cloud faded away.

The thin man in the passenger seat watched in horror as he saw the muzzle blast from the deputy's gun. He tried to fire his pistol again, but Jorge's bullets arrived first, one striking him in the throat and the other in the forehead. The sneer across his yellow teeth never changed.

A spray of blood and flesh blew into the pudgy face of the fat man sitting in the driver's seat before he could comprehend what happened. "Oh, my God," Fatso cried out. "I'm shot."

## 52
## INDIAN CULTURAL CENTER

Jonathon Blackeagle drove to the Indian Cultural Center and raced inside. He eased back in the old leather chair behind his desk and carefully took the rabbit skin pouch from his pocket. Setting the little fur bag on his desk, he stared at it, tenderly caressing the velvety fleece.

"You are the answer to an eternal mystery," he spoke to it. "That deputy said your mist was the same as the blue hooded cult's mist, but where do the images come from?" He was still muttering to the pouch when he heard the front door open and close.

"Who is there?"

"Jonathon, why are you here so late?" Laura asked, straightening her long dark braids.

He half smiled. "Perhaps, I should ask you the same,"

"I was worried about you." She leaned over the desk, looking into his eyes. "I called your house and no one answered, so I came here. Sandra is fine. She is with her mother."

Jonathon held up the pouch and motioned her to sit. "Please take a seat and I will tell you. Earlier tonight I went to one of the vortex sites and used the granules in the rabbit skin. They gave me a vision of the past far beyond the Ancient Ones to the ones who came before, then on beyond them perhaps to the gods." He wiped the sweat that began to form on his face.

"What is it, Jonathon?" her eyes pleaded. She reached out a small hand and rested it firmly on his.

"I am not sure whether I was playing with good or evil." He wrung his hands together. "It is the same vision the blue robes are creating."

"You know I care more for you than just respect." She tightened her soft hand on his and gazed tenderly into his eyes. "Nothing you would do could be evil. You are too good a person. The Great Spirit would protect you."

"I must ask the Great Spirit for guidance. Will I be able to use the pouch to overcome the evil within the clan? Do I have the authority?"

She lifted her hand from his, caressing it as she did. "Now that I know you are safe, I will leave and let you meditate. You will find the answer." She stepped out of the office and shut the door behind her.

Jonathon placed his elbows on the table, closed his eyes, covered them with his hands, and willed his mind from all outside activities. *Tonight I must follow the cult to the vortex,* he thought as the thick black braids fell across the front of his turquoise trimmed shirt. He stared into the watchful eyes of his forefathers painted in ornate frames hanging on the beige walls of his office. He glanced from one to another seeking an answer to the question revolving in his mind. His head stopped at one stately ancestor directly across from his large wooden desk, then looking deeply into the black eyes of the painting, he spoke aloud.

"Grandfather, a long time ago you took me to your knee and said that if I needed you, I only had to ask. Now is the time for asking. Something evil has entered our land and I fear something even more evil is on its way."

He raised his troubled head and began to chant softly to the Great Spirit. Closing his eyes, he started recalling the events of yesterday at the vortex site when he tossed the powders from the fur pouch skyward and watched the images appear. Over and over, he relived the events at the vortex, learning from them as they repeated in his mind until he felt a peaceful calm within him.

Jonathon opened his eyes. "Thank you Great Spirit," he said as he lowered his tired gaze to the noble face before him. "Thank you, Grandfather, I see the answer plainly. Tonight, I will challenge the vortex."

The big Indian stood and stepped around his desk until he faced the colorful painting of his grandfather. "Tonight I may see you, Grandfather, in the mists of the Great Spirit," he spoke in a tone loud enough for anyone in the Cultural Center to hear, but no one was there to listen.

He opened a nearby closet door within in his office and passed his hand over several personal ceremonial robes. He paused momentarily as he touched and thoughtfully contemplated the purpose of each garment. *I must wear the exact one tonight,* he thought. *I wore this one to the last Pow Wow and this to the Harvest Festival. This was the garment for the ceremony honoring veterans and here's the one for the installation ceremony of our new Chief.* He continued through the wardrobe, reminding himself of the purpose for each robe. He slowly ran his hands over each bit of cloth waiting for some sign telling him it was the necessary one, but when he reached the end of the closet, he knew the one he would wear was not hanging there.

Jonathon slowly closed the door and leaned his back against its oak paneling. He rubbed his hand over the thoughtful wrinkles that creased his forehead. *I know the robe is somewhere in the Cultural Center, but all my ceremonial garments are hanging here.* He glanced around his office one more time, muttering, "Where, where is it? Can you tell me, Grandfather?" His gaze swept upward, then a smile broke his troubled face. "As always, you have the answer."

He quickly turned and dashed from the office, down the hallway to a side room, and opened the door. As Jonathon raced into the room, he could feel the pull from some unseen force dragging him to the far end of the room. He raced past artifacts of local tribes that filled the space, crowding into every corner. Weapons for hunting and war hung along one wall while gathering and cooking utensils lined another side. Homemade clothing for men, women and children were displayed next to the cooking items.

The big Indian never saw any of the displays. His eyes were focused on the far corner of the room, locked on the freestanding forms where ceremonial clothing of past chiefs and shamans hung in all shades of the rainbow.

Jonathon never hesitated. He raced to the last ceremonial robe worn by his grandparent. "Yes, Grandfather, your robe is the one needed for tonight." He reached out his hands and touched the shoulders of the buckskin robe tinted in red and gold. He allowed his fingers to rest for a moment on the cloth when suddenly a hot sensation entered his palms. He tried to remove his hands, but they refused to be released from the robe. The heat ran quickly up his arm until it centered on his breast. A flood of warmth consumed his body and he collapsed to the floor, dragging the ceremonial garment with him.

# 53

## CABIN NUMBER FIVE

The moon was rising when they led Neanna from the storeroom with her hands bound behind her back and stripped to her bra and panties. She had a black hood over head, but that didn't prevent her from talking or fighting. She twisted her body trying to release the grip of her captors.

"Let me go," she shouted, trying to rub the dark hood from her head on the shoulder of the man to her left. "Let me go. Now! And I'll see the police go easy on you. Kidnapping is a death sentence in this country, or didn't you know?"

"Shut up, Chosen One," the Keeper screeched from the front of the room, "or I will have you gagged."

"By God, you'll let me loose now." She raised her leg and jammed her heel down on the instep of one of the men holding her.

The clansman screamed and released his grip. He fell to the floor grasping his foot, moaning.

Neanna turned, drove her shoulder into the other member, and whirled free. She tried to push the hood off with her bound hands, but failed. Turning her head from side to side, she tried to get her bearings. *Where are you old man? I know you're somewhere in this room.*

"Stop her," his high-pitched yell echoed across the cabin.

*Oh, there you are.* Neanna homed in on the sound. She bent her head as she charged to the front of the room, directly toward the shouting man.

A startled Keeper stared open-mouthed. "Grab her, you useless idiots."

Neanna felt a chair crash to the floor as her panic charge carried her closer to the whine of the Keeper's voice.

"Stop, Chosen One or I will use force," he shrieked and lifted his staff in the air.

As he brought the staff down, Neanna's head slammed into his midriff like the force of a battering ram. His stomach caved in and he staggered backwards toward the gold chair. The sharp edge of the carved wooden arm struck him in the lower back just outside the kidney. The chair buckled under the weight, flipping backwards to the floor.

The cloth hood fell from Neanna's head as she regained her feet. She leaped up and raced for the rear entrance once more as the cult members watched in strange fascination.

## Gateway to Another Dimension

"I'm out of here," she called as she burst out the door only to fall into a thick multitude of blue robes. Dozens surrounded her like an army of ants attacking its prey, sweeping her off her feet and holding her high in the air as a treasure for their queen. She struggled vigorously, but the shear size of the crowd overwhelmed her meager strength. In desperation, she collapsed into their arms, hands still tied behind her back, shivering in the cool night air.

The Keeper appeared at the rear door. He raised one hand, but held the other to the deep pain in his kidney. "Take her," he shrilled, shaking his raised fist, "Take her to the vortex. Tonight is the night. We can no longer wait." "Keeper, Keeper, Keeper," the gathering clansmen chanted.

The Keeper turned to one of blue-robed assistants in the cabin and handed him a red robe. "Brother Charles, dress her in this ceremonial robe and keep her hands tied behind her back. Then lead the members to the vortex site and wait for me." He leaned against his staff to steady himself, gritting his teeth against the pain in his side.

As the door closed behind the assistant, the Keeper settled in his golden chair, clutching his hand to his side trying to relieve the agony. He turned to his elite members in the cabin. "Tonight will be the coming of those beyond the Ancient Ones. We now have the Chosen One to share with them and they will release the Ancient Ones to fulfill the prophecy. The Ones Before will give me the answer and we will have the strength we need to control all the vortexes."

"But what will that provide us, Master?" spoke one of the clansmen meekly.

"Brother Joseph, it will give us the power to use the vortex to come and go to the places beyond. It will give us power over the people here until we grow in numbers so large no one can stop us. Those who came before the Ancient Ones made that promise to me."

"Yes, Master," the brother answered, shaking his head. Beneath his blue hood, creases lined his forehead and his eyes questioned the Keeper where his mouth could not.

"Now to the vortex site. We shall see the wonder of the wonders tonight." He stood, ignoring the pain, picked up his carved wooden staff, and marched out the cabin door. His members followed as he started the long procession to the place of the mystical vortex.

## 54

ON TO SEDONA

In the meager moonlight, Deputy Carasco quickly slipped to the rear of the black sedan and then to the driver's side. He yelled at the fat man sitting terrified in the front seat, wiping his bloody face. "Get out with your hands in the air and then on the ground. Quick! Or you'll get what your friend did."

Fatso, his skin paled-white, slowly opened the car door. "Don't shoot. I'm not armed."

"Out," Jorge shouted. "Get your hands in the air."

"Okay, they're up" He stepped from the car and stood beside it.

"Now, on your belly."

"Hey, man, I'll get all dirty. Ain't this okay?"

"On your belly. Hands behind your head. Now!

The fat man dropped to his knees in the red dust, and then to the ground as Jorge searched him for weapons.

"He's clean," the deputy yelled to Michael. "Come on over. I'm calling for backup to get him and the dead one. I'll cuff him to the steering wheel, then we'll go find Neanna."

"Hey man, you can't leave me out here with this dead guy. It's against the law."

"Look whose talking. Come on, Michael, let's go."

The archeologist hesitated. "I think you should look in the back of your car first."

"Oh God," Jorge exclaimed as he glanced at the back seat. "He missed me and shot my prisoner." The bearded man from the mine lay dead on the floor of the SUV.

"Now what?"

"Give me a hand and we'll put him in the Lincoln. The backup can take him, too." In a few minutes, Jorge slammed the door of the black sedan shut. "Now, let's get out of here?"

"I'm with you. We need to find Neanna before that cult kills her. You told me they already sacrificed one girl and tried to kill another."

"We need to find that cult first. I heard by the grapevine they're going to the vortex site tonight. If they have Neanna, we've got to be there before anything happens to her."

"Too bad we don't know which hotel room that guy Wallace is in."

"I think we can find that number." Jorge whirled back to the black Lincoln and grabbed Fatso by the throat. "Know a fellow named Wallace in Sedona?"

"I don't know nuth'n," the fat man blubbered.

"Maybe you'd like to join your partner." Jorge jerked his revolver from the holster and shoved it in Fatso's face.

"Okay. Room 201, the Kachina Hotel. Scarface and the guys at the mine brought him the gems. They handle the problems there, like that desert snoop. Slim and I take care of problems in town."

The deputy lowered his gun and shoved the fat man back in the sedan, then called to report the shooting and the location of the black sedan. He asked for backup at the Kachina Hotel.

Jorge started the SUV and drove out of Red Canyon roaring down the blacktop highway toward Sedona. He drove the Sheriff's patrol vehicle wildly through the night, watching the flickering lights of the city appear ahead of him.

Shadows of nearby buildings flashed past as they drove into Sedona. Here and there a few nightlights reflected back at them.

"How are you doing, Michael?"

"I'm getting stronger every minute we get closer to that hotel. I can't wait to get my hands on Wallace, whoever the hell he is."

*The Mystical Vortex*

"It's just ahead. I'll pull to the front and we'll go upstairs and roust this guy out." He jumped from the SUV, gave a high sign to the black and white sitting at the curb, and headed for the front door. "Come on, Michael."

Jorge bounded up the flight two steps at a time as Michael struggled to follow. The deputy knocked on Room 201 at the top of the stairs, then pounded when no one answered.

A loud voice from inside yelled, "Whose knocking on the damn door. Don't you know what time it is?"

"This is Deputy Carasco. A friend of yours got hurt tonight. Says he needs your help." He stood in front of the door peephole so Wallace could see him.

"Yeah, I see you. Who did you say was hurt?"

"Some guy called Scarface. He gave us your room number. Are you Wallace?"

"Yeah, I'm Wallace. Let me get the door open."

As Jorge heard the latches release, he jammed his shoulder against it, knocking the man inside to the floor. The deputy was above him in an instant with his revolver pointed at the man's face. "No need to get up. This is no social call. Where's the blonde girl?"

"What girl? I don't know what hell you're talking about."

"It's over, Wallace. Your henchmen are dead and the fat one is singing. The Sheriff's office is closing down your mining operation right now." He grabbed the man's throat and shoved the gun in one nostril. "Where's the girl?"

"All right," he growled. Wallace choked down the lump in his throat. "You got me. Scarface took the girl to those cabins where that blue-robed cult hangs out." His eyes flashed around the room until he saw Michael. "You're the damned archeologist. I thought you were dead."

"Not as dead as you'll be if anything happens to Neanna. Let's take him down to the cops and get out of here before it's too late, Jorge."

The deputy turned Wallace over to the city police waiting in the black and white cruiser. "Get a search warrant and go over those rooms with fine comb." He looked at Michael, "Let's go find Neanna."

## 55

### THE VORTEX SITE

At the airport vortex, the blue-robed crowd surrounded the flat top peak chanting quietly in anticipation of the Keeper's arrival. Neanna stood calmly in the thin red robe between several clansmen, her small hands loosely bound behind her back and a blindfold covering her eyes. She had given up struggling and waited for her strength to return.

Above them, whispy clouds drifted below a pale moon and nocturnal animals made their nightly calls, when suddenly the chanting stopped. The crowd began the whisper. "The Keeper is coming. I can see the Keeper. What will the Keeper do tonight?"

Almost magically, the Keeper appeared in their midst. "What are you waiting for?" he screamed at the nearest one. "Get the Chosen One to the top."

"But we thought only you took them up there, Master."

"Do I have to do everything myself?" his high pitched voice demanded. "If you are going to be part of the new order, you need to start thinking for yourself." He stared into the face of the member who held Neanna's right arm. "Brother Charles tonight you are the Keeper's right hand."

"I am the right hand," repeated Brother Charles. "What do I do next?"

The crowd began to mumble. "Do we have another Keeper? What do we do next? What do we do next?"

"Shut up," the Keeper shrieked back at the stammering clansmen, then hesitated, raised his wooden staff, and calmed his voice. "Quiet everyone. Listen. For months now, you have followed me. You have seen the images in the vortex. You have heard the voices. Tonight you will see why we waited so long."

"Waited so long," the clan muttered."

"Now, Brother Charles, take the girl to the top."

The right hand clansman pulled Neanna through the crowd toward the opening in the base of the tall sandstone formation.

They led Neanna into the dark passageway and as she started up the rough-hewn stairs, she stumbled and fell to the rocky floor.

"On your feet, Chosen One," the soft voice of Brother Charles spoke as he pulled her to a standing position.

*The Mystical Vortex*

As they continued, Neanna dragged her shoes on the stone steps to slow their progress. She sagged and fell limp in their arms, leaning against Brother Charles.

"What's going on?" the Keeper shouted behind them. "Can't you do anything right? Must I do everything myself?"

"I am the right hand. I have her," called Brother Charles.

"You are the Keeper. We are the followers," the others mumbled softly, relaxing their grip on the blonde-haired girl as a dazed look passed across their faces.

Neanna squirmed from Brother Charles grasp, trying to decide which way to go. The tightly bound blindfold prevented her from seeing. *They said up.* She felt for the steps.

"No, sometimes you must think for yourself," the cult leader yelled.

"Think for ourselves. Think for ourselves. How?"

"Just take the girl to the top," the Keeper screeched at them banging his staff on the stone steps. "Brother Charles, do you hear me."

"The girl is not here," Brother Charles called back.

"The girl is not here," the others repeated.

"Where's the damn girl?" the Keeper yelled, his high trilling voice echoing up the passageway. "Go to the top and find her, you idiots."

Stumbling upward into the dark unknown, Neanna heard the cry. She shivered in the cool night air as the sheer scarlet robe and hood flapped in the breeze flowing up the tunnel toward the stone plateau above. *I've got to keep going,* she thought as she tripped up the rough stone stairway. *Thank God they left my boots on.*

She stopped momentarily, trying to rub the blindfold from her eyes on the smooth stone wall. It didn't budge. *There must be a place to hide once I get to the top.* She stifled a cry as her toe caught the next step, slamming her knees against the rocky stairs. Tears of pain formed in her eyes, but she told herself to be strong as she gained her feet and plunged upward listening for the sounds of those following.

Below Neanna, the Keeper harangued his clansmen, pushing the nearest to move up the tunnel. "Get up there, you idiots," he screamed at them again. "Find the Chosen One or you will be the sacrifice."

"Find the Chosen One," they cried out and clambered up the passageway. "Chosen One. Chosen One."

Neanna could hear the clansmen getting closer in the dimly lit tunnel. *Dear God, they can see and I can't. Where's the top?* She leaned along one wall to help guide her as she worked her way upward and felt the tunnel curving to the right as she climbed higher. She momentarily stopped to listen again and hoped she would hear something from above, but the calling below drowned any sound coming from the top.

"The Chosen One is just above us. I can see her shadow," Brother Charles yelled.

As Neanna made the next upward step, the wall she followed on her left dropped away to nothing. Caught off balance by the disappearance of her support, she fell into a narrow crevice. Her left shoulder hit the ground, stunning her for a second. "Oh my God, not again," she cried out, swallowing the rest of the words as she painfully crawled deeper into the tiny sanctuary.

Just outside the small hideaway, she heard her adversaries calling. "Come Chosen One, the Keeper wants you. Come to us."

# 56
## INDIAN CULTURAL CENTER

As Jonathon Blackeagle lay on the hard floor of the museum, images began to fill his imagination. The painting that hung across from his office desk floated in space above him as the ornate frame dissolved into nothing, and the tall proud Indian in ceremonial garb stood before him. Long braids hung down from under a tall headdress surrounding a dark bronze face etched with age. The large headdress stood high on his head like the face of a tiara with colorful feathers reaching upward in a great vertical semicircle. Colorful beaded designs were sewn into his buckskin clothing and moccasins. The elderly Indian reached down a weathered hand and pulled Jonathon to his feet, then turned toward the door beckoning him to follow. The big Indian straightened himself and followed the Great Chief out of the room.

Instead of the Cultural Center hallway, Jonathon found himself outside on a long grassy plain. In the distance, red sandstone cliffs rose skyward, pockmarked with massive lodges built of flat stones. The old Chief strode rapidly toward the cliff dwellings and Jonathon raced to follow. The distance across the wide plain disappeared and they soon passed through thick lush cornfields until they stood below the cliff. Looking up, he saw many Indian men, women, and children filling the stone-walled structures above and circular ceremonial chambers below. Each individual seemed to have a purpose in the community as he went peacefully about his business.

His grandfather turned and looked at Jonathon, pointing back the way they had come, but Jonathon could only stare at the aged man.

"Grandfather," he stuttered. "Where did you come from? Why did you bring me to this place?"

"Look, my son, and you will know," he pointed behind Jonathon.

The big Indian turned his head back toward the grassy plain, but saw only sand blowing across shifting dunes stained with dead grass. The bleached bones of bighorn sheep and other animals dotted the barren land. "What does this mean, Grandfather?" He turned to find desolate dry corn stocks and a deserted cliff dwelling.

The harsh wind blew dust through the abandoned homes, and the roofs of the ceremonial buildings had collapsed on themselves. Weathered poles jutted upward at odd angles from the center. Ugly redheaded turkey buzzards sat on wooden beams protruding from the neglected structures, and scorpions hid in the meager shade.

The old chief pointed back at the dusty plain and Jonathon turned his head. Soldiers in strange helmets and armor rode horseback across the blowing sand toward them.

When Jonathon turned to question the old man, the Chief was staring back at the dwellings. Puzzled, Jonathon saw a strange mist slowly covering the site and within the cloudy haze, a bizarre movement transpired. Hooded beings in blue robes beckoned as an endless line of ancient Indians, men, women, and children disappeared into the thick fog.

"Who are they, Grandfather?" Jonathon turned to face him, but the old chieftain was gone. He had faded away like the people in the mist. As the vapor dissolved, Jonathon realized he lay on the floor of the Cultural Center with his grandfather's ceremonial garb in his grasp.

Grasping his head as the vision disappeared, he recalled the legend of his people rising from the water of Montezuma's Well. Now he realized they came from some other world. He knew the beings who brought his ancestors had taken the Anasazi back to their world, and were coming in the vortex to claim others.

## 57

### SCHNEBLY CABINS

"How close are we? Michael glanced over at Jorge. "I knew something was evil about those cabins the first night I dropped her off. Neanna's in Number Seven. Let's check there first in case she escaped."

The deputy hardly stopped the SUV in front of the wooden building when Michael leaped from the vehicle. He raced to the door and pounded on it. "Neanna! Are you in there?" No one answered and he tried the lock. It was secure.

"Is she there?" Jorge called from his open window.

"No, I'm going to Five. She said that's where they seemed to be gathering." He dashed past Six and on to the next cabin.

Jorge jumped out, his 12-gauge shotgun in hand. "Wait!"

Michael slowed his pace as he arrived at the corner of Cabin Number Five. Jorge slipped behind him and handed

## Gateway to Another Dimension

Michael his service revolver. "You might need this once we get inside." They edged around the building toward the front door.

"See anything?" the deputy whispered.

"No, but I hear voices inside."

"Let me try the door," Jorge spoke softly. "If it's unlocked, I'm going in first." The deputy carefully pushed down on the lever and felt the mechanism inside pull the latch to the open position. He turned back to Michael. "Ready."

Michael nodded.

Jorge slammed the door open and burst into the room. He slid to one side to allow Michael to clear the opening and swung the shotgun across the room. The archeologist followed and dropped on the opposite side of the door.

Directly across from them, two cult members in blue hoods and robes leaped to their feet from a cross-legged position on the floor. They started to stutter when Jorge yelled. "Down on the floor, on your bellies, hands behind your head."

They continued to look at him with a trance-like stare without moving. "Who are you?" one of them spoke softly.

"Deputy Sheriff," Jorge dropped his voice, waving the shotgun as he approached the two.

The clansmen backed toward the wall, hands hanging at their sides. "We will tell the Keeper you came by."

Jorge pushed them facing the wooden interior and ran his hands over the robes searching for weapons. "They're clean," he nodded to Michael.

The archeologist couldn't wait any longer. He jumped forward and grabbed the closest one by the man's reddish throat. "Where is the blonde girl?" His voice echoed through the room.

"Blonde girl?" he muttered softly.

"Yes, blonde girl," Michael shouted tightening his savage grip on the man's neck and squeezed in on the Adam's apple. "Where is she?"

"Blonde girl," the other man whispered.

Michael whirled to face him, never releasing his hold on the first one. "Where is she?" he yelled in the man's face.

The blank look never changed "She is gone with the Keeper."

"Yes," the first one repeated, "the Keeper."

"Where is the Keeper?" Michael increased the pressure.

The clansman squirmed, but could not break the grip on his neck. Tears poured down the man's cheeks and thin stream of snot ran from his nose as his eyes pleaded for help. The second man spoke as if sharing the pain of the first. "The vortex, they have gone to the vortex. Soon the Ones Before will come and we will all be saved."

"We will be saved," the man in Michael's grasp, slobbered, "at the vortex."

"Which vortex?" Michael demanded tightening his grip as the clansman slumped to the floor unconscious. "Damn," he yelled wiping the snot on his ripped pants.

"I know which vortex, Michael. Let's go."

# 58

## THE VORTEX SITE

Neanna Miller squeezed deeper into the tiny stone crevice without knowing if she could be seen or not. Outside, she heard the members of the blue-robed cult calling.

"Come, Chosen One, we are taking you to see the Keeper. If you are hiding, come out. The Keeper needs you."

Neanna could hear their slow plodding feet scraping and dragging on the rocky stairs as they passed her sanctuary. She started to move when she heard more confident footsteps approaching.

"Brother Charles, do you have her?" The Keeper called up the narrow passageway as he passed Neanna's nearby hideout.

"No, Master," Brother Charles whispered, "we are searching the top."

"What the hell is taking you so long?" screamed the Keeper. "You know damn well I need her presence and I need it now."

"Yes, Master, we will find the Chosen One for you."

Neanna sat up in the narrow crack and rubbed the blindfold on the gritty sandstone surface until it fell at her feet. She blinked her eyes and quickly glanced around as if expecting someone to be staring at her. *Good,* she thought, *no one's here. They must be looking for me at the top.* She rubbed the cords that bound her hands on a sharp rock jutting from the side of the crevice until they slid over her fingers.

She eased herself down on the cold rocky floor of the small sanctuary. An uneasy ripple shook her body as she thought about her captors. *They must have gone to the top. Maybe, I'll be safe for awhile.*

She willed her body to be still when Sabrina's words passed through her mind. *A rift in the family needs healing and I must have touched a sore spot,* she remembered what the girl at the New Age store had said. *Yes, but those things happened a long time ago. Why am I so concerned now? Maybe, I do need to share this experience with you, Mom, if I get out of here alive. God, I need to share it with someone. Will you listen, Dad, if I come to you?* A trickle of tears welled from her eyes and ran down her tired cheeks. *Surely, you must have time now. I know I do.* She wiped the wetness from her face with dirt stained fingers.

Suddenly, the Keeper's sharp edged voice echoed down the tunnel, breaking her thoughts. From the top of the stony plateau, he screeched. "She is not here you imbeciles. You let her get past you." He rushed to the edge and looked down on the crowd below. "Block the entrance and send five members up the passageway. Find the Chosen One or the wrath of the Ones Before will be on your souls."

Creeping from the hole where she had been hiding, Neanna started back down the narrow tunnel. Near the entrance, she saw a multitude of clansmen, some standing close to the opening, preventing her from leaving. *I'm trapped,* flashed through her mind.

The members below swarmed around the opening to the stairway and five clansmen, acting like part of a giant ant colony, flowed into the dark tunnel. They carefully climbed up the stairs, some side by side where possible, and the others following. They filled the rocky corridor from wall to wall. Above, the Keeper sent Brother Charles and several others down the tunnel preventing any escape in that direction. Neanna fled back into her secret hideout.

The clansmen worked their way down from above and up from the bottom. The members on the end of each row slid their hands along the walls. When they reached the crevice, the clansman's hand slipped into nothingness.

"Stop," he whispered softly, "we must stop here."

"Are we here?" the ones beside him spoke.

Neanna pressed her back to the far wall and waited for the chance to break free of her tiny prison. The cult members lengthened their width to include the depth of the dark crevice. The outside man scraped his hands along the inside wall. Neanna ducked her head under the outstretched hand and tried to pass the clansman, but her shoulder jammed into his hip. The man brought his hand down on her blonde hair, screaming, "I have found something. Help me."

Neanna straightened, bringing her open palm up rapidly, catching the man under the chin, knocking his head back into the stone wall. He collapsed to the rocky floor, rolling down the steps. She grasped the hood of the next one, twisting it, and shoving the man into the member beside him. The clansmen stumbled back, bumping into one another like dominos falling, clearing the way to the entrance below.

Down the stairs she raced, several steps at a time, directly at the bunch guarding the opening. As Neanna reached the crowd, she shouted. "The Keeper is coming. Move aside."

The group melted backwards and Neanna jumped through the opening. *Dear God, let me out of here.*

# 59
## INDIAN CULTURAL CENTER

Jonathon gently pulled himself upright and lifted his grandfather's ceremonial robe. He held it to his chest, and looking upward, thanked his Great Spirit. "Tonight I know the meaning and what I must do."

He quickly dressed in the clothes of his ancestor, amazed that he could fit into them, strolled to his desk to retrieve the rabbit skin pouch, then outside to the center's van. He drove rapidly through the night shadows toward the airport vortex site. "I hope I am not too late," he told the stars above as he steered the white vehicle into the darkness.

It was not long before he left the van, and carrying his grandfather's headdress, rushed up the path to the hilltop rock formation. Soon he could hear the distant rumbling of the circling clansmen. His moccasins were silent as he glided across the rough sand and gravel pathway toward the noise that trickled down the hill on a soft breeze. When he reached the group circling and milling around the stone pinnacle, he stopped and slipped into the shadows looking for some way through the mingling crowd.

Suddenly, the Keeper appeared above, lifting an ornately carved staff. The crowd fell silent. "Quiet," he shrieked down at his followers. "Get her. Get the Chosen One." He raised the wooden staff and began to chant.

The cult below picked up the monotone adding, "The Chosen One. The Chosen One is coming."

Jonathon put on the chieftain's tall headdress and joined in the chant, trying to blend into the darkness with the cult. "Keeper, Keeper," he softly repeated as he worked his way closer to the tunnel opening. Suddenly, he noticed a commotion at the entrance and heard Neanna shouting.

"Make way for the Keeper. The Keeper is coming," she repeated.

He watched as the crowd spread, making an opening for the blonde girl to escape. He pushed members aside in an effort to reach her when a loud voice penetrated the sky above. The clansmen froze in their tracks creating a barrier that Jonathon could not break through. He heard them chanting.

"The Keeper is coming," the crowd murmured.

Jonathon looked up at the tall blue-robed man that appeared over the sharp edge of the immense sandstone mound above him. The moon's glow encircled his figure, making him appear much larger than normal. Jonathon could not believe the words he heard, as the high plateau amplified the man's shrill voice pounding down on those below.

"Capture her, you idiots," he screamed. "Damn you, capture her."

Jonathon listened as the Keeper's voice thundered down on the transfixed crowd. He watched in amazement as Neanna leaped through the opening created by the confused clansmen only to see them close the tunnel entrance again.

Some members, glancing at the girl rushing toward them chanted, "The Keeper is coming." Others, looking up toward the top of the stone pinnacle, chanted, "Capture her, capture her."

Jonathon watched the girl in red plow into the dazed crowd. *Help her Great Spirit.* The big Indian prayed as he tried to push his way through the cult members to help her.

Above, the Keeper continued to yell, "Capture her, you idiots, capture her."

Then Jonathon watched in horror as the mass of blue robes came alive and swarmed around Neanna like beetles on a prey, blocking any possible escape. He saw her kick and fight until they subdued the girl and carried her limp body twisted in the red robe into the tunnel.

As the interference diverted the crowd's attention, the Indian slipped quietly through them toward the passageway. Nearing the opening, several members turned toward him. "Are you one of us?" they asked, pressing in on him.

"You do not belong here," said another as he grasped Jonathon's arms.

"We must take you to the Keeper." They crowded around forcefully pinning his arms to his sides as Jonathon tried to resist.

# 60

## OUT OF SEDONA

As they raced out of Cabin Number Five, Michael began to feel his strength return. Years of hiking through the deserts and mountains of the Southwest had conditioned his body to endure pain and heal injured and bruised muscles. He jumped into the passenger seat of the sheriff's SUV as Jorge started the engine and they roared away from Schnebly Cabins onto the highway leading to the airport vortex.

"Pour it on, Jorge, we've got to get there on time."

"I know it too well. I saw what they did to other girls. We'll make it," he slapped his friend on the knee.

They parked the SUV just off the road, oblivious of the white van parked behind nearby juniper trees, and hurried quietly up the hill toward the vortex site. Light desert brush hindered their way as they strayed off the worn trail. In the distance ahead of them, they could hear the cult chanting.

Jorge whispered, "Strange, isn't it. There's not a coyote howling, a cricket chirping, or a nighthawk flying. It's dead silence, except for the cult."

"Eerie,"

"It's just ahead. I've been here many times." He stopped, motioning Michael down. "See, in the moonlight, that flat top pinnacle with people on it. That's where we have to go."

"My God, how do we get up there?"

Jorge made signs with his hands showing the way to reach the passageway entrance. "The opening is on the other side. We've got to pass through the crowd below, then enter the tunnel and follow the stairs to the top."

"That's going to be tough without anyone seeing us. There must be over two hundred of them milling around the bottom of that rock formation."

"Last time, I just grabbed one of the cult, dispatched him with a chop to the neck and used his robe to reach the top. I also wore dark clothes, which I don't have this time."

"Damn, you're thorough, Jorge, but I can't do that. When we get near the cliff, I'm going up the backside. I've climbed steeper rock piles than that. I'll meet you at the summit. Where do you think they've got Neanna?"

"Probably on top next to the leader. I'll meet you there." He disappeared into the darkness.

Michael worked his way in the shadows around the outside of the ring of clansman until he approached the rear of the stone tower. He could hear the Keeper haranguing the members below, keeping the cult under his spell by chanting some long lost phrases over and over. The archeologist pulled his tattered field jacket over his head in a makeshift hood and slowly moved through the mesmerized crowd, telling himself to keep calm, until he reached the rocky cliff. He leaned into the shadow of the wall, pulled his coat from his head, and bent down to wipe the moisture from his hands on the dry soil at his feet.

"I can do this," he muttered as he looked for finger and footholds on the rough sandstone surface.

Jorge slipped around the chanting crowd in the opposite direction until he was across from the tunnel entrance. He slowly crept behind an isolated cult member, grabbing the man's throat from behind with one hand and covering his mouth with the other. As he pulled him down, he struck the man with the butt of his revolver. The clansman slumped to the ground unconscious. Jorge dragged him behind some meager brush, removed his hat, and donned the man's robe. *Perfect fit*, he thought, as he pulled it over his head and tied the cord around his waist. "Keeper, Keeper," he chanted as he joined the crowd surrounding the stone plateau.

Gently shoving the blue-robed people aside, he made his way though the gallery until he arrived at the tunnel. Several cult members in a mesmerized state blocked his way. As he tried to pass, they moved in his direction, and never talking or raising their heads, but moving in unison. "Whoa," Jorge mumbled and backed away. "There has to be another way."

# 61

## CAPTURED

Neanna kicked and struggled with the swarm of blue robes that engulfed her almost to the point of suffocation. They quickly wrapped her in the cords to their clothing until she was bound like a cocoon and carried her above their heads up the narrow corridor to the surface.

The Keeper screamed at his followers from the rocky surface of the plateau. "Bring her up here, you idiots. Do I have to do everything myself?"

Those standing next to him repeated. "Do everything myself."

He quickly turned and yelled at them. "Shut up that nonsense and make way for the Chosen One. Where are you, Brother Charles?"

"I am here, Master. What is your bidding?"

"You will meet the Chosen One at the top of the stairs and bring her to me. Go."

"Yes, I will bring the Chosen One."

In the dark tunnel below, Neanna screamed, "Help, help me anyone," hoping someone other than the cult would hear her, but her terrified voice bounced off deaf walls and up the empty passageway. She continued to yell as they arrived at the upper portal and out into the cool night air.

"I will take the Chosen One," Brother Charles, spoke softly to those carrying Neanna. They put her down next to the Keeper's right hand and she fell against him, unable to stand in the cords that bound her. "Help me," she pleaded, staring into his expressionless face.

Brother Charles ignored her desperate words and motioned to have her bonds removed. He twisted Neanna's hands firmly behind her back and marched the girl across the stone plateau toward the Keeper.

"Chosen One, I see you have returned to be with us once again." The Keeper's soft high pitched voice ended with a sneer. "Hold her," he spoke motioning two other disciples to Neanna's side. The three clansmen tightened their grip on the blonde-haired girl.

"I am not your Chosen One!" Neanna shouted, stomping her feet on the stone surface and struggling to break their hold.

"Be quiet. You are indeed the Chosen One," the shrill words blurted from his mouth. "One more outbreak and I will have you gagged."

The Keeper turned toward the crowd below and began to chant softly, first in English and then in some strange tongue that Neanna had never heard. Below him, the cult wandered in circles around the base of the flat-topped pinnacle, repeating his incantation with the words, "Keeper, Keeper," interspersed.

The tall hooded cult leader turned back to Neanna. "Your time will come very soon, Chosen One," his lips sneered whispering to her. The moonlight flickered over the twisted smile that played across his wrinkled face.

......

Near the lower tunnel entrance, Jonathon's face strained in anger as he tried to hold back the crowd of blue robes shoving him against the sandstone wall. As he struggled, their weight pressed in, squeezing him against its rocky surface. As more swarmed over him some cult members pushed others until even those next to him were being crushed in the onslaught.

"Why do you wish to injure the Ancient One who has come to redeem you?" he shouted to those around him. "Look, see my headdress. The headdress from the mist."

First one and then another began to murmur. "The Ancient One. He is the Ancient One from the mist."

The pressure on Jonathon slowly subsided as he spoke pleasantly to the crowd. "I have come from the mist to be

## Gateway to Another Dimension

among you. To share your desire. To help bring you to the Ones Before."

The crowd drifted back until they freed the big Indian of his human prison. He leaned back against the stone wall and took a deep breath. *I have to finish here and get to the top,* he thought, filling his lungs with air.

"Look up," he pointed. "I will soon be there with the Keeper. Look up, look up," he repeated.

Jonathon distracted most of them, but some clansmen followed him to the entrance of the tunnel blocked by a solid line of other cult members. "The Ancient One comes," they chanted behind him as Jonathon bravely approached the entrance guards.

"Ancient One," the guardians echoed the words of those following the Indian and opened the wall of blue like a swinging door.

Jonathon passed through the opening and into the dark tunnel.

Jorge watched in amazement at the ploy by the tall Indian. *He's good,* he thought, as he moved to stand at the end of the blue line that became the open door. *It's my turn now.* He watched as Jonathon passed through and the clansmen started swinging themselves around to close the human door. Undetected, Jorge swung with the blue robes and squeezed inside as the door jammed shut. "Made it,"

335

he murmured, and quickly hid in the dark shadows along the rocky stairs.

*I don't dare call Jonathon,* he thought, *the tunnel may be lined with other guardian clansmen.* He crept upward, trying to hide the thud of leather boot heels on the stone steps.

On the other side of the plateau, Michael climbed silently up the faded red sandstone pillar. He paused to rest his straining fingers periodically. *I'm not quite as strong as I thought,* passed through his head as he tried to lean in against the cold rock. *I'm about half way up there. Hang on, Neanna, I'm coming for you.* He edged himself on when suddenly his tired foot slipped and he lost his grip with his left hand. He swung out from the wall, clinging by his right fingertips. Dust and crumbled rock scoured down from the stone face onto the hoods of the clansmen below. Several of them reached up as the sand ran down their capes.

"Are you up there, Keeper?" they chanted. "Are you up there?"

Michael pulled his body back to the shadows of the cliff and regained his foothold. The leverage allowed him to reach with his left hand and find the tiny crevice where his fingers had slipped. Digging deeper into the crack, he pulled himself upward until he sensed the Keeper chanting from above. As the sound drifted over the edge, he heard

"Chosen One, Chosen." *Damn, the archeologist thought, the guy must be talking about Neanna.*

# 62

## THE MYSTICAL VORTEX

The Keeper raised his long wooden staff and arms into the air as he increased his chanting. The crowd below stood entranced by his words. They too began the repetition, increasing the volume as the Keeper pumped his carved staff up and down. "Now is the time to call the Ones Before," he shrieked.

"The Ones Before," the excited members picked up the call, "The Ones Before."

"Are you ready to receive them?" His shrill voice flowed down on the crowd.

"We are ready," the mass of blue robes chanted. "We are ready for them; we are ready for them."

Holding his staff high, the Keeper reached beneath his robe with his other hand and pulled out a long slim quartz crystal tapered at each end. He held it in the air and tightened his grip on the glassy surface. As the pressure from his hand squeezed the clear gem, a tiny scarlet glow

## Gateway to Another Dimension

flickered at the pointed tips. He clenched it tighter and the faint light brightened to a darker red, dancing from one end of the jewel to the other. "We are almost ready, little one," he whispered and dropped the crystal back inside his robe.

"Are we still ready, ready, ready?" he chanted down at the crowd.

"Ready, Master, ready, ready," the incantation from below echoed around and around the stone plateau.

The Keeper reached again inside his robe and produced a small rabbit fur pouch. He rested his wooden staff on the ground and opened the soft velvety bag. From inside, a silver mist began to form. It spread upward, rotating as the hazy fog climbed higher above the Keeper and the others standing behind him. It swirled upward, creating a misty vortex. The Keeper continued chanting, "Come to us, oh Ancient Ones. Bring with you the Ones Before." He held the small fur pouch and turned around in harmony with the swirling mist. His chanting words changed to some strange tongue. Those below picked up the words and chanted back to him.

Figures of recent Indians danced through the silver haze flowing around the plateau in ever enlarging circles. Then the Indians of ancient times took the place of the newer Indians. "Ancient Ones, we see you," chanted the Keeper in English and then in the language of the Ancient

Ones. Soon, people in strange helmets and uniforms drifted swiftly through the mist as it thickened, almost hiding the Keeper from those below. The rotating cloud expanded covering the stone pinnacle to the ground below.

The cult members screamed as the helmeted figures passed around and through them. Some clansmen fell to the ground crying out to their god of the past. "Help me, Oh Lord, I should not be here." Another moaned, "God, take me away from this evil place."

The Keeper seemed to hear them as he called down from above. "Arise you nonbelievers," he shrieked. "Stand to receive the Ones Before."

As he spoke, the uniformed people disappeared and eerie luminescent orbs bobbed around inside the silver mist like misshapen balloons or globs of liquid floating within a lava lamp. As they bounced and rotated though the haze, glistening faces appeared and disappeared in the glow, some with features of men and women, and others of children. Some expressions showed signs of happiness with smiles crossing the faint mouths, while others displayed signs of terror with wrinkled faces and mouths twisted in pain.

The members screamed and withered further into the earth trying to escape from the bobbing translucent heads fading into faint lustrous shapes that danced in the thickening mist.

The Keeper looked up at the globules of light bobbling above and around him as he put the rabbit fur pouch away and picked up his staff once again. "Oh mystical spirits, I have brought the Chosen One as you have asked. I have her beside me."

The lights brightened inside the liquid balls as they danced faster. Some paused before the Keeper causing him to stumble back in amazement. The glow inside flickered as if trying to communicate with the man in front of them. "I have her as you requested," he stuttered fearfully. "I have brought her to fulfill the promise you made to me, to share your power with me." His voice trailed to a gasping whisper as he stared into the blinking globes before him.

They twinkled in tune to some thought process as the Keeper gently rested his staff and pulled Neanna to him. "See, here she is, the Chosen One." He reached inside his flowing blue robe and pulled out the slender quartz crystal. The glow on each end brightened to the redness of a hot steel rod.

"No," Neanna screamed. "I am not the Chosen One. He is mistaken. He is evil."

Some glowing spheres took on faint colors as they rotated toward each other and the lights within danced and sparkled, then turned back to the Keeper. The flickering increased as the colors gradually changed in tune to the blinking lights.

"Thank you, Ones Before," a pleasant smile erupted across the Keeper's wrinkled face. He grabbed Neanna's throat in a steel grip and pulled her across in front of him. His ugly grin leered from under his hood at her terrified face as he lowered the glowing crystal to her bare forehead. He hesitated for a moment, glancing up at the orbiting globules, then carefully lowered it again.

Neanna looked up at the quartz gem inches from her head and watched as the Keeper lowered the throbbing red-pointed tip to her brow. She closed her eyes tight, straining in hopes to find the old woman. She willed herself to visualize her inner mind and began to ask for help. "Grandmother, I know you're in there and I need you now more than ever. Tell me what I must do. Physically, I am powerless, but I know my strength lies inside."

Suddenly, the voice within answered. "Concentrate on the charka; concentrate on the energy site within your forehead. It is the center where your strength begins."

Neanna squeezed her eyes tighter and willed herself further inward. Her body slowly warmed, and seemed to evaporate until only her mind existed as she appeared to be inside looking out. Concentrating on her forehead, she watched the stain within her grow, first as a tiny red mark, and then larger and thicker building a dark crimson barrier across her brow. She could see the glow brighten to a fiery hot coal beneath her thin white skin.

## Gateway to Another Dimension

The Keeper looked down at the pale forehead of the girl he held in his arms. He knew he had but to touch the crystal to her head and she would be in his control, but he wanted the moment to linger. Once in his control, he could present her to the Ones Before and, as promised, they would transfer the power of the vortex to him.

He looked up at the soft glowing orbs with their flickering lights as if waiting for a signal from them. "Ones Before," he chanted in a slow squeaky monotone, his wrinkled face twisted in desperation and his eyes closed to narrow slits with red lines flickering across the glassy surface. "What is your desire? Give me a sign to follow tonight."

The illuminated shapes rotated as if looking at each other and vibrated the lights within until they blinked in harmony.

The frantic Keeper nodded his head at each revolution and flicker of the dimly lighted globules trying to read something out of their movement. "Oh, Great Ones," he continued his shrill chant. "I can feel your desire to receive this Chosen One. The moment of truth is here." The painful look on his deeply grooved face slowly changed to a peaceful one, almost saintly.

Around him and below, his disciples picked up his call. "Oh, Great Ones," they muttered, "Oh, Great Ones. We too can feel your desire. Come to us."

"Open your eyes, Chosen One," the Keeper squeaked, smiling softly down at Neanna. "Now is the time to receive the Ones Before. Open your eyes so you can witness the coming." He slowly lowered the bright red point of the quartz crystal toward Neanna's forehead.

## 63

ON THE PINNACLE

Jonathon walked confidently up the stone steps toward the opening above. Every few minutes he repeated, "The Ancient One is coming." As he neared the top, he could hear the Keeper chanting, but resisted the desire to charge up the stairs and free Neanna. *I need to use the element of surprise when I reach the surface.*

As the big Indian stepped through the upper portal, he was amazed to find himself enveloped in thick white mist. *I'm too late,* quickly flashed through his mind. *I must do something in a hurry.* He raised his hands to the heavens and strode to the center of the plateau. "I am the Ancient One. I have come to save you. I am the Ancient One."

The blue-robed followers, faintly visible in the rotating haze, surrounded Jonathon. "We are the guardians. Who comes to seek the Keeper?" As the clansmen approached the big Indian, they began to listen to him.

Jonathon repeated, "I am the Ancient One. The Keeper sent for me. I have come to save you."

The ring of cult members opened as they echoed Jonathon's chant. "The Ancient One. The Ancient one comes."

On the far side of the flat-topped tower, a bruised hand slipped over the ledge as Michael Adams pulled his aching body to the rim. His eyes peered over the edge and glanced around. He heard the Keeper's sing song melody and the cult members repeating the words, but the thick mist prevented him from seeing any of them. As he stood to get a better look, two robed clansmen grabbed him from each side.

"You are not one of us," the first one spoke.

"We must take you to the Keeper," spoke the second, tugging on Michael's arms as they tried to pull him to the center of the plateau.

"I'm not going anywhere," Michael shouted, dropping to his knees and pulling the blue-robes with him. He broke loose from one of them and grappled with the other in the mist. The archeologist rolled over the surface trying to break the grip of the first man. Twice he felt the hand of the second one searching for him in the thick fog. Then suddenly, his hand reached out into empty space. "Oh hell," he muttered, "we're going over the edge." He dug his heels into the rough stone surface and rolled the clansman across

## Gateway to Another Dimension

his body and out into the empty darkness. The man's cry faded away in the distance below.

Michael lay still on the cold stone surface listening for the other cult member, but only the Keeper's chanting reached his ears. He crept carefully across the rough plateau toward the high pitched voice until he saw the cult members standing in a semicircle around a tall man with his back toward Michael. He looked in amazement at the glowing liquid orbs dancing in the mist before the chanting man. *Where's Neanna?*

Deputy Carasco slipped out the upper end of the tunnel into the night air and the whirling haze soon after Jonathon passed through the opening. He caught a quick glimpse of the big Indian's figure as it disappeared into the fog, and recognized the deep voice repeating, "I am the Ancient One."

"My God, he's smart," Jorge murmured to himself as he crouched and started to circle the dimly visible group of cult members. From the left and then the right, the clan moved to block his approach. *I'm safe,* he thought, *I'm wearing one of their robes.*

"No one is to approach the Keeper at this time except his assistants. We are the guardians and you are no one we recognize. You must go back. You must go below."

"The Keeper. I go to the Keeper," Jorge muttered softly.

"No. We are the guardians. You are no one. You must go below. The clansmen, using only their bodies, forced Jorge back toward the upper tunnel entrance. Several members dropped away until only two leaned against the deputy. Jorge resisted the weight of the men until they reached the tunnel with his back to the opening. Just before he arrived at the top step, the lawman dropped down, grabbing the open throats of the blue-robed capes. The stunned clansmen were too startled to resist as Jorge jerked them over his head and down the tunnel behind him. He heard the thud of their bodies crashing down the rock stairs and into the stone walls until only silence reached his ears.

He stood and crept around the remaining members working his way toward the center of the plateau. Jorge hesitated as he heard the Keeper chanting in some unknown tongue. *I've got to get closer,* the deputy thought.

## 64

ACROSS THE PINNACLE

Jonathon Blackeagle strode through the cloudy mist toward the large group of cult members standing behind the preoccupied Keeper. As he approached them, they turned with apprehension and surprise, then reached out to block his approach. He raised his hands, the high headdress bobbing above giving the appearance of a taller than normal figure, and repeated, "I am the Ancient One; I am the Ancient One."

The followers bowed and opened for his passing as they too chanted, "Oh, Ancient One."

As the last row of clansmen stepped aside, Jonathon noticed the Keeper holding Neanna across his waist, hand on her throat, and the gleaming crystal poised above her head. Directly in front of them, the glowing orbs danced and flickered in harmony with some high pitched tone that only the cult leader could hear.

"They're calling for the Chosen One," he muttered to himself. "They're calling for the Chosen One's return." As the tone pounded in the Indian's head, he reached to cover his ears crying loudly, "Great Spirit, help me. Help this poor girl."

The Keeper glanced over his shoulder at Jonathon's cry. "You are too late, Old Chief. Look, see your ancestors coming." He pointed into the mist filling the sky over the edge of the sandstone tower.

Jonathon watched in amazement, as lines of ancient Indians passed across his view. "Grandfather," he called as the great chief followed the others into the distance. "Come back. There is so much I need to learn from you."

The great chief waved his hand, smiled, and vanished in the mist.

Then chiefs of other tribes following their procession passed through the haze. At the rear, Laura Running Deer's sister appeared, dressed in the clothing of a chief's daughter. Her form flickered in and out until it disappeared, no longer following the others.

*She still lives,* thought Jonathon.

"See, Old Chief," the Keeper wailed. "The ceremony has already started. The Ones Before are here to receive the Chosen One. They will prevent any and all interference."

The intensity of the muted sound increased, driving Jonathon to his knees. He struggled to his feet, raising his

## Gateway to Another Dimension

face to the heavens, "Great Spirit, stop this infidel from the evil he is about to bring to your people. Stop him before it is too late."

"No, Old Chief, you are the one who is too late," the cult leader's shrill voice cried out.

The high pitched sound continued to drum in Jonathon's head. "You will not win, Evil One," he cried out as the intensity of the pain twisted in his mind. "The coming you expect is not the one you will receive. You will lose."

"Goodbye, Old Chief." The Keeper slowly lowered his dark bleary eyes and then his head as if to drive Jonathon down into the mist.

The big Indian collapsed to his knees and then to the cold surface. He groveled on the floor of the stone plateau clamping his hands tightly around his ears. The thick mist enveloped his body as the sound penetrated his skull.

The Keeper's leering mouth smiled as he continued to lower the red-tipped crystal slowly toward Neanna's exposed skin.

Around the far side of the high plateau, Michael Adams crept through the thickening haze and approached the group of clansmen gathered near the Keeper. *Neanna must be in the center of that bunch somewhere,* he thought. *I've got to get closer to see through this fog.* As he flanked the crowd, he noticed their attention concentrated on the vibrating balls of lights that seemed to change color and move in some strange harmonic dance. He ducked around the end of the pack and faintly saw the Keeper, his hand raised with the glowing crystal tinted scarlet on both ends.

Michael watched as the clan leader chanted and slowly lowered the pointed gem. At that moment, as his eyes followed the crystal downward and through the cloudy mist, he saw Neanna's blonde hair cascading over the Keeper's arm. "Damn," he cried, "it's the death crystal Jorge described to me." He jumped forward to save her. Two clansmen turned to block his way, but Michael stuck them with his shoulder, bowling them down as he bounded across the mist-covered surface. He reached out to knock the glowing crystal from the Keeper's hand only to smash head-on into a solid clear impenetrable wall.

"Not today young man, not ever." The cult leader turned in his direction and a cruel smile crossed his wrinkled face.

Michael flattened against the invisible barrier, his arms outstretched, his face twisted in agony, and his nose jammed to one side. He slid down into the drifting mist.

Deputy Carasco, dressed in the blue robe of the cult, had caught up with Jonathon and followed him across the stone plateau toward the gathering clansmen. He chanted, "Oh, Ancient One, Oh, Ancient One," in tone with the clan, bowing when they bowed. Then he watched in horror as the big Indian collapsed to the floor of the stone plateau, disappearing into the thick mist floating across the surface.

As Jorge glanced around, he noticed everyone staring at the Keeper and the dancing globes. *Whatever they are, the cult never brought them here,* he thought. *They must have emerged from this mist.* He slipped around the cult members, approaching the Keeper on the opposite side from Michael's calamity.

"The death crystal," he whispered to himself as he saw the glowing gem in the Keeper's hand. "He must be holding Neanna. If only I could see better through this cloud." He eased his revolver from the holster and stepped closer. Not a single clansman moved or paid attention to him. *Odd,* he thought. As he reached for the Keeper's shoulder, his hand struck an invisible wall.

Jorge never hesitated. He stepped back, raised his gun, and fired two shots directly at the Keeper. The lead bullets flattened against the barrier and slid to the rocky floor. Undaunted, he fired two more rounds with the same result.

Once again, the Keeper turned and hideously smiled at Jorge, his red-tinged eyes blazing. "You also are too late to save the Chosen One," then gazed back at Neanna. The evil smile spread across his rutted face as the scarlet tipped jewel inched closer to her head.

Deputy Carasco stared in unbelievable amazement as the flattened lead slugs slid down some invisible surface and disappeared into the mist-covered floor. His mind raced for some solution when he thought of Jonathon. *He will have the answer.* He glanced around, looking for the form of the tall Indian. The clansmen appeared to be oblivious of what happened and continued chanting.

Jorge ran to the place where he saw Jonathon fall and felt for his body in the thick mist flowing over the floor of the stone plateau. When at last the toe of his boot touched something soft, he knelt and pulled the Indian's body to a sitting position. The man still held his hands tightly around his ears.

Jorge pulled at his arms and yelled in his face. "Jonathon, can you hear me?" but only silence answered him. He slapped him across the cheek and was surprised to see the Indian's eyes suddenly open. He shouted again, "Are you in there, Jonathon? Speak to me."

His mouth moved, but no words flowed as the Indian strained to speak.

Jorge shook his shoulders. "Come on, big guy, we don't have much time."

Jonathon's mouth twitched again and squeaky words formed on his lips. "The pouch, you must use the pouch." He nodded to his waist, his eyes flickering in that direction.

"The pouch?" Jorge repeated.

"Use the pouch before it is too late," his eyes pleaded as he twisted his face in agony.

Jorge looked down at the Indian's waist and spotted the small rabbit fur bag tucked into Jonathon's beaded waistband. He pulled it loose and held it up as the big Indian nodded again and again.

"Open it, now," he strained to speak.

The deputy raised the dainty fur treasure in his hand as if it were all the gold in the world. He pulled the leather thong to open the pouch and watched in amazement as a silver glow slowly emerged, surrounding the little bag.

## 65

## THE POWER OF THE CHAKRA

Neanna sensed the glowing red-tipped crystal moving closer.

"Soon it will be over, Chosen One," the Keeper whispered to her, as a dutiful father would talk to a child. "I will release you to your destiny." The crimson color within the jewel raced from one point to the other increasing in brightness.

Neanna's face reflected back the brilliant red glow like a crimson beacon flashing over her face. Within her mind, she asked the old lady for reassurance. "Grandmother, now is the time for action. Somewhere within my body I feel my strength building. What is it?"

"You have always had the power, my child, but there was never a time you needed it. It gave you the independence to succeed where others have failed. It gave you the independence to strike out on your own. And now it will give you the force to save yourself. Think, Neanna, just think."

She closed her eyes even tighter and allowed her thoughts to concentrate on the red spot within her forehead. "Okay, Old Lady, I'm thinking. I can see the redness spread. I can see it grow. I'm concentrating on it, okay."

"You will succeed as before, Neanna. Goodbye."

"No. Wait. Don't leave me. Tell me about my parents."

"The answer is in your heart."

"What is it? What is the answer, Grandmother? Don't give me riddles."

"Ask your heart Neanna. Do you love them?"

"Yes, I've always loved them, but do they love me?"

"Again, ask your heart. You are their daughter."

"I know they do. I've always known they loved me. Maybe more than I loved them. Thank you, Grandmother."

"Then goodbye, My Dear. My presence is no longer required. I have given you what you need."

"Wait," Neanna cried out, then she heard herself answer, "She is no longer needed. She has given me herself. I must concentrate." Inwardly she looked at her charka as a sudden burst of energy released from it.

Outside, the Keeper watched in fascination as a bright red beam leaped from the girl's forehead to the glowing crystal. "I've done it," he shrieked. "I have taken control of the Chosen One."

The beam grew until it engulfed the tapered jewel in the Keeper's thin white hand. The glow within the crystal widened until the complete gem beamed in a bright crimson color radiating out in all directions. As the intensity of the red light increased, so did the heat within the crystal.

The Keeper shook his head and looked uneasy at the gem as the heat increased. Hesitantly, he spoke, "I now have you in my control, Chosen One," his speech faltering. "Stand and obey my commands."

Neanna rose beside the tall man in blue as he held her upright with the crystal still poised next to her golden head. As he looked down at her, she suddenly opened her eyes. The emerald light within them flashed up into the deep sunken red-streaked eyes of the Keeper. "Who is in control?" she asked.

The Keeper opened his trembling mouth to speak, but the heat within the crystal seared into his thin palm sending a shock wave of pain up his arm and into his body. "What is happening?" he stammered. "What is happening to me?"

"Now is the time of reckoning, Old Man. You have sacrificed your last victim." Neanna stepped away from his grip, as the Keeper staggered backward screaming at the pain.

"Get her, you idiots," he shrieked through clenched teeth at the clansmen surrounding him. "Get her now."

Brother Charles and the other blue-robed cult members charged at Neanna, when suddenly a red glow radiated from her body. The first clansman to reach her screamed in pain as his robes burst into flames. The next tried to stop his forward motion, but he too fell into the heat wave radiating from Neanna's body. The mass of blue robes behind the first pushed others forward until the stone floor before her reeled with screaming bodies. The remaining cult members raced to the passageway, stumbling and falling to the bottom.

In front of Neanna, the glowing orbs suddenly began to vibrate in a variety of soft colors. The harmonious flickering lights within changed from one globule to another. They rotated toward each other as if communicating. She raised her arms, watching the glowing objects follow the motion of her hands. Blue-white jagged streaks of electrical energy raced from her fingers to the dancing orbs.

The pain within Jonathon's head instantly disappeared. "Now," he cried to Jorge. "Release the powders."

The deputy reached into the fur pouch and extracted a handful of the strange sand and threw it in the air. Within the Keeper's hazy vortex, a second whirling mist of pinks and blues appeared. It swirled up and around filling and surrounding the red rock mountaintop. Once again Indians of the recent past appeared and drifted through the cloud, then men in strange armor on tall horses rode though. Next came the Ancient Ones in their primitive Indian clothing,

*The Mystical Vortex*

and finally the faceless liquid blobs danced and bobbed among the orbs summoned by the Keeper.

The lighted globules blinked off and on. They circled one another.

The glow radiating from Neanna's body dissipated as she watched the vortex experience. Her face changed to a peaceful calm as she lowered her arms and her fierce glare dropped from the Keeper's eyes. Suddenly, the light within the crystal faded and the heat vanished.

The Keeper stepped back, fear filling his wrinkled face. He raised his feeble arms as if to ward off some invisible foe. "No, no," he shrieked as the crystal dropped from his heat-seared fingers, falling to the stone plateau, shattering into a myriad of tiny fragments. Gently holding his scarred hand to his chest, he stared blankly, his red-stained eyes trying to follow the rotating orbs.

Neanna turned as Michael burst across the stone plateau and grabbed her in his arms. She wrapped herself around him, burying her head in his chest.

"Neanna, I can't believe what I just saw," he stammered pushing her back and staring into her eyes. "What did you do to them?"

She looked at him, laughing. "We're not through yet."

Pulling Jonathon's big arm around his shoulder, the deputy escorted him to Michael's and Neanna's side as they watched the past and future enfold before them.

"What's happening?" Jorge shook his head at the big Indian.

"They came for a Chosen One and they will not leave without one," Jonathon answered.

"But the Keeper called Neanna the Chosen One," Michael broke in, "and we don't intend to let her go."

"Watch." Neanna smiled, brushing the thin blonde hair from across her left eye, and pointed.

The glowing liquid orbs had now balanced in harmony. The lights within changed colors and flickered in symmetry. They vibrated back and forth across the stone plateau until they formed a semicircle that moved across the rocky surface until it encircled the Keeper.

"No, not me," he cried. "She is the Chosen One." He raised his terrified face upward and waved his thin white hands as if to chase them away.

The luminescent globules brightened into a steady glow as they circled the sandstone tower one more time, then evaporated into a gas that just drifted upward.

The Keeper disappeared with them.

# 66

Indian Cultural Center

Jonathon Blackeagle sat at his large wooden desk fingering a small rabbit fur bag. He tossed it slightly in the air several times, nodding his head methodically. As he toyed with the pouch, he looked up at the painting of an old Indian Chief.

"What do you think, Grandfather?"

The figure in the painting never answered.

"That is what I thought, Grandfather." Jonathon smiled. "Thank you for the advice and, of course, the use of your ceremonial robe."

The big Indian strode over to a large wooden box, weathered by time, and bound with copper corners, hinges, and hasp, each coated with a pale green patina. Using a brass key, he unlocked the ancient padlock and opened the box. Peering in at the empty space, he dropped the small fur pouch inside. It looked small and insignificant lying on the wooden bottom. "Rest there for another century, small mystery." He locked the padlock and, as he strolled back to his desk, he heard the door bell ring.

"Come in," he called down the hall. "The door is open."

"Is that you, Jonathon," Neanna answered.

"In here, in my office."

"I'm so glad we caught you," the blonde girl replied.

The big Indian stood behind his desk. "And I'm glad to see both of you. I missed your smiling face, Neanna. Please sit. Tell me what you have been doing."

"And I missed your warm hands, but first, have you heard from Jorge."

"Let's see. He said the FBI picked up the men from the cave and the sheriff's department rounded up the blue-robed cult. They are being sent to a reprogramming center and tribal members are helping with our people."

"Neanna twisted an errant strand of hair behind her left ear. "Well, we're getting ready to leave Sedona. Michael and I have been talking almost steadily for the last three days. In the past, I think we only had a physical appeal for each other. Now, I believe it is more of an emotional attraction."

"Yes," Michael cut in, "Neanna and I are closer than ever."

The blonde girl slid her chair near Michael and hugged his arm.

Michael continued. "We have been recuperating from one of the most horrendous experiences I, we, have ever lived through. I still don't know what happened on that mountain top, do you?"

"Yes," Neanna spoke up. "We've been trying to understand what has taken place here since we arrived."

"I too have wondered." Jonathon shook his head. "I have asked the Great Spirit to help explain it, but I received no answers." He looked up from his desk into Neanna eyes. "But I do know there is something spiritual in you, Neanna, something special."

"That's why we're leaving. Too many weird things have happened to me since I came to Sedona. I feel it's presence in me, in my soul. I need to leave."

"What about you, Michael. Do you feel the same?"

"No, but some strange things have occurred here that I can't explain. It's Neanna I'm really concerned about. I believe she needs to leave this place."

"Have you learned anything while here," the big Indian asked. "Or should I say, have you overcome any difficulties that you brought with you."

"I brought the problems I had with my parents and that seemed to burden every decision I made." Neanna nervously played with a strand of blonde hair that drifted over her left eye. "Even the girl who took me to the vortex site seemed to sense it. After the night on the mountain, my mind seemed to clear." She pushed the hair away from her face. "And would you believe this, Jonathon, I called my Mom last night." Suddenly she sobbed, and raised her hand to her mouth as tears rolled down her cheeks. "And we talked for a long time." She choked away the lump in her throat. "It was wonderful."

"Are you all right?"

"Yes." Neanna wiped the tears from her eyes. "You know I feel at peace now. Maybe I just misunderstood my mother these last few years. We talked like it was the first time, like I just met some wonderful person. I could hear my sister, Naomi, talking in the background. Even she seemed interested in what Mom and I were saying. It was such an incredible experience, Jonathon."

"And your father?"

"Mom's been talking to him. Mostly about Naomi, but Mom said he did ask about me. Made me feel good." She giggled.

"And how about you, Michael?"

"Neanna and I have made some important decisions. I'll be going back to the university and she'll be going back to her work. If we decide to do any exploring, we'll make arrangements to do it together."

"What about the treasure you said you found? Will you still be looking for it?"

## The Mystical Vortex

"We went back to the cave," Neanna spoke up, "and found the old Spanish helmet that Michael carried out of the gallery."

"That helmet' Michael continued, "will provide me with the evidence I need to prove Antoino de Espejo's expedition came here. The paper will perhaps get me a grant for more searching, with Neanna of course." He smiled at her and squeezed her hand.

By now, Jonathon had a big grin on his face. "So, do I detect wedding bells in the future?"

Neanna snuggled closer to Michael, and looked into his face. "Maybe." She turned and looked at Jonathon. "What about you? That young woman, Laura, seems to be more than an assistant. I believe she needs you and you sure need her. You said I had some special powers. That's what they tell me right now."

A faint crimson glow slipped behind Jonathon's bronze complexion. "Your powers reveal too much, Neanna."

"I'm sorry, dear friend." She stood and reached her hand across the table. As Jonathon grasped her fingers, Neanna could feel the warmth move up her arm. She quickly withdrew her hand. "If I ever need your help, I'll be back. Maybe treasure hunting this time"

They stood and walked toward the door.

Printed in the United States
48738LVS00006B/1-78